The Wiccan Wheel Series
by JENNIFER DAVID HESSE

Midsummer Night's Mischief

Bell, Book & Candlemas

Yuletide Homicide

Samhain Secrets

May Day Murder

MAY DAY MURDER

Jennifer David Hesse

KENSINGTON BOOKS
KENSINGTON PUBLISHING CORP.
www.kensingtonbooks.com

KENSINGTON BOOKS are published by

Kensington Publishing Corp.
119 West 40th Street
New York, NY 10018

All Kensington titles, imprints, and distributed lines are available at special quantity discounts for bulk purchases for sales
promotion, premiums, fund-raising, educational, or institu-
tional use.

Special book excerpts or customized printings can also be created to fit specific needs. For details, write or phone the office
of the Kensington Sales Manager: Attn.: Sales Department.
Kensington Publishing Corp., 119 West 40th Street, New York, NY
10018. Phone: 1-800-221-2647.

Kensington and the K logo Reg. U.S. Pat. & TM Off.

First Printing: April 2019
ISBN-13: 978-1-4967-1773-3
ISBN-10: 1-4967-1773-2

ISBN-13: 978-1-4967-1774-0 (eBook)
ISBN-10: 1-4967-1774-0 (eBook)

10 9 8 7 6 5 4 3 2 1

Printed in the United States of America

For Sage,
my springtime daughter,
who wears flowers in her hair
and always makes me smile

Beltane, also known as **May Day**: An ancient fertility festival, long celebrated by Pagans to honor the abundance of the blossoming earth. Falling midway between the spring equinox and the summer solstice, Beltane is a cross-quarter holiday on the Wheel of the Year, marking the sacred union of the god and goddess with a fiery, passionate, and festive energy.

Oh I must pass nothing by
Without loving it much,
The raindrop try with my lips,
The grass with my touch;

For how can I be sure
I shall see again
The world on the first of May
Shining after the rain?

—Sara Teasdale, "May Day"

CHAPTER ONE

My trouble always begins in the most innocent of places. I was in the back of my friend Mila's New Age gift shop, Moonstone Treasures, intently examining a bowlful of polished stones, when her bubbly, tinkling laugh carried from the front of the store. I peeked around a row of shelves to see Mila chatting at the checkout counter with a nice-looking guy I had never seen before. He wore a loose-fitting fatigue jacket over a brown T-shirt. Judging from the laugh lines around his eyes and the silver glints in his dark blond hair, I guessed him to be in his early forties.

I ducked behind the shelves and resumed my quiet browsing. As usual, I tried not to draw too much attention to myself when shopping at Moonstone. Since it was Saturday morning—and a wet and chilly April morning at that—I was fairly certain I wouldn't see any other lawyers. But if I did happen to bump into any clients or acquaintances, I had my excuse at the ready: I would say I was trying to find a gift for my twelve-year-old niece. No one needed to know the real reason for my visit to Moonstone Treasures—that I was searching for the last ingredient I needed for the magic spell I planned to cast at the stroke of midnight tonight. No, that would never do. My Wiccan religious practices were my own business and no one else's.

"Keli!"

I jumped at the sound of my name.

"Keli, can you come over here for a minute? Maybe you can help."

I closed my eyes and allowed myself a brief sigh, then I came out from behind the shelter of the shelves. "What's up?" I asked, as I tentatively approached the pair.

"Erik is trying to sell these books." Mila lifted a stack of five hardcover books, the sleeves of her peasant blouse fluttering back to reveal colorful bangles on both of her wrists. "As much as I'd like to, I don't buy used books for Moonstone. But I remembered you know someone who does, don't you?"

I nodded. "Sure. T.C. Satterly. He deals primarily in rare books, but not exclusively." I tilted my head to read the titles on the counter: *Dark Secrets of the Occult*; *Rise of the Golden Dawn*; *The Shamanic Way*; *Old Spells for a New Age*; and *Fairies, Sprites, & Other Magical Creatures*. "He might be interested in these. I can ask him if you'd like. I'm actually heading that way next. I have an errand near his bookstore."

"Oh, yeah?" said Erik. "Think I could catch a ride with you? My car is in the shop and my buddy Billy dropped me off here. I have a few hours to kill before he can pick me up again. I live over in Fynn Hollow, so I don't know a whole lot of people here in Edindale."

"Um . . ." I hesitated and glanced at Mila.

She clapped her hands together and beamed. "How serendipitous! I love it. Erik, would you excuse us for one second? I just remembered something I have to show Keli."

Feeling confused, but not too surprised considering Mila's spontaneity, I followed her through the tinkling, beaded curtain into her divination parlor in the back room. "What is it?" I asked, looking around.

"Oh, there's nothing. I just didn't want to put you on the spot. Would you mind giving Erik a ride to the bookstore? He's an awfully sweet guy, and I'd like to help him out. Plus, it's too perfect that you're heading there anyway. As I always say, everything happens for a reason."

I had to smile. She and a whole host of other people say everything happens for a reason. But I trusted her instincts. "Okay, sure. It's no problem."

We returned to the front where Erik stood flipping through one of his old books. His face lit up when I agreed to give him a ride. Of course, I could have pointed out that it would have been a short walk for him to the bus stop, then a short ride to the old business district. But, as it happened, it was raining buckets outside—April showers in power spray mode—and I was feeling charitable. I even offered to share my umbrella with the guy after Mila had rung up my purchase and he had shoved his books into a recycled plastic shopping bag. Since he was taller than me, Erik held the umbrella. We dodged puddles and laughed at the futility of trying to stay dry in the midst of the sideways rain shower. As we dried off in the confines of my car, I had the fleeting thought that my live-in boyfriend might not appreciate the humor of the situation.

Nah. Wes trusted me. Besides, there was nothing to be jealous about.

Starting up the car, I flicked on the windshield

wipers and looked over at Erik. "Did your books stay dry?"

He peeked into his bag. "Yeah, thank goodness. I kind of hate to sell these, but I need the money. Anyway, I haven't read most of them in ages. Not since I was a much younger man, trying to find the right path for me."

We stopped at a stoplight, and I spared another glance at him. He flashed me a crooked smile. "I'm a Druid, in case you were wondering—land lover and follower of the Celtic Virtues. How about you?"

"Me? Oh, I'm a . . . Wiccan. I practice solo, sort of my own brand, rather than any particular tradition."

Did I really just say that? I could count on one hand the number of people who knew I was Wiccan. Well, make that two hands now, counting Erik. There was something about him that made me feel comfortable opening up.

"I've studied Wicca," he said. "It's pretty similar to Druidry. We follow the Wheel of the Year, too. In fact, my ex-girlfriend is a Witch." He chuckled. "I mean that in the nicest possible way, even though she hasn't been very nice to me. It's her fault I'm broke. She hexed me."

"She hexed you?"

"Yeah, that's kind of her specialty. I should have known better than to cross a Witch who makes her living dealing in curses and dark magic."

I glanced at him to see if he was joking. He stared straight ahead, a somber expression on his face. "First, I was laid off from my job," he continued. "Then, just when I had a line on a new job, my car broke down. So, I missed the interview."

"Bad luck," I said sympathetically.

Erik shook his head. "Bad mojo. I knew it was

Denise's spellwork when the first dead bird appeared on my doorstep. That's so like her."

"The *first* dead bird? How many have there been?"

"Just two so far. I'm going to have to go see her and pay back the money I owe her. Hopefully, that's all she wants."

I pulled into a parking spot in front of Satterly's Rare Books and cut the engine. "Here we are. It looks like the rain is letting up. Maybe your luck is starting to turn around."

Erik grinned at me. "Well, it was certainly lucky meeting you. Thank you for the ride."

We got out of the car and stood for a moment on the sidewalk. I peered in the window of the bookstore and saw my old friend, T.C. Satterly, perched on his stool behind the counter. He appeared to be flipping through a graphic novel. He always did strike me as someone who would be more at home selling comics than rare books. I smiled as I made out the C.S. Lewis quote printed on the T-shirt straining over T.C.'s ample midsection: EATING AND READING ARE TWO PLEASURES THAT COMBINE ADMIRABLY. I turned back to Erik. "That's T.C. He's a good guy. I'm sure he'll help you if he can. I'd stop in and say hi, but I need to get going to the civic center. I want to make sure I catch the community director before she leaves for lunch." I gave Erik a little wave and started to leave.

"Hey, are you going to the Beltane Fire Festival?"

I paused, confused. "The one in Scotland?"

He laughed. "No, a little closer than that. It's at a private nature sanctuary outside Craneville. It's loads of fun. My Druid fellowship is leading the drum circle this year. There will be a maypole ritual, of course, and a bonfire. Lots of good food and music, too."

I knew Beltane, otherwise known as May Day, was only two weeks away, and that many Pagans celebrated with bonfires. After all, the word *Beltane* came from the Celtic word *Bel-Fire*, referring to the bright fire of Bel, the god of light. But as a solitary practitioner, I usually stuck with candles or torches to honor the start of the bright half of the year.

"I don't usually attend public rituals—"

"Everyone's friendly," he said. "But it can be kind of tricky to find the place if you've never been. If you give me your email address, I'll send you directions." He pulled out his phone and looked at me expectantly.

I opened my mouth to protest, then shrugged. "I doubt if I can make it, but you can send me the info." I gave him my email address, then we shook hands and parted.

I took off down the sidewalk thinking it wasn't likely I'd ever see the out-of-town Druid again. By the time I reached the civic center, a sprawling two-story brick building that housed a banquet hall, recreation facilities, and several meeting rooms, my mind had turned to my job and the presentation I was scheduled to give that evening. Since I had opened my own law office at the start of the year, I was trying to be more visible in the community. I needed to actively seek new clients and promote my services—a responsibility that was proving to be much more time-consuming than I had anticipated. As much as I enjoyed working with clients and handling their legal matters, I didn't exactly relish the idea of spending my Saturday evening giving a lecture on estate planning and will preparation.

Stop complaining, I told myself. *You're your own boss now. Put on your big girl pants and play the part already!*

I found the community director, Chelsea Owen, in her office on the second floor. I gave her the handouts I had prepared and confirmed the details for the presentation that evening. Nearly forty people had preregistered, which, Chelsea assured me, was an impressive number. She then showed me the meeting space and explained the room's technology system. After testing the microphone and projection screen, I thanked her and headed for the exit. I was almost to the door when I heard a noise behind me. Then someone touched my shoulder, and I jumped.

"Whoa, there! I didn't mean to scare you."

I whirled around and found myself face-to-face with Erik the Druid. He pushed his sandy hair away from his eyes and gave me a sheepish grin. "Sorry about that. I wanted to catch you before you left."

"Oh. Okay. What's up? Did T.C. buy your books?"

"He did! And I have you to thank for that. He said he normally offers store credit for used books that aren't particularly valuable, but he made an exception since I'm a friend of yours."

"That's nice." Inside I was thinking, *A friend of mine? We only just met.*

"Unfortunately, I'm in a bit of a jam now," Erik went on. "My friend Billy called and said he can't come back for me. None of my other friends are answering their phones, and I can't get a taxi to drive me out to Fynn Hollow. Of course, ride-sharing services haven't made it to Edin County yet. I hate to impose, but is there any chance you have time . . . ?" He trailed off, apparently too embarrassed to finish the question.

Time? Time was the one thing most lacking in my life lately. I started to shake my head, but then I remembered something. "Fynn Hollow is on Rural Route 17, isn't it?"

"Yeah. It's only about fifteen miles from here. Pretty drive, too." He batted his eyelashes, making me laugh.

"I have a client who lives out that way," I said. I knew it was difficult for Mrs. Millhorn to leave her house, and I didn't have access to a courier anymore. Use of a messenger service was just one of the perks I'd lost by leaving the firm. I had to be more frugal now. Every dollar spent on my business was a dollar out of my own pocket. "I told her I'd bring her some papers I need her to sign. I've been carrying them in my briefcase for the past few days." I checked my watch. "If we go now, I can make this work."

"Thanks! You're the best."

We exited the civic center and headed toward my car. We hadn't gotten very far when a gust of wind shook the branches of the boulevard trees, spraying our faces with a stream of water droplets. We stopped in our tracks and laughed as we wiped ourselves off.

"Mother Nature will not be ignored," Erik joked.

"She can't accuse *me* of ignoring her," I retorted. "Before the rain rolled in this morning, I was barefoot in the woods, welcoming the sun's first rays." Once more, I surprised myself at my openness with this guy. Mentioning a nature ritual wasn't something I'd do with most people I'd known for years, let alone someone I'd just met.

Erik gave me an approving smile. Then he turned his head and sniffed the air. Someone had opened the door of the diner we happened to be passing, releasing the tantalizing scent of salty French fries.

"This place is supposed to have good Portobello sandwiches. I'd love to treat you, only I don't have any spare cash . . ." He trailed off with a sigh, as he rubbed his stomach.

I checked my watch again. "You know what? Let's pop in and grab a bite. It's on me."

"You sure you have time?"

"I'll make time. I don't function very well when I skip meals."

During lunch, Erik regaled me with stories of his pilgrimage to Stonehenge and a shamanic vision quest that led him to pursue a career in the healing arts. Before I could ask him what that meant, the check came, and I realized we should get going. This day was getting away from me.

As we left the restaurant, I called Mrs. Millhorn to let her know I was coming. A short while later, we finally pulled up to her charming old farmhouse on a gravel lane about a mile off the highway. Erik waited while I went inside to take care of business. Of course, everything took longer than expected. I emerged from the house twenty minutes later with the signed papers in one hand and a bunch of cut tulips in the other. My clients tend to be very sweet people.

"At least that's one less item on my never-ending to-do list," I said, as I handed Erik the flowers.

Regarding them thoughtfully, he remarked, "'And 'tis my faith that every flower enjoys the air it breathes.'"

I faced him in surprise.

He shrugged. "I read it someplace."

"You read it in a poem by Wordsworth." I'd read lots of poetry in college. It was rare to encounter anyone else who remembered those old lines. *Interesting guy,* I thought, as I shifted into reverse and returned to the highway.

The sky had cleared, allowing the afternoon sun to cast a pleasant light on the newly sprouted fields and colorful wildflowers along the side of the road. To make conversation, I asked Erik about his friend Billy who had driven him to Edindale.

"So, he just left you high and dry, huh? That doesn't seem very nice."

"Well, it wasn't really his fault. He had to bail out our other friend, Viper."

"Viper?"

Erik snickered. "It's a nickname, based on his power animal. Lately, he's been short on power, though. Viper is another victim of Denise's curses—Denise is the ex-girlfriend I was telling you about. Viper was pulled over this morning for speeding, even though he swears his speedometer showed he wasn't. It was his third strike. On top of that, he was busted for possession of weed."

"Wait a minute. So, when you said Billy had to 'bail out' Viper, you meant that literally?"

"Yep."

Nice friends. "So, Erik, how long have you known Mila?"

"Who?"

"Mila. Mila Douglas? Owner of Moonstone Treasures?"

"Oh, I didn't know that was her name. I've been in the shop only a couple times."

Suddenly I felt a strange sinking sensation in the pit of my stomach, and my earlier warm feelings toward Erik rapidly cooled. Wasn't he a friend of Mila's? I could have sworn . . . If he wasn't, then that meant I was giving a ride to a complete stranger. On a lonely country road. How could I have made such a dumb mistake? That was so unlike me. Usually I was much more cautious.

It was all Mila's fault.

I trusted her like a sister. After all, she was a Wiccan High Priestess and natural-born psychic, not to mention a close friend. Of course, she was also friendly with everyone she met and always eager to be of service. In hindsight, I probably shouldn't have been so quick to assume the stranger in her shop was anything more than a pleasantly charming customer in need.

I peeked at Erik, who was drumming his fingers on the dashboard, oblivious to my sudden nervousness. Luckily, we were nearing the village. We passed a cluster of signs advertising Fynn Hollow's attractions, which included a covered bridge, a dairy farm with an ice cream stand, a stable offering horseback riding lessons, a winery, and several churches. Another small sign informed us the population was 4,100.

"Which way?" I asked, as we stopped at a four-way intersection.

"Go on into town and take a left at the first stoplight. I'm going to have you drop me at Denise's place. I want to pay her back as soon as possible, so she'll lift the hex."

I followed the directions he gave me and soon pulled up in front of a neat one-story ranch featuring bright purple shutters with crescent moon cutouts. The astronomy theme continued with the moon-and-stars wind chimes hanging on the front porch and the star-speckled purple forsythia twig wreath on the front door. The whole place had a whimsical air—in stark contrast to my image of Denise as a vengeful practitioner of the dark arts.

Once again, Erik turned to me in the front seat. "Do you mind coming in with me? I could use a buffer."

I hesitated, torn between a sudden impatience to be rid of the likable-yet-pesky stranger—and my piqued curiosity about this woman who cursed people.

"It will only take a minute," he promised. "Then I'll walk home from here and you can get back to Edindale." He flashed me another one of his engaging smiles.

I caved. "Okay. But just for a minute."

I followed him to the front door and stood back as he rang the bell. When there was no answer, he rang it again and rapped on the door.

"Guess she's not home," I said, stating the obvious.

"All the better," said Erik. He reached down, tipped up a flowerpot, and peeled off the key that was taped to the bottom. "I'll leave her the money with a note."

He unlocked the door, and we went inside. "Are you sure this is okay?" I looked around. The small entryway opened to a living room-dining room combo overstuffed with mismatched furniture, assorted knickknacks, and several unframed oil paintings leaning against the walls. "Is Denise an artist?"

"She dabbles." Erik went into the kitchen and helped himself to a can of soda from the fridge. "Want a drink?"

"No, thanks." I knew I should get going, but instead I kept looking around, trying to get a sense of

Denise from her decorating choices and refrigerator magnets. What kind of a modern witch used magic to curse people? It was unethical, an abuse of the famous Wiccan moral code to "harm none."

I picked up a painted skull to examine the intricate symbols drawn all over it. In the process, I accidentally knocked over a stack of books. "Darn it!" I replaced the skull and straightened the books, while Erik sat down on the sofa and took a pad of paper and pen from an end table drawer.

Suddenly, he looked up. "Do you smell that?"

As soon as he said it, I noticed a pungent odor in the air. "It smells like bleach," I said. "Or ammonia. Or . . . both?"

Erik jumped up and raced down the hall, with me at his heels. He stopped short at a bathroom, which was dark and empty, then turned to look at a closed door on the other side of the hall.

"Is that her bedroom?"

"No. Her bedroom's the next one. This is her workroom." Erik opened the door. The acrid odor hit our senses like a bulldozer. We backed away, coughing. Then, Erik took a deep breath, pulled his T-shirt up over his mouth and nose, and rushed inside.

Through watering eyes, I peeked around the doorway. Erik was opening the windows as wide as they would go. A strong breeze billowed the curtains, helping to reduce the noxious fumes. I entered the room to see if I could help. In an instant, I took in the room's disarray. Some of the clutter, such as the towering stacks of magazines, excessive floor pillows, and multicolored candles on every surface, seemed to be more evidence of Denise's pack rat tendency. But the tipped-over ladder-back chair and spilled potion bottles indicated that something was amiss.

Then Erik cried out. "Denise!"

I looked to where he was staring and clapped my hand over my mouth. On the floor behind the table was the body of a young woman. She was curled up in a fetal position, her face frozen in a contorted mask of pain. Erik ran over and felt for a pulse, but I knew it was no use.

It was clear—Denise was dead.

CHAPTER TWO

Erik pushed back Denise's purple-streaked dark hair and shook her gently, as if he could wake her up. I walked over and put my hand on his arm. "We need to get out of here and call the police."

He looked up at me and nodded. Then he stood and started to lift the overturned chair.

"Leave it, Erik," I said. "Don't touch anything."

Unfortunately, I had come across more than one crime scene in my time. While it was quite possible Denise's death was an accident, something told me there was more here than met the eye. Maybe it was the position of the body, which made me think she must have ingested something that gave her a horrible stomach pain—rather than inhaled toxic fumes as I first assumed. Or maybe it was the fact that the tarot cards spread across the table faced away from Denise's chair, as if there had been another person sitting across from her.

I reached for Erik's hand to lead him out of the room. As I did, I took one more glimpse of the poor woman on the floor. That's when I noticed that her hands weren't empty. Clutched between her fingers was some sort of card. Carefully, I crouched down for a closer look. It appeared to be an oracle card, though not from any deck I had ever seen. The image on the card depicted a Viking. I made a mental note of the picture, then turned back to Erik and nudged him out the door.

Once we were outside, Erik leaned over and put his hands on his knees. He took a few gulping breaths of air. I felt a little woozy myself.

"Let's walk over there," I said, pointing to a flowering redbud tree.

He nodded and followed me to the edge of the front yard. We both pulled out our phones. While Erik called 9-1-1, I turned my back and called my boyfriend. He didn't pick up, so I had to leave a message.

"Wes, you're not going to believe this. I had to run to Fynn Hollow, and I'm at this lady's house, and she's *dead.*" My words came out in a tangled rush. I knew Wes would have a million questions. I had quite a few myself. "Anyway, the cops are on the way, so I'll probably be home late."

I hung up and took a deep breath before making my next phone call, to a colleague at my old law firm. I winced as I punched in his number. "Crenshaw Davenport, the Third," I said, under my breath, as the phone rang. "A suitable name for a guy who fancies himself a Regency gentleman—even though he's as American as I am."

Crenshaw and I had made partner together—a role that suited him well but only gave me heartburn. I had tried to tell myself it was because he had no social life—unless you counted business dinners and networking events. Crenshaw lived and breathed work, whether it was his law practice or his amateur acting gigs. I, on the other hand, had found life as a partner oppressive and stifling. Too often I was frazzled and crunched for time.

Kind of like now. There was no way I was going to make it back to Edindale in time to go home, change clothes, and arrive at the civic center before 7:00.

Crenshaw's resonant voice cut into my worried thoughts. "Ms. Milanni. To what do I owe this pleasure on a Saturday afternoon?" Whether he was being genuine or snarky, I had no idea. Sometimes I wondered if he even knew himself.

"Hello, Crenshaw. I need to ask you a really big favor." Without giving him the specifics, I told him I was tied up handling an out-of-town emergency. I had just finished explaining the details of my lecture when a police car zoomed down the street and screeched to a halt right behind my car.

"Is that a police siren I hear?" Crenshaw asked. "Is everything all right?"

"Oh, yes," I said quickly. "Everything's fine. Just a little matter I need to attend to. Thanks for covering for me tonight. I owe you one."

I hung up and wrung my hands as I watched Erik lead two cops into Denise's house. "How do I get myself into these situations?" I muttered. I hugged my arms against the wind, which had suddenly turned chilly.

"This can't be good," said a voice behind me. I spun around to see a pale woman with raven hair and heavy eyeliner. She appeared to be a few years older than me, maybe just shy of forty, and wore a black leather jacket and artfully torn blue jeans.

"No," I said, agreeing with her. "It's not."

Just then, the coroner arrived, so identified by a placard on the side of his brown sedan. I was grateful. This saved me from having to break the news of Denise's death to the black-haired woman—or to any of the other neighbors who had started trickling out of their homes up and down the street.

But the woman didn't appear terribly upset. "How did it happen?" she asked.

"I don't know. We found her on the floor."

"So, she finally went too far," the woman commented philosophically. She stared at the gaping front door the coroner had just entered. "I'm not surprised. It's a wonder it didn't happen sooner."

"What do you mean?"

"Some people call it karma. What goes around comes around. It's the threefold law: what you put out comes back to you times three—if you're not careful, that is. Denise messed around with some dark energies. Obviously, it came back to bite her."

"Did you know her well?" I asked, thinking it seemed mighty callous to speak of the recently departed in that way.

She tilted her head. "Well enough. We've been neighbors for a couple years." The woman turned to face me and stretched her mouth into a grim smile. "I'm Thorna, by the way."

"Keli," I responded. "I'm . . . with Erik."

Thorna gazed at me with a curious look and might have said more, if she wasn't distracted by the appearance of an agitated young woman hurrying up the sidewalk. The girl wore a bright yellow slicker and polka-dot galoshes. Her strawberry-blond hair was pulled into a messy ponytail at the top of her head.

"What's all this?" asked the newcomer in a loud, high-pitched voice. "Has Denise been revealed as the fraud she is? Did someone press charges?"

Just then another police car arrived. The officer who stepped out, a burly man with a thick mustache, was buttoning up his jacket as if he had put it on only moments ago. He went into the house, then came out a minute later and went back to his car where he opened his trunk and retrieved a megaphone and a clipboard. After blowing into the megaphone a couple times, he spoke at full volume. "Okay, people! Everybody, and I mean everybody, line up over here. Be ready with your I.D. if you have it on you. Otherwise, give me your name and address."

So, the police must also think the death is suspicious.

Before I could take a single step, a dozen people had lined up to speak with the officer. First in line was the brightly clad woman who had called Denise a fraud. From what I could tell, she seemed to be asking more questions than answering them. Suddenly, she let out a wail and dropped to her knees. The officer patted her shoulder awkwardly.

"Poor Poppy," said Thorna. "I better go help console her."

Thorna left me standing alone under the tree. I made a move to join the crowd on the sidewalk, when I noticed a rusty old Camaro rolling slowly up the street. The two men in the front seat stared at the scene in front of Denise's house. Then the car pulled into an adjacent driveway, turned around, and left. As I stared after them, I noticed the man in the passenger seat had his arm crooked out of the open window. Coiled around his forearm was a vivid green snake tattoo.

Must be Billy and Viper, I guessed. Once again I marveled at what shady friends Erik seemed to have. *And he seemed so nice and normal himself.* I looked at my watch. Speaking of friends, I was supposed to check in on one of my own at some point today. Farrah Anderson, my fun-loving, adventure-seeking BFF, broke her ankle in a skiing accident during a recent trip she took up north. She had been hobbling around on crutches for the past two weeks, so I promised I'd go grocery shopping for her this weekend. Instead, here I was in a stranger's front yard waiting for my turn to give a witness statement to one of Fynn Hollow's finest.

Erik came out of the house and called me over. "The cops want to talk to you inside."

I sighed and nodded. Returning to the dead woman's house gave me the heebie-jeebies. Still, I was anxious to give my statement and be done with the whole mess.

It was nearly dark when I turned onto Springfield Lane and parked my car along the curb. I grabbed my briefcase and purse from the backseat and headed toward my cozy two-story brick town house. I paused on the sidewalk and breathed in the fresh, damp air, laden with the sweet scent of the honeysuckle taking over my neighbor's shrubbery. After the afternoon I'd had, the peace and quiet of my neighborhood was comforting, even with the distant cheers and yells from a baseball game over at Fieldstone Park.

My mood improved even more at the sight of

my sexy, dark-haired boyfriend standing in the open doorway. He wore indigo jeans and a faded button-down shirt rolled up at the sleeves. His black eyebrows narrowed in a slight frown.

"You would not believe the day I had," I said, kicking off my shoes. I went to the kitchen and poured myself a glass of iced tea, then turned to Wes with a hopeful, slightly nervous smile.

"Your text was pretty vague," he said. "You gave some guy a ride to Fynn Hollow and ended up finding a dead body? Who was this guy? And what about your talk at the civic center?" He looked pointedly at the digital clock on the microwave, which ticked over to 7:20.

"I got Crenshaw to cover for me." I set down my glass and approached Wes. He leaned against the doorjamb with his arms folded across his chest. "Look, please don't give me a hard time. I feel bad enough as it is. I didn't want to miss that talk. I would have much rather answered questions about trusts and estates than about finding a dead woman on the floor of her house. It was awful."

He immediately softened and pulled me into his arms. He held me close and rubbed my back. *Now that's more like it.*

After a moment, he pulled back and searched my face. "Who was she, the woman who died?" he asked. "How did it happen that you found her? Were you . . . led to her? Like, in a supernatural way?"

"Hmm. I hadn't really thought of that. She was a Witch, though I don't know if she was Wiccan. It was really kind of a bizarre turn of events that led me there."

We sat down at the kitchen table for a dinner of reheated leftovers, and I told him everything. The muscles in his face twitched when I explained about the second time I agreed to give Erik a ride. And when I got to the part about following Erik inside an empty house by myself, Wes clenched his jaw so hard I was afraid he would break a tooth.

To his credit, he didn't scold me. He didn't have to. I knew I had been reckless. I wondered if all the extra hours I was putting in at my new job were beginning to take their toll. Was I overdoing it so much that my judgment was impaired?

I pushed back from the table and took my plate to the sink. "I'm going to take a bath and then go to my room for a bit."

Wes looked over at me and nodded. "Yeah, all right." He knew what I meant when I said "my room." While the bedroom—like the rest of the house—was ours to share, the spare room had become my personal haven. It was where I kept my altar and Wiccan supplies—and where I cast my most private, indoor spells. I was itching to cast one now.

First, however, I retreated to the bathroom where I lit some candles and drew a warm bath. Then I gathered some items from beneath the sink: a square of cheesecloth, a piece of twine, and assorted dried herbs. In a few practiced motions, I fashioned an herbal sachet to infuse the water with magical properties. Lavender, chamomile, and calendula were all good for relaxation, healing, and cleansing—both physically and psychically. After what I'd seen today, I needed a good psychic cleansing.

With the tub full and steaming, I tossed in a handful

of Epsom salts. Using the first two fingers of my right hand, I swished the water in a circular motion, and murmured a blessing:

Mother Goddess, bless this water,
That it may purify, heal, and cleanse my being.
Extract all negative energies,
And bring me to a state of clarity and peace.
So mote it be.

I stepped into the warm, fragrant water and took a deep breath in and out. After several more calming breaths, I reached for a bar of soap. As I washed, I envisioned the suds capturing up any negative energies, so that by the time I pulled the plug it was easy to imagine my stress and worry flowing down the drain with the bathwater. I toweled off, slipped on a robe, and headed to the altar room.

My black cat, Josie, followed me in. She'd lived with us for only six months, but I felt I'd known her forever. She had the run of the house, but seemed most comfortable in this room. I often found her curled up on the quilt-covered bed or perched on the wide windowsill above the altar. Now, she watched me with apparent curiosity, as if she knew something was up.

"You're right, Josie," I said. "Today was not what I expected. Not at all."

I glanced at the Moonstone Treasures shopping bag I'd set on the chair beside the door. It could wait. I wasn't feeling up to casting the midnight abundance spell I had planned oh-so-many hours ago.

Was it just this morning that I had happily browsed among the crystals in the back of Mila's store?

I shook my head. *No.* Abundance wasn't what I needed right now. To cap off my ritual bath, I opted for a healing spell instead—along with a peace prayer for the recently departed and her family.

Given how tired I was, I conducted the short version of casting a circle—I picked up my wand, flicked my wrist, and used my imagination to conjure a shimmering, silvery sphere all around me. Then I placed the wand on the right side of the altar next to a small statue of the Green Man, a Pan-like figure with a face of leaves, and placed my chalice on the left side next to a statue of the Goddess Diana. I lit a white candle in the center and raised my hands in supplication.

> *Goddess and God, I stand here in sorrow*
> *For pain, for death . . . a girl's lost tomorrow.*
> *In the midst of such sadness, grant solace and ease.*
> *By your power, send light, love, and peace.*

I dropped my arms and pressed my palms together, as I continued my appeal.

> *Bring peace and healing to the ones left behind.*
> *Bless family and friends, soothe their hearts and*
> *   their minds.*
>
> *Bring peace and healing to the one who is gone.*
> *Bless Denise. Free her spirit, guide her soul,*
> *Help her to move on.*

I paused, staring at the flame, as I contemplated the death of this woman I didn't know. I didn't know her, or Erik, or any of the people who had gathered at her home. But I did know death. I had seen it before. Almost without thinking, I tacked on an addendum to my prayer:

Where darkness has fallen, bring truth to light.
Where evil was done, bring justice and might.

I brought my hands to my heart and let my eyelids fall closed. Almost immediately I found myself in the midst of a dreamlike vision.

I was in a dark, empty room. The walls were moving, like undulating waves. Upon closer inspection, they appeared to be the heavy velvet curtains of an opera house. I turned and noticed something in the center of the stage—a raised coffin. It was open but not empty. I approached with tentative steps and beheld a woman in repose, with her arms folded peacefully, like Snow White in her poisoned sleep. I fixated on the woman's flowing skirts of purple and silver gauze, and I understood that this was Denise. Fighting back fear, I forced myself to look at her face—only, I couldn't see it. She was wearing a mask, a hard, flat golden mask.

Suddenly, I realized I wasn't the only spectator in the room. From out of the shadows emerged a group of strangers holding candles. They were all wearing masks—fantastical Venetian masks, with sharp noses and gilded trim. I stared, mesmerized.

Something touched my legs. I gasped and the

vision dissolved. Looking down, I saw Josie circling my feet, mewing. I exhaled.

"It's okay, Josie. It's over now."

As I extinguished the candle and closed the circle, my mind returned to the masked strangers. And the masked dead woman. As a symbol, a mask left no room for misunderstanding. It meant secrets and deception. It meant Denise had been hiding something. And so were the people around her.

CHAPTER THREE

The next morning I awoke to the smell of freshly brewed coffee and sizzling bacon and smiled. It was kind of ironic that the scent of bacon should make me happy, I mused. As an ethical vegan, I never touched the stuff myself. But it was still a homey smell. And it reminded me that, for almost eight months now, I shared a home with the man I love.

I tied on a short, satin robe and padded downstairs to the kitchen. Wes was shredding potatoes for hash browns and bobbing his head to the rock music blaring from his i-Pad speaker. I turned it down and wagged my finger in a teasing way.

"You're gonna have the neighbors knocking on our door again."

Wes looked up. "Who? The St. Johns?"

"Of course. They have a low tolerance level for loud music, remember? They say it excites Chompy and makes him too nervous to eat."

Wes rolled his eyes. "Everything excites that pup. He's the most excitable dog I've ever met, and pugs are supposed to be mellow. It must be the way he was raised."

"True." I chuckled and poured myself some coffee. Then I prepared a bowl of granola cereal with sliced banana and almond milk and sat down to watch Wes cook. He looked so natural at the kitchen counter.

"Want me to make enough for you?" he asked, holding up a potato.

"No, thanks. I don't have much time."

Although it was Sunday, I needed to go into the office. I had made an appointment with a prospective client who couldn't come in during the week. With my business so new, I found myself making a lot of accommodations like that. I was still building my clientele and couldn't afford to turn anyone away. The thought made me check the clock. I needed to get a move on.

After a quick shower, I pulled on some white trousers and a floral blouse, applied a little makeup, and twisted my long hair into a low, loose bun. Back downstairs, I took my coffee cup to the sink and glanced at Wes, who was now editing photos on his laptop. I was starting to regret my decision to go into work. What was the point of being my own boss, if I never had any time off?

I was gathering up my things when my phone buzzed. It was a text from Farrah: Hey, busy chick, she wrote. My neighbor said she'd pick up groceries for me. You didn't already do that, did ya?

"Dang it! I suck," I said to Wes. "I was supposed to go to the store for Farrah." I texted her back: So sorry!!! I'm heading to the office, but I'll stop by later. Promise. I have lots to tell you.

Just then the house phone rang. Wes answered. A few seconds later he handed me the phone. "It's a cop," he said.

I frowned as I took the phone. This couldn't be good. The person on the line identified himself as Deputy Ike Langham. He said the county was taking over the Fynn Hollow investigation, and he wanted to ask me a few questions. He asked if I would stop by the sheriff's office sometime today, the sooner the better. I said that I would.

"Now what?" asked Wes, after I'd hung up.

"Now I need some aspirin. It's not even eight-thirty, and I already feel a tension headache coming on."

I scarcely had the words out when there was a tap at the patio door, followed by the shrill voice of Mrs. St. John. "Yoo-hoo!" she called.

"Ugh," I sighed, rubbing my temple.

"You go," said Wes. He handed me my trench coat. "I'll take care of her."

I raised an eyebrow at that, and he laughed. "I mean, I'll duly apologize and make nice and all that."

I smiled and kissed him good-bye. *Everything's fine,* I told myself, as I stepped out into the brisk morning. *I need to relax. There's nothing to worry about.*

The knot in the pit of my stomach didn't mean anything. Not a thing at all.

As it happened, Carol Peters, my new client, was half an hour late and then could stay for only twenty minutes. She was a single, working mother whose ex-husband was suing her for full custody of their children. "Between raising my kids and working two jobs," she said, "I feel like I'm stretched thinner than the elastic in my old underwear." She laughed out loud and tugged nervously at the collar of her waitress uniform.

I smiled. "It's no problem, Carol. We can chat for

a few minutes now and talk again later by phone. I
charge a flat rate for this kind of case, so you don't
have to worry about extra fees every time we speak."

She relaxed a little and handed me a copy of her
custody agreement. As she explained, ever since
her divorce a year ago, she's had primary custody
of her two school-aged kids, while her ex-husband
took them on most weekends. However, he had recently remarried and joined his new wife's church,
and now he was arguing that the kids would be better
off with him full-time.

"My kids are perfectly fine with me," she insisted.
"They're well cared for. They're happy. Their lives
were disrupted enough with the divorce last year.
They don't need to be disrupted again."

I nodded and jotted a note on my legal pad. "You
raise a good point. Usually, judges aren't inclined to
revise a previously agreed upon custody arrangement so soon without a significant change in circumstances. Has anything changed other than your
ex-husband's new marriage?"

She shook her head. "It's this new wife of his. I know
it. She's convinced him that I'm a bad influence."

"In what way?"

"Well, you know."

I stared at her. *I know?*

Her confused expression must have mirrored
my own. "I thought I mentioned it," she said. "Mila
Douglas referred me to you, because you're Wiccan,
too. My ex was never bothered about my religious
practices, but his new wife is something else. She's
the type who thinks witches consort with the devil
and such nonsense. I'm afraid of what they'll say to
the judge." She pulled at her collar again. "I can't
lose my kids, Keli. I just can't. I think I'd die."

I assured her that I'd do everything I could and briefly explained the next steps. She was in a hurry to get to her job, so she signed the retention agreement and stood up to leave. I promised to be in touch as soon as I'd drafted a response to the lawsuit. She said she had faith in me.

As soon as she left, I could only shake my head. Without knowing it, Carol had dropped quite a revelation on me. To think—I'd just been hired based on the exact thing I'd kept hidden from my colleagues my whole professional life!

I didn't have time to dwell on it. I was eager to get to my next appointment—and get it over with. As I exited the boxy brick building that housed my new office, I wondered what the local news was reporting about the murder in Fynn Hollow. I hadn't been contacted by any reporters, which was always a good sign. I pulled sunglasses from my purse and put them on against the bright sun filtering through the newly budded trees along the boulevard. *Who knows? Maybe my name won't come up at all.* I tried to garner some optimism, but that nervous feeling in my stomach refused to go away.

The sheriff's office was across the street from the courthouse, which was just a few blocks from my office. I entered the building quickly and looked around. Almost immediately, Deputy Langham came out to meet me. He shook my hand, thanked me for stopping by, and asked me to follow him.

I couldn't contain my curiosity as he escorted me through a steel door and past a warren of cubicles. "Do you have the toxicology results back yet?" I asked. "Do you think the death could have been accidental?"

He ignored my questions and led me to a small

interrogation room. Shutting the door behind him, he motioned toward a sturdy metal chair at a plain, narrow table with a scratched and marred surface. He took the chair facing me.

As I sat down, I found myself wishing I'd put on a business suit that morning and skipped the open-toed sandals. Then I might not feel at such a disadvantage with the stern officer. With his buttoned-up uniform, trim mustache, and military-style buzz cut, he gave me the impression of a general about to declare war. Either that, or a drill sergeant.

He opened a notepad and took several seconds to read whatever was written there. Then, scowling, he flipped back a page to reread something he had already read. All the while I sat there feeling increasingly on edge. Was he doing this on purpose? Finally, he looked up at me and cleared his throat. "How long have you lived in Edindale, Miss Milanni?"

"Oh, um, about eight, almost nine, years."

He nodded curtly. "What brought you here?"

"I came here for law school and decided to stay when I was offered a job at Olsen, Sykes, and Rafferty. I really liked it here. This is a lovely town."

"Mm-hmm. And when did you first meet Denise Crowley?"

"I never met her."

"You didn't know her before yesterday?"

"I didn't know her at all."

"Had you ever been to her house before?"

"No."

"What were you doing there yesterday afternoon?"

"As I told the Fynn Hollow police, I had just given Erik a ride to her house. I was dropping him off, but he invited me inside to meet Denise."

"Why is that?"

"Because, he was afraid—I mean, I guess he didn't want to be alone with her. They had recently broken up, and he thought she . . ." I trailed off. Why was I having to explain this? Shouldn't he be asking Erik these questions?

"He thought she what?" asked the deputy.

"He thought she wasn't very happy with him because he owed her money. He had sold some books in Edindale and had the money to pay her back. That's why he wanted to stop at her house."

"How long have you been seeing Erik?"

"Seeing him?"

"Dating him."

"I'm not dating him. I barely know him."

"Hmm." He flipped through his notebook again. "Apparently a couple neighbors seem to think you and he are friends."

"Oh. Well, I might have said we were friends. But we actually just met yesterday morning."

He frowned and looked at the notebook again. "Sounds like he thinks you're friends, too. He said as much to the bookstore owner. A Mr. Satterly?"

I didn't say anything. What could I say?

Langham stared at me. "Do you often give rides to men you've just met?"

I felt a flush rise up my neck and into my cheeks. I shook my head. "No. I thought Erik was a friend of a friend."

"You thought? Who did you think he was friends with?"

"Mila Douglas. She owns Moonstone Treasures. That's where I met Erik."

Langham wrote something in his notebook, presumably Mila's name. Then he stared at me again. "What time were you at Moonstone Treasures?"

I tried to think. "I got there around ten o'clock, and left a little after ten-thirty or so."

"Did you buy anything?"

"Yes. I bought—" I stopped myself. He didn't need to know about the magickal crystals and powdered High John the Conqueror root. "I bought something. Why?"

He wasn't going to let me off the hook that easily. "What did you buy?"

Suddenly, I felt my hackles raise and I sat up a little straighter. "I'm sorry. I didn't realize I was going to be treated like a suspect. I thought you just had a question or two about the statement I gave yesterday. Unless I'm being charged with something, I think I'm finished answering your questions."

My heart thrummed in my chest and my palms felt slick, but I held my ground. I knew my rights. Still, I didn't want to seem uncooperative. The last thing I wanted to do was come across as suspicious to the deputy.

"You're not being charged with anything," he said coolly. "Let's see, I do want to confirm something from your previous statement." He looked at the notebook again. "How long were you in Ms. Crowley's house before you found her body?"

I licked my lips, then internally kicked myself for acting guilty. I couldn't help it. I *felt* guilty. "About ten or fifteen minutes, I think. Erik was going to leave her a note."

"Did you touch anything while you were in there?"

"Yes. While I was waiting for Erik, I looked at some of Denise's things." I cringed, thinking how that sounded. "Only things she had on display," I hastened to add.

"Okay. We'll have to take your fingerprints to compare with all the prints found on site."

I nodded. *Terrific.*

"One other thing. Just to confirm. You were with Erik for five hours yesterday? From about ten thirty A.M. until the time he called 9-1-1 at 3:25 P.M.?"

I thought about it. *Was that right?* "Not the whole time." I mentioned my meeting with the community director at the civic center. Langham wanted to know what happened after that, and I told him about running into Erik. I explained that we had walked to my car and headed out of town, stopping off first for a quick bite of lunch. I also told him about having papers signed at my client's house.

"Seems kinda chummy for two people who just met," he commented, after writing in the notebook again. Before I could respond, he asked another question. "Was Denise expecting Erik to drop by?"

"Not that I know of."

"What do you know about Denise's line of work?"

"Nothing. I don't think Erik mentioned her job. Unless you mean—" I broke off. I didn't want to go there, but it seemed I had just been lured.

"Unless I mean what?" he prompted.

"Nothing. I don't know what she did for a living."

"Several of the neighbors said she called herself a witch and sold potions and spells and the like. Did you know about that?"

"Erik might have mentioned something like that. But I don't know anything about it."

"This Moonstone Treasures shop, where you met Erik. They sell potions and the like there, don't they?"

I took a deep breath. "Deputy Langham, I have an appointment I need to keep. I really don't think I can be of much more help to you. So, can we do the fingerprints now?"

He regarded me for a moment, then shut his notebook. "You bet. Wait here and the tech will come to you." He stood up and opened the door, then paused. "By the way, you don't have any vacations planned in the near future?"

"No," I said, bleakly.

"Good. Do me a favor and don't take any overnight trips outside the county without giving me a heads-up first."

From the sheriff's office, I retrieved my car and went straight to Farrah's apartment complex. I rang the bell and waited as she unlocked the door with some difficulty. When the door finally swung inward I saw why: she had crutches wedged under both armpits, a bottle of wine in one hand, and a wineglass in the other. She handed the bottle to me.

"She lives," she said, tapping the side of my leg with a crutch. Her normally rosy skin appeared wan, and her light golden hair was frizzy and unbrushed.

"I'm a terrible friend." I shut the door behind me and followed Farrah to her living room. "I'm so sorry. I wanted to get here a lot sooner. What's with the wine?"

"No worries," she said. "I was just bringing the wine from the kitchen to the living room when you rang. I'm having dinner in my recliner. It's where I spend most of my time lately."

I helped Farrah into her chair and looked around. "What dinner? Just the wine?"

"I have crackers, too." She pointed to a box on the coffee table.

"Oh, honey." I *tsk*ed at her. "Are you that bad off? Let me make you some food."

I opened the wine and poured Farrah a glass, then rummaged through her kitchen until I found the ingredients for Mexican beans and rice. While the stew simmered on the stovetop, I helped myself to a glass of wine and joined Farrah in the living room.

"How does your ankle feel?" I asked.

"Itchy." She tossed aside the magazine she had been perusing.

"When will the cast come off?"

"Not soon enough, but I can't really complain. It's my own dang fault I ended up this way. Luckily, I haven't had to miss too much work." As a legal software salesperson, Farrah was able to conduct a good portion of her business from home.

"But enough about me," she continued. "What's your news? Something's got you upset. I can tell by how fast you drank that glass of wine."

I looked at my empty glass and laughed without humor. "Let's eat first." I stood up to check on dinner. It was only 4:00, but I had skipped lunch, so I was famished. A few minutes later, with steaming bowls on our laps, I brought Farrah up to speed on my adventures with Erik the Druid.

"What does he look like?" asked Farrah, cutting right to the chase. "Was he so hot that you just agreed to whatever he asked without thinking?" She said it without judgment.

"No!" I made a face at her. "I mean, he's okay looking, but I wasn't swooning or anything. He's in his forties, average build. Blondish with a bit of gray." I paused, reflecting on why it was I had felt so comfortable with the man. "He was really friendly. Seemed normal. He's a Pagan and knows all about Wicca."

"Ah," said Farrah. "That explains it."

"What do you mean 'That explains it'?"

"Nothing. Just that you probably have a lot in common with him." She gave me an innocent look.

Before I could ask her just what she was implying, my phone jingled in my purse. I reached for it, expecting it to be Wes. When I saw the display, I groaned. "It's Crenshaw. He probably wants to tell me about the workshop he covered for me."

I adopted a cheerful voice when I answered. "Hi, Crenshaw! What's up?"

"Keli, I had two very interesting phone calls this afternoon. As a result, I can't help but feel you weren't entirely forthright with me yesterday."

Crap. How was it that, after six years of working side by side with this guy, he was still able to make me feel like a teenager in trouble with my parents? I could just picture his ginger-bearded chin jutting forward in that smug way of his.

"Who called you?" I asked.

"First, I heard from an acquaintance at the coroner's office, who informed me that one of my former colleagues was on the scene of a murder yesterday. Evidently, a woman had been poisoned? Then I heard from a contact at the public defender's office who had just come from the sheriff's station. She said she happened to see one Keli Milanni enter the interrogation room with the lead detective assigned to investigate said murder. I said to myself: *Keli Milanni? The same Keli Milanni who assured me yesterday that all was well?*" His voice was even, but I could tell he was perturbed. I was starting to feel annoyed myself. Crenshaw seemed to be more informed about the case than I was.

"I was going to tell you," I said defensively. "But I was a bit preoccupied."

"I'll say."

For the next five minutes, I listened to Crenshaw chide me. His attitude ran the gamut from annoyance to concern to curiosity. In the end, I managed to convince him that I was simply an innocent bystander, nothing more. When I hung up, I looked over at Farrah, red-faced.

"What was that all about?" she asked.

"Word travels fast," I said. "And the word on the street is that . . . I'm a murder suspect."

CHAPTER FOUR

Farrah pointed to the kitchen. "Go grab another bottle from the wine rack."

I obeyed, selecting another crisp white and pouring a generous amount into both of our glasses.

"Are you really a suspect?" she asked. "Or is that just the gossip?"

"I don't know. The way Deputy Langham acted, I think he thought I was hiding something."

"Why would he think that?"

I shrugged. "I was nervous. And embarrassed. And I might have gotten a little defensive when I felt his questions were getting too personal."

Farrah looked thoughtful. "I can hook you up with a good criminal attorney, but you might want to hold off on that for now. Appearances, you know."

"Oh, I know. Believe me, I know."

She assumed a reassuring expression. "I'm sure they'll find the murderer before too long. From the way you described the scene, the killer must not have been very careful."

We were both silent for a moment, each absorbed in our own thoughts. When Farrah spoke again, I knew her line of thinking had paralleled my own. We had both transitioned to detective mode.

"What do you know about the victim?" she asked.

"Nothing—except that she liked the color purple." I recalled what I had seen in her house. "Also, she painted landscapes, collected various witchy objects, and had a special workroom where she gave tarot readings and performed magic spells. Oh, and she had a habit of cursing people."

"Interesting. So, anybody she cursed is a potential suspect. Take your boy, Erik, for example, and—"

"*My* boy?"

"And the other guy. What's his name? Snakebite? Cobra?"

I laughed. "Viper."

"Right. Now there's a guy I wouldn't mind meeting."

"I'm sure he's a real prince. But about those curses. I'm not sure Denise was always the one who cast them. I got the impression that people could buy curses from her."

"She sold spells? Was she like a village witch, doling out love charms and secret potions to back-door customers?"

"I'm not sure. But this one chick who showed up yesterday called her a fraud. Her name was Poppy, I believe."

"A dissatisfied customer maybe? Sounds like another possible motive."

"Your guess is as good as mine."

"You know what you should do?" said Farrah. "You should get together with the ex-boyfriend, Erik. See what you can learn from him."

"I don't know if that's such a great idea. Langham made a big deal about me being Erik's friend. I don't want to be associated with him or his kooky pals any more than I already am."

Farrah shifted in her recliner. "Ugh. I hate being cooped up in here, helpless as a baby. How am I going to help you snoop around and tail suspicious characters?"

I smiled in spite of myself as I recalled some of our past exploits. "I don't think there's any snooping to be done this time. I need to stay out of this and let the police do their job. They'll probably catch the culprit on their own, without any help from us."

"Well, that's no fun." Farrah pouted. She grabbed a pencil from the end table and used it to scratch beneath her cast. Then she tapped the pencil on the top of her thigh. "Grab my laptop, will you? Let's look these people up. I want to see what your Druid looks like."

I hesitated for half a second, then reached for the laptop. I supposed it couldn't hurt to look. To tell the truth, I was curious to learn a little more about the guy myself.

It was nearly dusk when I left Farrah's place. As I sped down Lincoln Boulevard, my eyes kept flicking to the sky, awash in layers of purple, pink, and orange above the setting sun. It filled me with a sense of peace and serenity. In fact, it was such a breathtaking display I almost pulled over. Mother Nature always did have a way of pulling me outside of myself and my petty problems.

Farrah and I hadn't gotten very far in our attempts at Internet stalking. We found Erik's profile on a professional networking site and learned that he had been a lab technician for a pharmaceutical company for a number of years. With one click, we learned the company was recently bought out and downsized. That explained why he was laid off. No curse necessary there.

I noticed Erik looked a little neater and more clean-cut in his profile picture than when I'd met him the day before. He also appeared younger. I guessed the photo was at least ten years old. To Farrah's disappointment, we didn't find anything connecting him to Druidism or any other Pagan practices.

When we searched Denise's name, we found she had a shop on a popular online marketplace for handmade and vintage items. She sold prints of her paintings, as well as calendars, journals, and other handcrafted items—all with whimsical, witchy designs. There was nothing dark or sinister in her offerings.

I glanced in my rearview mirror and caught sight of a cop car. Suddenly, my idle reveries careened to a halt.

Shoot! I abruptly let up on the gas. "Please don't let him pull me over," I said out loud. My mind started spinning terrible possibilities.

What if the cop smells wine on my breath? I had stopped drinking an hour before leaving Farrah's place and didn't even feel buzzed, but would that matter? What if I started babbling from sheer nervousness? Would he ask me to step out of the car and walk on a line? Would he run my plates and find out I was a suspect in a murder investigation?

I cracked the window to let in some fresh air and started to tap the brake when the police car zoomed past me. The officer at the wheel didn't even look my way. I let out my breath and fanned my face.

Jeesh. I had never felt so anxious around the police. What was wrong with me?

At the next intersection, instead of turning left toward home, I turned right. I needed to speak to Mila. Ten minutes later, I parked in front of her house and pulled out my phone to give her a quick heads-up before showing up at her door. But I needn't have bothered. Before I even pressed the first button, she stepped onto her front porch and waved at me. Her sixth sense was as reliable as any telephone.

As I hurried up her front sidewalk, I saw the look of concern on her face. "I suppose you know what happened," I said.

Her worry lines deepened. "No. I only felt that you were near. What's happened?"

I felt my shoulders slump. "Got a few minutes?"

Mila led me to her cozy living room, redolent with the faint scent of patchouli and sandalwood. I sank into her velvet sofa and sighed. I was a little bummed I was going to have to repeat the whole sordid tale. This would make the fourth telling.

She sat next to me and took both of my hands in hers, wordlessly sending me a blessing. Instantly, I felt calmer and safer. Mila's intuition might not provide her with all the details, but she was an expert at picking up on moods. She knew when something was amiss—and what to do to help make it better.

"Want to hear a funny story?" I began.

She listened quietly as I told her all about mistaking Erik for a friend of hers, giving him a ride to Fynn Hollow, finding the body of his ex-girlfriend, and, ultimately, being questioned by the cops.

"Why did you make me think Erik was your friend?"

I asked. "I thought I was doing you a favor by giving him a ride."

"Oh, my. I'm so sorry. He's been in the shop a few times, and I always got a good vibe from him. I didn't mean to imply I knew him other than as an acquaintance."

"Well, now I know him a lot more than I ever wanted to," I said ruefully. "Going through a trauma together will have that effect."

"You poor thing," Mila soothed. "What a dreadful experience you had."

I paused, reflecting on her words, then decided I was done feeling sorry for myself. "It was more dreadful for the victim. Did you know her? Her name was Denise Crowley. She was a tarot reader and artist. I'd guess her to be in her early- to midtwenties."

Mila shook her head. "I don't think so. But Catrina might have known her. She's more up on the younger Pagan crowds than I am. I'll ask her in the morning." Catrina was Mila's assistant at Moonstone Treasures, as well as a member of Mila's coven.

"I'll try to stop by the shop tomorrow," I said. "I'm interested in hearing Catrina's impressions. Evidently, Denise specialized in curses. One of her neighbors implied her death might have been blowback from delving into dark magic."

"Oh, dear. You think she was attacked for being a witch?"

I considered the possibility. As Mila and I both knew, there was a lot of misunderstanding about Wicca. In spite of the strides Wiccans had made over the years in gaining public acceptance, and even being legally recognized as a legitimate religion, plenty of people still harbored fears. Mila herself had been targeted by a group of scaremongers who believed witchcraft was evil. Yet, I didn't hear that kind of rhetoric from the people who had gathered outside Denise's house.

"I don't really know what to think," I said. "Except that more than one person talked about Denise's curses."

"Ah. That's not surprising. To curse or not to curse—a question that can have Pagans arguing for hours. As you know, most Wiccans avoid baneful magic if they can help it. Ours is one of the most peaceful world religions ever practiced. On the other hand, some witches feel there are circumstances that warrant the use of a hexing spell."

"Like for self-defense, right?"

"Sometimes."

"I've heard such spells can be dangerous, because they require you to draw up so much negative energy. It would be hard not to feel the effects yourself, even if you're trying to direct it at another person."

"True. Of course, there are ways to protect yourself, but you have to know what you're doing. In general, I would advise against the use of negative magic."

I thought about Denise's cute and cluttered house and wondered how often she really worked dark magic there. Then I shook myself. Whether she did or didn't was really beside the point. The idea that her death might have been the result of a curse gone awry didn't sit well with me.

"You know," I said, "I'm all for personal responsibility. That's one of the things that first attracted me to Wicca, its emphasis on self-governance and personal accountability. But to bring up karma when a woman has been murdered . . . I mean, talk about victim blaming."

"Definitely in poor taste," Mila agreed. "People often misunderstand the principle of karma as some sort of cosmic system of justice. In fact, although the concept has many interpretations by its varied adherents, I think of it more as a teacher. We're meant to learn from our experiences, not to be punished by them."

"That makes sense. Punishment is definitely a human thing, not a spiritual thing." My mind flashed to poor Denise lying on the floor of her workroom. I remembered the Viking card in her hand and asked Mila if it sounded familiar to her.

She closed her eyes in thought. "Yes. I do recall an oracle deck that might have a Viking card. When you stop by tomorrow, we'll take a look."

I thanked her for the chat and told her good night. It wasn't until I was halfway home that I remembered Carol, my new client. I'd meant to thank Mila for the recommendation—and also kid her about referring someone to me without letting me know. And a fellow Wiccan, no less.

Oh, well. After all the talk about curses and death and retribution, it didn't seem so important anymore.

The house was dark when I got home. Wes was working late at the newspaper office, as he sometimes did when a late-day assignment had to be readied for print the following morning. I didn't mind the quiet. After talking all day, it felt good to give my voice a rest.

I puttered about the kitchen, unloading the dishwasher and getting dinner for Josie. She was good company—sweet, intelligent, and strangely inspiring. I always seemed to have fresh insights and unexpected ideas when she was around. Watching her now, I thought about the spell I had been wanting to cast. Ever since striking out on my own as a solo practitioner, I had wanted to plant the seeds of intention for my business—namely, that it would grow bountifully and be a great success. In other words, I wanted to cast an abundance spell.

But I had been putting it off. It was never the right phase of the moon or perfect day of the week. Or I didn't have the best ingredients, the right frame of mind, or enough time.

"Well, I have time now," I said to myself. Josie gave me an arch look, as if to say: *Okay, so what are you waiting for?*

I walked to the patio door and gazed out at the dark backyard. For the spell I had in mind, I wanted to plant some literal seeds in my garden. It was only a day past the new moon, so the timing was still ripe for setting intentions. And I didn't mind working in the dark. All the better for privacy and seclusion. Still I hesitated.

Maybe it was all the talk earlier about karma and unintended consequences. As the old saying goes, be careful what you wish for. What if I cast a spell for lots of new clients and ended up with more than I could handle? I could end up busier than I was before I'd left the law firm.

The jangling of the house phone interrupted my waffling thoughts. I liked to keep a landline for emergencies, but it rarely rang. When it did, it was usually either a telemarketer or my mother.

"Hello," I answered cheerily. There was silence on the other end. "Hello?" I waited a couple seconds, then hung up. As I started to walk away, the phone rang again. I answered to more silence.

"Hello!" I said loudly. "Is anyone there? I can't hear you." No response.

Exasperated, I hung up for the second time. A few seconds later, it rang again. This time, I decided to let the answering machine get it. When it picked up, I expected there to be silence once again. Instead, there was music.

I walked over to the phone and stared at the speaker. The music sounded tinny and distant, like an old music box. My skin prickled as I listened to the strange melody. It was familiar, but I couldn't place it.

When the music stopped, silence filled the room once more. I grabbed the receiver. "Who is this?" I demanded. I heard a click, then a dial tone. Immediately, I dialed *69, but the last call to my number was "unavailable."

I paced the living room for the next ten minutes, but the phone didn't ring again.

"What was that all about?" I wondered aloud.

Josie mewed in response.

I looked out the window again, but I'd lost my nerve. I didn't much feel like going outside into the darkness anymore. Instead, I got ready for bed and curled up under the covers with a good book. But first, I turned the ringer off on the house phone.

CHAPTER FIVE

The next morning, I walked to work as I often liked to do. Fieldstone Park was damp and glistening from overnight showers. Skirting puddles and dripping leaves, I followed the meandering walkway, admiring tulips, bluebells, and lily of the valley along the way. When I exited the park, I continued a couple more blocks until I reached quaint downtown Edindale, where blossoming trees of pink, white, and yellow lined the boulevards. Before I knew it, I found myself standing in front of the glass windows of the four-story building that housed the venerable mid-sized law firm of Olsen, Sykes, and Rafferty. For a moment, I felt confused. I had been so lost in thought, I'd followed a well-worn path and wound up at my old office building. I didn't work here anymore.

Footsteps clicked up the sidewalk behind me, and I heard a familiar voice. "Keli! Imagine! I was just talking about you!"

I turned to see Julie Barnes, the firm's young receptionist. A petite woman with fuchsia lipstick and trendy tortoiseshell glasses, she had always lent a lighthearted, youthful energy to the law office. She held a cardboard to-go carrier with four tall paper cups of coffee. Seeing my look of surprise, she chuckled. "Crenshaw blew up the coffeepot. I offered to make a run for the partners."

The partners. Those would be my former colleagues, Beverly, Kris, Randall, and Crenshaw. I glanced at the entry door and felt a small pang of longing. I missed the old gang.

"Going in?" asked Julie.

"Oh, no. I'm just passing by. I—Did you say you were just talking about me?"

"Yeah. First thing this morning, before I'd even turned on my computer, a guy from the sheriff's office called to ask about you. He wanted to know how long you worked here and who your boss was. Stuff like that. I transferred him to Beverly. Why do you think he was asking?" She leaned forward and gazed at me with bright eyes. Julie was always eager for the latest gossip.

I tried to keep my voice light. "Oh, it's nothing. Standard procedure. I was a witness—that is, I and another person found a woman who had died. So, you know . . ." I trailed off. There was just no good way to explain it.

"So, it's true! You were one of the friends the newspaper was talking about. You found Denise Crowley's body? I didn't even know you knew her."

"I didn't know her. I happened to be with her ex-boyfriend and . . . It's a long story. But wait. Are you saying that *you* knew her?"

"Yeah. I grew up in Fynn Hollow. Nothing like this has ever happened there. I don't think there's been a murder in, like, a hundred years. Last time a crime made the news was when somebody stole some cash from an overturned armored truck—though kids do regularly lift candy from the general store. It's like a rite of passage or something." Julie laughed. "Denise was one year ahead of me in school."

"Oh! Interesting. I didn't realize she was that young." Not that it should matter to me, but that meant Erik was dating a girl at least fifteen years younger than he.

"Well, she always dressed a little out of time, if you know what I mean. In high school, she wore gypsy skirts and beads, stuff like that. She was a little odd."

Speaking of "a little odd," I thought about the people I had seen at Denise's house. "Did you know a woman named Thorna when you lived in Fynn Hollow?"

Julie shook her head. "I don't think so. Is that her real name?"

"I'm not sure. But she's older than you anyway. How about a woman named Poppy? Or a couple of guys named Billy and Viper?"

"Yep, them I remember. They all hung out in the same crowd as Denise. Kind of an artsy, misfit sort of vibe, you know? They were nice enough, I guess. Especially Billy Jones."

Any uneasiness I'd felt before was now overtaken by curiosity. "Why especially Billy?"

"He was just real sweet and caring. He was the only black kid in his class—small town, you know. But everybody liked him. Senior year, he got into fund-raising for charities and petition drives and stuff. One week it was "save the owls," and the next it might be "cure AIDS" or "help senior citizens" or some-thing else. He meant well." Julie tapped her chin, as she thought. "He was also kinda nerdy, into cosplay and reenactments and stuff. Probably still is, as far as I know."

"What about Viper? I heard he was busted for possession recently." I said it casually, as if just passing along a little gossip.

"Doesn't surprise me. He was always a stoner, and probably the least ambitious of that group. He was harmless, though. His real name is Edward Vikers."

"And Denise and Poppy? Were they close?"

"I didn't know them well, but I think they were pretty good friends. Poppy's real name is Penelope, by the way. Penelope Sheahan. She and Denise were both into art and New Age woo woo stuff."

I grinned at her choice of words. That was one way to describe it.

"Anyway, how's the new practice going?" Julie asked. "I still can't believe you left. It's not the same without you."

"Aw, that's sweet. I miss you guys, but I'm not far away. And the practice is going fine. Speaking of which, I need to get to work. Tell everyone 'hi' for me."

I hurried off to my new digs, which were located in a much older building on a narrow side street off the square. The rust-red brick structure, a former bank, had been converted to office space a number of years ago. I'd rented one of the smallest units, but it served me well.

My door, so noted by a shiny brass nameplate, was one of the first off a short interior hallway. I unlocked it and flipped on the light in the small waiting room, which was outfitted with two flea market armchairs and a couple of small wooden tables. There

were two doors off the waiting area, one to a closet
and the other to my inner office, where I spent most
of my time.

I liked my work space, in spite of the close quarters.
As I settled in at my tidy oak desk, I surveyed the cozy
room. The wall to my left held floor-to-ceiling book
shelves, while the one on my right featured my
framed law degree, various certificates, and artistic
photos taken by Wes. A small window behind me
overlooked an alley—not the greatest view, but at
least it let in some sun. I'd placed several plants on
the cabinet beneath the window.

I took a sip of coffee from my travel mug and
opened the morning paper. News of the Fynn
Hollow homicide was on the front page. I skimmed
it quickly to get the gist, then read it a second time
more closely. The paper described Denise as a free-
lance artist who lived alone and worked from home.
It quoted some unnamed friends, who described
Denise as "sweet" and "talented." Another friend,
Poppy Sheahan, said she had gone to see Denise earlier on Saturday morning, but there was no answer to
her knock.

Or was there? I wondered what time Poppy had supposedly tried to see Denise.

There was also a statement from a neighbor,
Vanessa "Thorna" Attley, who said she didn't see or
hear anything from Denise's house, but that it wasn't
unusual for Denise to receive visitors at all hours.

*Visitors looking to buy spells or curses? Or was something
else going on?*

I read on, but didn't learn much else that I didn't
already know. The county sheriff's department was
handling the case, and they made no comment other

than to say that the investigation was ongoing—and that they were in the process of questioning a number of persons of interest.

Persons of interest. I swallowed hard. Did that include me? I could understand being questioned as a material witness, but how could I be a person of interest? As far as the public was concerned, a person of interest was basically a suspect who hasn't been formally charged. One would never aspire to be a person of interest.

I folded the newspaper and set it aside. I was being paranoid. The cops had a procedure to follow. *They have to cross all their T's, et cetera, et cetera.* I couldn't fault them for doing their job.

For the next couple of hours I busied myself with client work, including Carol's custody case. When I finally looked up, I was surprised to see that it was only 11:30. It was amazing how much I could accomplish without interruptions. On the other hand, the absence of any phone calls was not necessarily a good thing. While some of my old clients had elected to stay with me when I left the firm, most of them did not have ongoing legal issues. My work was largely transactional—real estate closings, contracts, wills, and divorce work. In other words, one and done. I was going to have to find a way to attract new clients.

I stood up, stretched, and took a little walk down the hallway outside my office. It was eerily quiet. There were shared restrooms on each floor of the two-story building and numerous offices, but I didn't see a single person. All the doors were closed and many were dark. It appeared that my fellow tenants kept odd hours. There were a few therapists, an accountant, and a couple property management companies. I had a feeling half the offices were vacant.

When I returned to my desk, I checked my voice mail, which had zero messages, and my email, which had one new message. It was from Erik Grayson. Seeing his name filled me with a weird sense of dread mixed with solidarity. Because of our shared experience on Saturday, we had a connection now. And I kind of resented it.

I opened the message and read the brief note: Can you meet me for lunch today? I'll be at the Cozy Café from 12:00 to 1:00 or so.

I hesitated, then grabbed my purse. I needed to eat anyway.

As I entered the café, I scanned the room for signs of anyone who might know me. After Deputy Langham had made such a big deal of my supposed friendship with Erik—which I had firmly denied—it would be mighty embarrassing to be seen hanging out with him.

Luckily, I didn't see any familiar faces—except for Erik's, looking so downtrodden, I immediately forgot my concerns. He was slumped in his seat and wearing the same wrinkled jacket he'd worn two days ago. He appeared to have aged since I last saw him, though he brightened slightly when he saw me. "You came! I wasn't sure if you'd see my message in time."

I sat down across from him. "How are you holding up?"

He shook his head. "Man, it's been a rough couple of days. I still can't believe Denise is gone. Even though we'd split up, I figured we'd always be friends, you know? I wanted to make things right with her. Balance the scales, so to speak."

"I'm sorry for your loss. She sounded like a really interesting person, from what I've heard."

"Yeah. She was."

We sat silently for a minute, with Erik twisting a plastic straw and me trying to convey a sympathetic presence. I didn't know what else to say. I felt sure he'd asked me to meet him for a reason, but I didn't want to press him.

A waitress brought us drinks and took our orders—salad for me and a vegetarian burrito for Erik. I wondered if he was a vegetarian and almost asked but decided against it. It seemed too inconsequential under the circumstances. I took a sip of my iced tea and waited for Erik to speak.

He raked a hand through his hair, then sat back and heaved a sigh. "This is so crazy. I'm trying to process this horrible thing that's happened, and . . . and the cops are grilling me like I did it! I was at the station till midnight that night. And the next day they came to my house with more questions. They kept looking around like they wanted to search my place, but they didn't have a warrant. It was like they were hoping I'd trip up and confess or something. Unbelievable."

"Would you like help finding a lawyer?" I asked. "I don't practice criminal law, but I know a lot of lawyers."

"Nah. I don't think I can afford one right now. Besides, I have an alibi." He gave me a halfhearted smile, and I realized he was talking about me.

"Right. Except we don't know the time of death.

She might have been killed before you and I met at Moonstone." I grimaced and looked away.

"Oh. I didn't think of that. But it doesn't matter. I'm innocent. The cops have nothing on me."

At that moment, the waitress appeared with our orders. She stopped in her tracks at Erik's last statement but recovered quickly. As soon as she left, I asked Erik the question I'd been holding back.

"Erik, do you have any theories about Denise's death? Did she have any enemies?"

"Enemies? That's such a goofy word." He stared at his lunch plate as if lost in thought. "Denise could be . . . difficult. She was moody and opinionated. She argued with people, even her friends. Not long ago she had a falling-out with her best friend."

"Who was her best friend?"

"A girl named Poppy Sheahan. They went to school together."

I recalled that Poppy was the one who had called Denise a fraud, and then seemed upset when she learned Denise was dead. That made sense if they'd once been best friends. But if they were no longer friendly, why would Poppy have gone over to her house on Saturday morning? "What was the falling-out over?"

Erik shrugged. "Who knows? Like I said, Denise could be unreasonable. But I can't think of anyone who would consider her an enemy."

"The newspaper reported that a neighbor mentioned people coming and going from Denise's house at all hours. Do you know why that would be?"

Before Erik could answer, my phone buzzed in my purse. "Oh, sorry."

"That's okay." He waved away my apology. "Go ahead and take it."

Erik stuck a fork in his burrito and took a large bite. I saw that the call was from Wes, so I answered.

"Hi, there," I said. "What's up?"

"Hey, babe. Just checking in. I have a break before my next photo assignment. Have you had lunch yet?"

"Actually, I'm at lunch now. Sorry."

"Where are you? I can come and join you."

"Oh. Well, I'm at the Cozy Café, but I'm not alone."

"Got it. Client meeting?"

"Um, no. I'm having lunch with . . . Erik."

"Who?"

"You know. Erik Grayson?"

At this point, I could feel my face growing red hot. Erik looked up and regarded me curiously. Why was this so awkward?

"I have no idea who you're talking about," said Wes. Then it must have dawned on him. "Wait. Is that the guy you took to Fynn Hollow? The one whose girlfriend was murdered?"

"Yeah," I said shortly. "Anyway, I gotta go, hon. I'll talk to you later, okay?" I hung up and dropped the phone into my purse. I forked my salad and avoided meeting Erik's eyes. When I finally looked up, he appeared to be amused.

"So," he began, "there's something I wanted to tell you."

"Yes?"

"When the police were questioning me, they asked about you a couple times."

"That's not surprising. They questioned me, too, you know. What did they say?"

"Well, they were on a fishing expedition, like I

said. They wanted to know if we were a couple and wondered if there might be some jealousy between you and Denise."

"You're kidding. Where did they get that idea?"

"I assured them they were barking up the wrong tree. Although . . ." He trailed off, leaving me hanging.

"What?"

Just then, the café door opened, and a young guy entered and looked around. Erik stood up and waved at him. "Over here!" he called. To me, he said, "That's Billy. He's my ride today."

Billy approached and smiled at me. "You must be Keli. How nice to meet you."

Erik moved over to make room, and Billy sat down. He was a pleasant-looking guy, with dark brown, neatly trimmed hair, bright eyes behind black-framed glasses, and dimples when he smiled. He wore chinos and a navy polo shirt featuring the logo of a local electronics store.

"Do you have to get to work?" asked Erik.

"I've got a bit of time," said Billy. "You can finish your lunch."

"Thanks, man. If you ever get tired of fixing computers, you can always become a chauffeur. You already drive Viper everyplace, and now me."

"Viper doesn't have a car?" I asked.

"Oh, he has a car, but no license. At least, not at the moment."

"Ironic, isn't it?" said Billy. "A mechanic who can't drive."

For the next few minutes, we made small talk. I recalled Julie describing Billy as a nice, do-gooder type, and the description seemed accurate. When I told Billy I knew Julie from my old firm, his face lit up.

"Julie, Julie, Julie. She was such a cool girl. Tell her hi for me next time you see her."

Erik laughed. "Was she one of the popular kids? Amazing she remembers you." He grinned at his friend and winked at me. "I love him dearly, but Billy wears his nerd card like a badge of honor. I mean look at him—tucked in shirt, horn-rimmed glasses, a master of tabletop war games."

"Speaking of which," said Billy, apparently unfazed by Erik's ribbing, "don't forget game night tomorrow."

"Really?" said Erik. "Don't you think we should cancel, considering what happened?"

"Not at all. This is a good excuse to get together. It'll be something to distract us and maybe even cheer us up a bit. Keli, you should come, too. The more the merrier. We could use some fresh energy. What do you say?"

"Thanks," I said. "That's nice of you, but I don't think I can make it."

"Well, it's a standing invitation, if you change your mind."

As I finished my salad, I wondered if it would be in poor taste to bring up Denise again. It was nice to see Erik in better spirits. On the other hand, since I was already mixed up in her murder investigation . . .

"How often do you have these game nights?" I asked.

"Once a week, if we can. Sometimes we miss a week, but not if I can help it."

"It's the highlight of his life," Erik said wryly.

"Did Denise participate in the games?"

There was a palpable change in the mood around the table. Both men dropped their smiles and grew silent. Billy was the first to speak.

"She came a couple times, especially back when she and Erik first started dating. In fact, I'm the one who introduced her to Erik."

"Yeah," said Erik. "But she didn't really like the games."

Billy looked away, and I had the strong sense he was holding something back. It was clear I'd struck a nerve. I wanted to ask more, but Billy checked his watch, and Erik pulled out his wallet.

There's definitely more to learn from these guys, I thought. *Maybe I should accept that game night invitation after all.*

CHAPTER SIX

Back at the office, I checked my calendar and realized I didn't have any appointments until Wednesday. I really needed to work on a marketing plan. I spent some time brainstorming and came up with a few possibilities, none of which I could implement at the moment. I decided I might as well go to see Mila at her shop.

As far as I was concerned, Moonstone Treasures could have been called "Edindale's Treasure," because it was a true gem. Part gift boutique, part witch's emporium, the store carried a multitude of charms, supplies, tools, and decorations. With the divination parlor in the back and the exotic ambience throughout, it was chockful of Mila's warm, wise, and wonderful witchy personality.

She greeted me with a hug when I entered, even though I'd just seen her the day before.

"Hello and merry meet! Come on back. Catrina and I were just unpacking a shipment we received from Haiti. Fredeline hooked us up with this wonderful jewelry maker. Fantastic stuff."

I followed Mila through the beaded curtain to the

back room. Today the Japanese screens that usually separated the two sides of the large, open space were set aside. Mila headed to the tea tray sitting on a bureau on the right-hand wall in the divination parlor. I glanced to the left where Mila's office desk sat in the corner next to a tall worktable and shelves of inventory. Catrina, Mila's spiky-haired, multi-pierced assistant, perched on a bar stool at the worktable, where she was surrounded by a stack of small jewelry boxes. She looked up when we entered.

"Hey, Catrina. How's it going?" I pulled out a chair at the round, cloth-covered table where Mila gave palm readings and tarot interpretations. As I sat down, I noticed Catrina seemed to be gazing at a point above my head. I twisted around but couldn't figure out what had captured her attention. "Um, what's up?" I asked.

She set down her pricing gun and joined us at the table. "Sorry. I was trying to read your aura."

Mila poured steaming herbal tea into painted fortune-telling teacups. "Keli might not want her aura read," she admonished gently.

"Oh, I don't mind," I said. "What do you see?"

Catrina squinted at the space around me. "It's not entirely clear. It's kind of a brownish gold." She glanced at Mila for confirmation.

Like Catrina, Mila gazed at the space around the border of my head. Then she looked into my eyes. "Your underlying divinity is apparent, as is your own strong intuitive abilities. But it appears you're also experiencing some stress right now. I see some insecurity, particularly over material matters." She paused and smiled. "I'm sure you didn't need me to tell you that."

"No," I murmured. "That all sounds about right." I took a sip of tea and winced as I burnt my tongue.

"You know what?" said Mila. "You need something to take your mind off such grave matters. With spring on the horizon, this should be a joyful, playful season. Maybe you could plan a fun getaway with your boyfriend. Oh! And definitely come to the Beltane Fire Festival on the first of May. My coven is leading the maypole ritual."

"Beltane Festival? You're the second person to mention that to me."

Suddenly the beaded curtain parted, and a frecklefaced young man stuck in his head. "Mila, can you help me out for a second?"

Mila excused herself, and I looked at Catrina for an explanation.

"That was Steve," she said. "He's a college student working here part-time. Nice kid, but a bit slow on the uptake." She snickered, then leaned forward. "Hey, I heard you were at the scene of the Fynn Hollow murder."

I flinched, but she didn't seem to notice.

"So, are we talking about an isolated incident here?" she asked. "Or was it the work of a serial killer? Should we be worried?"

"I have no idea. I haven't heard anything about other murders."

"That's good. The Witches' Web has been going crazy with rumors and speculations. You never know what to believe."

"The Witches' Web? What's that?"

"Are you joking?"

"Um, no."

"You are such a loner, aren't you?" teased Catrina. "The Witches' Web is an online social network for

Pagans. If you ever came out of your little solitary broom closet, you might know that."

"I like being a solitary," I said, feeling defensive. "My spirituality is personal. Besides, I have you and Mila for Wiccan socializing."

"I suppose. Well, for those of us who want to connect with even more Pagans, the Witches' Web is a great resource. It has chat rooms and message boards and stuff. You can ask questions on any topic or jump into an ongoing conversation. Do you want to see?"

"Yeah, sure. I'd like to see what they're saying about the murder. Are there people on there who actually knew Denise?"

"I think so. But nobody uses their real name, so you wouldn't necessarily know who's talking. It's all meant to be anonymous."

I dragged my chair over to the desk and joined Catrina at the computer. With a few clicks, she brought up the website. It had a spare design with a black background and very few pictures. Animated fairy lights along the margin provided a whimsical touch. After logging in, Catrina showed me the discussion chain that had begun as soon as word spread of Denise's death.

"See what I mean?" she asked. "People are freaking out. More than one person called the murder proof of a witch hunt. They're saying it's a sign of the Burning Times all over again." She angled the screen and slid the mouse toward me.

"Wow." I scrolled through the messages, looking for anyone who professed firsthand knowledge of Denise—or *DeeDeeStar*, as she was called on the website. I browsed some of the comments:

I knew DeeDee, and she was always nice to me . . .

I knew DeeDee, and she had some personal issues . . .

I knew DeeDee, and she messed around with dark forces . . .

I glanced at the username of the person who had mentioned "dark forces." *WickdThorn. Could that be Denise's neighbor, Thorna?* I clicked on the name and found myself on a page with a short profile of *WickdThorn* ("Female, Capricorn, member since 2015"), and links to all her comments and posts. Perusing each one would take a while.

"I need to get back to work," said Catrina, as she pushed back from the desk. "You can keep reading, if you want. Just don't post anything under my name. *FierceGoddess* has a reputation to uphold."

"I wouldn't dream of it," I said, with a smile. Then I returned to the original thread about Denise. I wanted to finish reading all the comments about her death before going down the rabbit hole of past conversations. After scrolling through a string of generic comments expressing astonishment, fear, and sadness, I paused at a brief exchange that stuck out from the rest:

DredShaman: Now you can sleep easy, BalderBoy.

BalderBoy: Don't. Not now.

DredShaman: But our problem is solved. You should be thanking me.

BalderBoy: Shut up, DredShaman. Just. Shut. Up.

"Hmm. Interesting." I clicked on *DredShaman*, whose profile was as sparse as *WickdThorn*'s. He wasn't a frequent poster. From what I could tell, his comments appeared primarily in a few discussions on drum circles, Shamanism, and magic mushrooms. Then I saw a snippet of text that included the names

DeeDeeStar and *BalderBoy*. I clicked on it and skimmed the conversation. They seemed to be debating the binding power of blood oaths.

DeeDeeStar: Of course oaths can be broken. There's always a way.

BalderBoy: Hey, a pact is a pact. It's very bad form to break a pact.

DredShaman: Not without dire consequences. I once knew a guy . . .

BalderBoy: Come on, guys. Don't even joke about this.

DeeDeeStar: Whatever.

That was the end of the conversation. Based on the date stamp, it had occurred a month ago. I stared at the words for a long moment. They seemed ominous considering what had happened to Denise. I wondered if Deputy Langham knew about the Witches' Web.

Mila returned to the back room. "I found that oracle deck I was thinking of yesterday. It's called Tarot of the Valkyries, and it's based on Old Norse mythology." She removed the plastic wrapping and handed me the deck.

I thumbed through the cards. The deck seemed to follow the classic Rider-Waite tarot system, but with Norse-themed images and symbols. I recognized the gods Thor and Odin and the goddess Freya, as well as the majestic site of Valhalla. There were also cards featuring elves and dwarves, and, of course, a Viking warrior. "This is it," I said, holding onto the Viking card. "This is what I saw in Denise's hand."

Catrina hurried over to take a look, as Mila peered over my shoulder. We studied the card in silence. It was the Knight of Swords, as portrayed by a heroic-looking blond Norseman, complete with long flowing hair and a full beard. Instead of riding on horseback, he wielded his sword from the bow of a ship before a background of stormy skies and sea. A stylized letter *V* was stamped in the lower right-hand corner of the card.

"Is this supposed to help identify her murderer?" asked Catrina, giving voice to the question in my mind.

"I don't know," I said. "Not necessarily. Maybe it just happened to be the last card she drew when the poison took effect." As a lawyer, I was used to looking at problems from all angles. But deep down I felt there must be some significance to the card. "Mila, what does this card usually represent in a reading?"

Mila sighed. "So much of tarot interpretation has more to do with the reader than with the card itself. I'd want to know what questions or concerns were on the reader's mind. Also, where did the card appear in the overall spread—and was it right-side up, or inverted? Cards have completely different meanings when reversed. However . . . the suit of swords often indicates delivery of a message related to change and conflict. As you can see, the image shows a hero figure, which stands for courage, adventure, loyalty, and truth. But heroes' quests can have both positive and negative results. And they sometimes involve violence."

Catrina scoffed. "It definitely involved violence in this case. The question is, who was the perpetrator?"

"As for this card," I said, holding it up, "the real question is, what did it represent for Denise?"

Of course, none of us could answer that question. Catrina headed back to her pricing gun, and Mila patted my shoulder. "Would you like me to warm up your tea?"

Before I could answer, Steve came rushing into the back room again. "Mila!" he hissed. "Could you please come out here? There's a policeman asking all kinds of questions I can't answer. He's really intense. And kinda judgy. He's making me nervous."

"Langham," I said.

"Do you want to leave out the back door?" asked Mila.

I hesitated, knowing that I absolutely wanted to leave out the back door—and feeling ridiculous about it. I bit the inside of my cheek. "No," I finally said. "It's okay. I should go, but there's no reason I shouldn't leave out the front door. Besides, I want to buy this tarot deck."

"You're not buying it. It's my gift to you." She squeezed my hand, then disappeared through the beaded curtain. I took a deep breath, then dropped the cards into my purse, and followed her.

Langham stood at the back of the store, scrutinizing the shelves of boxed herbs and potion bottles. He turned as Mila approached and flashed her a thin-lipped smile. Then he noticed me, and his eyes narrowed.

"Ms. Milanni. I'm surprised to see you here."

I ignored his baiting tone. "How's the investigation going, Deputy? Do you have any leads?"

His false smile twisted, and his eyes took on a cold, calculating gleam. "As a matter of fact, we do have leads. The autopsy report is still pending, of course, but we received some interesting information from the forensics team." He paused, waiting for my reaction. I was beginning to like the man less and less.

"What kind of information?" I asked.

"There were two teacups in the victim's sink. They had been rinsed, but not thoroughly enough. There was a substance stuck to the bottom of one of them. Turns out the substance contained atropine."

"Oh, dear," said Mila.

"What's atropine? Some kind of drug?"

"It's used in some drugs," said Langham. "But not in the form found in the teacup. No, this substance was pretty raw. Like mashed leaves and berries."

I glanced at Mila, whose face was flushed. "I don't sell—"

"You see, Ms. Milanni?" Langham interrupted. "Ms. Douglas knows what I'm talking about. Atropine is found in the belladonna plant, otherwise known as deadly nightshade. Ring any bells? It should. It's a classic ingredient for you witches."

CHAPTER SEVEN

It wasn't until I was seated behind my desk in the safety of my quiet little office that I finally breathed a sigh of relief. *What a jerk!* I knew Langham was sharing details of the case only to gauge our reactions, but he didn't have to be so gleeful about it. I had been so flustered after his provocative comment, I couldn't think of an appropriate comeback. At least, not a civil one. I mumbled something about having to get back to work and fairly flew out of the store. Now that I was alone I felt sheepish about running out on Mila like that. Some friend I was.

A tap on the outer door startled me from my thoughts.

"It's open!" I called, as I stepped into the small waiting area. The door opened, revealing an older woman with gray hair and cornflower-blue eyes. She sported slacks and a light sweater, and wore a pleasant, curious expression.

A new client!

"Hello!" I said. "Come on in! I'm Keli Milanni. Please have a seat. Can I get you a glass of water? Or a cup of coffee or tea? I have an electric kettle that heats water in a jiffy."

"Sounds nice, only I can't stay," she said briskly. "But I'm glad to finally meet you. I'm Annie, your next-door neighbor."

Oh. Not a client. I maintained my smile in spite of my disappointment. "It's great to meet you, Annie. I was beginning to think I was the only occupant in this building."

"There *are* a few vacancies," she admitted. "And the rest of us are mostly part-timers. I only come in when I have a scheduled appointment. Because of our odd hours, deliveries usually get dropped off with whoever happens to be here." She held out a bulky envelope. "This came for you last week."

"Thanks." I took the envelope and set it on the coffee table. I hadn't anticipated receiving packages that wouldn't fit through the mail slot. That could be a problem. "Are you sure you can't stay for a cup of tea? It's a slow afternoon for me."

"Another time. I'm on my way out for the day. Toodles!"

When she left, I dropped into one of my waiting room chairs and listened to the quiet. Then I picked up the package and turned it over. It had a local postmark, but no return address. "A mystery package, huh? How exciting. And now I'm talking to myself."

I rolled my eyes and ripped open the package. Reaching inside, I pulled out a plain white card that contained a one-line message written in flowing cursive script: *Congratulations on your new law practice.*

I turned it over, but there was nothing else. No signature. Reaching in a second time, I pulled out a small bundle of bubble wrap and tape. It took some doing, especially when I realized I didn't have any scissors in the office, but when I finally removed all the wrapping, I gasped in delight. In the palm of my hand was a lovely little figurine—a delicate fairy reclining on a knotty, carved tree branch.

"How pretty," I breathed.

I figured it must be from Mila. She was the most generous, thoughtful person I knew, and this was just the kind of thing she carried in her store. On the other hand, it wasn't like her to be mysterious. She'd be more likely to write a sweet, personal note than send an anonymous package.

There *was* someone else in my life who used to send me mysterious letters, postcards, and gifts. But it couldn't be from her. Aunt Josephine had died more than six months ago. Thinking of her now filled me with both fondness and sadness. I'd always felt a special connection to my aunt, even though I never really had a chance to get to know her.

Goose bumps prickled on my arms as an unlikely thought popped into my mind. Wouldn't it be something if Josephine had somehow arranged to send me this gift before she passed away? Like one last message from beyond the veil?

But no. That was impossible. I hadn't even decided to open my own law practice until after her death.

I stood up and carried the figurine to my office, where I placed it on a shelf near my desk. Whoever it was from, they had good taste.

After checking my messages one more time, and finding none, I decided to call it a day.

That evening over dinner I told Wes about my mysterious gift. He put his fork down and scowled.

"What's the matter?"

"A present from a secret admirer? Don't tell me it's that Fynn Hollow guy again. Why did you have lunch with him anyway?"

"Erik? We were just comparing notes about the police investigation. The package couldn't be from him. It was mailed before I even met him."

"Hmph," Wes grunted, evidently not convinced.

As we finished dinner, I pondered the possibilities. I had an old boyfriend who had once sent me some anonymous gifts in an effort to be cute and mysterious. But he lived in Virginia and, last I heard, had gotten married and started a family. The fairy gift had come with a local postmark. *Oh, well.* I decided it was probably from a colleague or client who had forgotten to sign their name, and put it out of my mind.

After we cleaned up, Wes settled in on the sofa in front of a baseball game, and I brought my laptop to the table. First I checked my email, then clicked over to the Witches' Web. Without Catrina's log-in information, I'd have to create my own account. I tapped my fingers on the table, then looked up as Wes came into the kitchen to get a drink from the refrigerator.

"What should I pick for my username? I want to make sure nobody can guess it's me."

He strolled over to look at the computer screen as he unscrewed a bottle of beer. "What are you signing up for?"

I told him about the social network site, and he wrinkled his forehead as if giving my question serious consideration. "I know! How about *Hot Witch*?" Seeing my look, he grinned. "What? Too descriptive?"

"Very funny. Let's see. I've always been partial to Aphrodite." The goddess of love and beauty evoked a fiery, passionate energy—useful for creating all kinds of magic. She also happened to be the goddess of fertility, which somehow seemed appropriate. Spring was in the air, after all.

I typed in *FlightyAphrodite,* which I hoped was sufficiently antithetical to my real personality, and found myself on the home page of the Witches' Web. I scanned the list of trending topics and saw that the upcoming Beltane Festival was at the top.

"Huh. A week ago I'd never even heard of this event. Now everybody's talking about it."

"What's that, babe?" asked Wes, who had drifted back to the living room.

"There's a May Day festival happening somewhere out in the boonies in a couple weeks. Mila's circle is leading the maypole dance."

"You gonna go?"

"Are you kidding? A public ritual? My so-called broom closet door might be open a crack, but I'm not quite ready to step all the way out."

Josie sauntered in and rubbed against my leg. I reached down to pet her head. "What do you think, kitty? Am I being paranoid? I know I'd be among friends, but still . . . I have my professional reputation to think of."

I turned back to the computer and clicked on the discussion of Denise's death. There were several new posts since this afternoon. Most were filled with the usual shock and dismay, with a few unhelpful speculations sprinkled throughout. Then I came to one that hit me with a whole new theory. Actually, it was a warning, posted by someone named *MadMedusa*: "Watch out, witches. The cops think it's an inside job—a witch-on-witch crime. They're questioning anyone even remotely connected to Paganism who might have had contact with DeeDee. So much for privacy."

All I could think of was the gleam in Langham's eyes when he talked about belladonna's association with witches. *Ugh.*

Just then the house phone rang, and I remembered the weird call from the night before. "Could you get that?" I called to Wes.

I hurried into the living room and watched as he muted the TV and reached for the telephone on the end table. "Hello. Hello?" He waited a moment, then hung up. "Nobody there."

"Did you hear any music?"

"What?"

"Like tinny, distant music?"

"No. Just silence, then a click. Must have been a wrong number. Why?"

He gave me a puzzled look, as I stared at the phone waiting for it to ring again. When it didn't, I shook myself. "Never mind. Scoot over. I'm done thinking about creepy things tonight."

CHAPTER EIGHT

The next morning, first thing after breakfast, I went straight to Moonstone Treasures. I wanted to apologize to Mila for bailing on her the day before. As I might have predicted, she brushed away my concerns.

"Don't be silly. You were already on your way out, and the deputy didn't stay very long anyway."

"So, was he here only to see if you sell any products containing belladonna?"

"No. Not exactly. He also wanted to confirm what time it was when you and Erik were in the shop on Saturday."

"Oh. Of course."

I followed Mila throughout the store as she straightened merchandise and arranged a new display of spring flowers surrounding a painted cauldron and faux deer antlers—feminine and masculine symbols of fertility. One of the central themes of Beltane was the coming together of the God and Goddess, whose sensual union brings life back to the earth.

But Mila's demeanor didn't match the cheerfulness of the display. I could tell she was worried. "Is there more?" I asked.

"Well, he was very interested in the time. He said it was vital to get it right. He even asked if I had any sales receipts that would corroborate the exact time you were here. I told him I'd have to look and get back to him. Of course, I wouldn't give him something like that without checking with you first. Though, I suppose he could come back with a warrant . . ." She trailed off, looking conflicted.

"It's okay," I said. "He already knows I shop here. At this point, it's probably best to go ahead and give him the receipts."

Mila nodded. "I agree. You have nothing to hide. Frankly, I don't understand why he's so interested in you. It's ludicrous, when you think about it."

"Uh, just how interested did he seem?"

"He wanted to know how you were acting that morning—and if I knew where you had been before you came to the store. It's back to the time question, I guess. He told me the time of death hadn't been pegged yet, but it might have happened earlier than they thought at first."

"Really?" I had a sinking feeling I wouldn't like where this was headed.

"I told him you most likely came from home and that your boyfriend could vouch for you. I mean, where else—" She broke off and peered into my eyes. "What's the matter? Did I say something wrong?"

"No, no. It's fine." I tried to erase the worried expression from my face. "Only, I didn't come here straight from home that morning. I actually drove out to Briar Creek for a private early-morning ritual. The weather was so nice, and I hadn't been out there in a while. It's always so quiet and peaceful. And secluded." Meaning, of course, that no one saw me.

The bell above the shop door jangled and a little girl came running toward us. Her shiny amber pigtails perfectly matched the loose ponytail on the woman who chased her inside. To my surprise, it was Carol Peters, harried and out of breath. "Slow down, Dorrie! And remember, don't touch *anything*!"

"Mila! Mila!" cried Dorrie, ignoring her mama.

Mila leaned down and gave the little girl a great big hug. "Hello, Dorrie, love! How nice to see you. But shouldn't you be in school?"

"No preschool today," said Carol. "We're on our way to a doctor's appointment, a routine check-up. I told Dorrie she could wear my lucky pendant, but she insisted she should have her own. So, I told her we'd pop in here and take a look if we had time, and we do—just barely."

"Smart girl," I said with a smile. "Of course she should have her own lucky charm."

"Absolutely," agreed Mila. "Come with me, Dorrie. I'll show you what we have. Do you like turtles?"

Mila took Dorrie's hand and led her to a jewelry case near the checkout counter. Carol came up to me and furrowed her brow in concern.

"Keli," she said softly, "I have to thank you again for meeting with me on Sunday. At the time, I had no idea what you'd been through the day before. How are you holding up?"

"I'm fine," I said, somewhat startled. "I mean, it was dreadful finding the poor woman, and I feel sorry for her friends and family. But I didn't know her myself." Something about the doubt in Carol's expression gave me pause. "I assume Mila told you I found that woman in Fynn Hollow?"

She shook her head. "I didn't hear it from Mila. I read about it in the paper this morning."

It was my worst nightmare come true: to be outed as a Wiccan in a public, and very negative, way. I couldn't believe this was happening.

After leaving Moonstone, I hurried across the square toward my new office. Along the way, I passed several acquaintances, none of whom said hello. Everyone either pretended not to see me or quickly averted their eyes. One or two gave me curious stares from a safe distance away.

Or maybe it was all in my imagination.

I let myself into the quiet, old building, which appeared deserted as usual, and went straight to the computer. I needed to see the article for myself.

When Carol had told me the newspaper mentioned me by name, I was shocked. Wes worked as a photographer and web designer for the *Edindale Gazette*. Surely they would have given him the courtesy of a heads-up—not to mention reaching out to me for a comment. Then Carol clarified what she'd meant.

"It was in the college newspaper, the *Daily Beat*. Another waitress where I work goes to school at the university. She knows I'm Wiccan and wondered if I know you. In fact, she asked if I thought you'd be willing to speak to her prelaw class. I guess they're closely following the case."

I blanched at that suggestion. This was all too much.

Now I tried to remain calm as I pulled up the website for the student-run newspaper. I was immediately struck by the sensational headline: FYNN HOLLOW MURDER TIED TO WITCHCRAFT. I skimmed the article, looking for my name. I found it in the second paragraph:

> The victim was a self-described witch, who dabbled in potion-making and other "dark arts." But her death was no accident. Sources say the cause of death was poisoning by a deadly drug found in the belladonna plant. According to folklore, witches would coat their broomsticks with belladonna salve to make them fly. It isn't known if Ms. Crowley was that kind of witch, but she did consort with a number of individuals who claim to practice modern witchcraft, also known as Wicca. This includes the victim's ex-boyfriend, Erik Grayson, a member of a secret society of nature worshippers called the Order of the Celtic Druids. It was Mr. Grayson and another friend, Edindale attorney Keli Milanni, who found Ms. Crowley's body.

I was torn between irritation and worry. I was irritated by the tasteless sensationalism and subtly patronizing tone of the article, as well as the factual errors in the piece—strictly speaking, Wicca was *not* another name for modern witchcraft. But I was more worried about the way the article used my name. It implied I was one of the other witches with whom Denise "consorted." Didn't it?

I reread the article. Maybe it wasn't as bad as I thought. It didn't actually come right out and say I'm a Wiccan. At worst, it only implied I was a friend of Denise's—a claim that was just plain untrue.

"Oh, who reads college newspapers anyway?" I said aloud. I closed the screen and straightened my desk. I needed to stop dwelling on matters outside my control and focus on drumming up new business.

Five minutes later my phone rang. It was Everett Macy, the client I had scheduled for the following afternoon. He was a referral from Crenshaw, who had said he was too busy to prepare an estate plan on Mr. Macy's short timetable. I wasn't sure if that was true, or if Crenshaw was just being nice by throwing me a bone—while also managing to brag about how busy he was. Either way, I was more than happy to meet with Mr. Macy as soon as he liked.

"Hello, Mr. Macy," I said, after he'd identified himself. "I'm all set for tomorrow. Do you have any questions about the new client questionnaire?"

"Er, no. That's not why I'm calling. Unfortunately, something has come up and I have to call off the appointment."

"Oh, that's no problem. I'm happy to reschedule. When would you like to come in?"

There was a long pause, as the truth sank in. He wasn't calling to reschedule. He was calling to cancel. Still, I wasn't ready to give up so easily. "I know how eager you are to have your estate plan updated, and you should be commended for that. That's very responsible of you. I'll tell you what—I do sometimes make house calls. I can come by your home anytime you'd like, day or evening. How does that sound?"

He cleared his throat. "That's very kind of you, but I've decided to go with someone else. Thanks anyway." With that, he hung up.

"Dang it." I deleted the appointment from my calendar, then stood up and paced my office. "I have to do something," I muttered. As long as the murder remained unsolved, there was the likelihood of more articles like the one in the *Daily Beat*. There would be more questions, more speculation, and more bad press for witchcraft. And no matter how many times I professed my innocence, in the back of some peoples' minds, I'd still be guilty by association.

I picked up the phone again and called Farrah. She picked up on the first ring. "Hey, lady! I'm glad you called. I am bored out of my mind."

"Things aren't exactly hopping here either," I said ruefully. "Except my mind is on overdrive. I need you to tell me I'm overreacting."

"You're overreacting."

"I mean *after* I tell you the latest." I filled her in on all that happened since we'd last spoken, including Langham's insinuations, the newspaper article, and my client cancellation. "Do you think I'm being too sensitive?"

She hesitated half a second, then spoke with care. "I think things probably aren't as bad as you imagine—though I don't blame you one bit for being upset. I'm sure I'd feel the same. Hey, can't you cast a curse on Langham? Give him the evil eye or something to make him stay away from you?"

I had to laugh. "Don't say 'curse'!"

"Too soon?"

"Yeah. Though I can't say I haven't been thinking

about casting some kind of spell to help with the whole situation. If only the murderer would be caught . . ." I trailed off, but Farrah jumped on the idea.

"We need to do some poking around. Is there going to be a funeral or anything? Some occasion to see all Denise's friends in one place?"

"I haven't heard anything about a funeral yet, but I do know where some of them will be tonight." I told Farrah about my invitation to Billy's game night.

"We have to go!"

"'We'?" I echoed. "You're not exactly mobile right now."

"I can get around well enough. I can certainly sit at a game table and watch for suspicious behavior."

"Are you sure?" I had to admit, the prospect of engaging in a little light snooping with Farrah at my side was starting to cheer me up. At least it was better than doing nothing at all.

"I'm positive. Now, what should we wear?"

CHAPTER NINE

Farrah and I stood at the foot of the steep, wooden porch stairs and squinted up at Billy's front door. There were probably eight or nine steps between us and the entrance to his apartment, but they might as well have been the rocky crags of Mount Everest.

I turned to Farrah and sighed. "This was a mistake."

She lifted one crutch and tapped it on the bottom step as if to test it out. "Yeah. I gotta say I'm not especially eager to break my other leg, too. Darn it."

"Maybe the back door—"

Before I could finish the thought, the front door swung open and two men clambered down the stairs to meet us. It was Billy and Viper.

"Oh, man!" said Billy. "I'm sorry about this. I wish I had a ramp or something. What can we do? Can I offer you my arm?"

Farrah smiled doubtfully. I was about to bow out from game night, when Viper took matters into his own hands. Literally.

"I got this," he said, his voice raspy and confident, like some kind of movie mobster. Before anyone could react, he grabbed Farrah around the waist and hurled her over his shoulder. She cried out in surprise, as her crutches clattered to the sidewalk. In a matter of seconds, he hauled her up the steps and set her down by the door. Farrah gawked at him with wide eyes as she struggled to find words. Evidently, she couldn't decide whether to be indignant or grateful. Or impressed.

Viper smirked as he looked down at Billy and me. "What are y'all waitin' for? C'mon, Billy. Let's get these ladies inside and get 'em a drink."

Billy grabbed Farrah's crutches and motioned me to proceed upstairs. "After you," he said.

"Alrighty, then."

Billy's apartment occupied one-third of a converted Victorian mansion. It was slightly shabby in the way aging rental properties often were, but it was clean and not without its charms. He led us through the small living room and into what was presumably intended to be a formal dining room. For Billy, it was a game room dominated by a large round table and six black leather chairs. A glass-doored cabinet against the far wall contained stacks of boxed games on top and a minibar inside.

As we entered, Erik emerged from the adjoining kitchen holding a tall mixed drink. He leaned in to give me a one-armed hug and, to my surprise, a kiss on the cheek. "Good to see you again, Keli. I'm glad you could make it." He looked better than he had the day before, in a nice button-up denim shirt and black jeans. His hair was slightly damp, as if he'd just gotten out of the shower, making it look more brown than blond.

As I introduced Erik to Farrah, I noticed someone standing behind him. When he stepped aside, I saw that it was Thorna Attley, Denise's neighbor. She had on the same black eyeliner as the other day, but had dressed up her appearance with dark red lipstick, a short black mini-skirt, and a lacy black top. The outfit seemed slightly formal for game night, but who was I to judge? Farrah and I had opted for casual Boho chic—she in a long suede skirt and knotted baby-blue T-shirt and me in skinny jeans and a light, off-the-shoulder sweater.

Billy fussed over Farrah to help her get settled into the nearest chair, while Erik poured us drinks. Viper slid into the seat to Farrah's left, and I took the one to her right. Erik pulled out the chair on my other side. Thorna seemed to angle for the seat on Erik's right, but Billy got there first. He was too busy opening up a game box to notice her scowl, as she settled into the chair between Billy and Viper.

"I hope we didn't take someone else's place tonight," I said, realizing there was only enough space for six players.

"Not at all," said Billy. "A couple guys from work had agreed to come if we needed them, but they were fine with skipping out." He pushed up his glasses and flashed his dimples. "Lucky for you, Thorna. Right? Now you're not surrounded by a bunch of dorky men."

"Speak for yourself," said Viper, as he slouched in his chair.

Thorna gave Billy a tight-lipped smile and didn't say anything. Farrah and I exchanged a glance, and Farrah cleared her throat. "So, what is in this delicious-looking concoction, if I might ask?" She held up her drink to have a taste.

"House special," said Erik. "Seven and seven without the garnish."

"No frills," said Viper. He raised his highball toward Farrah. "Here's to simplicity." They clinked glasses, then he drained his.

"Pace yourself, Vipe," said Erik. "The night is young."

Billy had set up the game board and was now passing out tokens, cards, and game pieces. He slid a character list between Farrah and me. "Whenever we have new players, we let them choose their characters from the list. We're in the middle of an ongoing campaign, so I've made a note of the characters that are already taken."

The list looked like the cast of an epic fantasy series. I saw that Erik was a monk, Viper was a dragon slayer, and Billy was a Viking. "I don't see you on here, Thorna," I said. "Aren't you a regular?"

She dug a piece of ice from her glass and popped it in her mouth. "I guess not. I'll be the mage."

Farrah wrinkled her forehead at the complicated-looking game board. "Do you have an instruction booklet I can read?"

"It's easy," said Thorna, sounding bored already. "All you gotta do is roll the dice. The boys will take care of the rest. As they should. Isn't that right, Erik?"

"I can give you the backstory," said Billy. "The year is fourteen-twelve, and the kingdom of—"

"You can explain as we go along," interrupted Viper. "We don't have all night."

"I'll be an elf," said Farrah. "Elves are cute. Keli?"

"Um, I don't know. I'll be a giant. That sounds powerful."

"You'd think so," said Billy, with a snicker. Clearly, he had played this game many, many times.

For the next hour, the game slogged along, with Billy's nonstop commentary. Only he and Erik seemed to be having fun. Every now and then, Erik turned to me and grinned like a little boy. Thorna was sulky all evening. It was obvious she wasn't there for the game.

As for Viper, he drank nonstop and became increasingly loud and sloppy, knocking over game pieces and dropping his dice on the floor. Finally, in the middle of Thorna's turn, he stood up and said, "Break time!" He left the room abruptly, bumping my chair on the way out.

Billy checked his watch. "Yeah, okay. We should take a break. Does anyone want snacks? I have all kinds of appetizers in the freezer: pizza rolls, mozzarella sticks, potato skins. You name it."

Thorna pushed back from the table. "I'll go make a platter."

"Thanks," said Billy. "I'll come help in a minute." He straightened the cards and jotted some notes in a spiral notebook, presumably so we wouldn't lose our place in the game.

Erik excused himself, and I turned toward Farrah. I was hoping to speak to her in private for a minute. We really needed to formulate our own game plan, because so far we'd learned absolutely nothing. But then Viper returned and scooted his chair closer to Farrah's. He leaned over and whispered into her ear.

She rolled her eyes, but curled her lips into a smile. "No thanks," she said.

He sat back and shrugged, then pulled a joint from his jacket pocket. He lit it, took a drag, and then offered it to me. "No thanks," I said, echoing Farrah's words.

Erik came up behind me and placed a hand on my shoulder. "Want me to tell him to put it away? You'd think he'd learned his lesson after being arrested."

"Hey, it's practically legal now," said Viper. "As long as you don't carry too much at once."

"It's okay," I said to Erik. We were there to observe the natives in their natural habitat, I mused. Might as well let them do what they normally did.

Viper reached down and tickled Farrah's toes. "Hey!" she protested. "No fair. I'm at a bit of a disadvantage here."

"Sorry," he mumbled, his red eyes glistening. "How'd you break your leg?"

"I had a disagreement with the side of a ski slope. The slope won."

"Harsh," he said. "Got a pen?"

"I beg your pardon?"

"So I can sign your cast."

"There's a whole cup of pens on the cabinet," said Billy, returning to the room with a fresh bottle of 7 Up.

I turned to Billy. "Could you show me the washroom?"

"Sure thing." He led me through the living room and down a short hall, where he pointed out the door to the bathroom. Once I was alone, I took my phone from my purse and texted Wes.

Wish you were here. This is a strange scene.

He replied immediately. Want me to join you? I can leave now.

Sweet man. That's ok. Probably won't be here much longer.

I took a quick peek around the bathroom, scanning the contents of the medicine cabinet and the cupboard beneath the sink. No clues there. I ran my fingers through my hair and touched up my lipstick, then opened the bathroom door—only to come face-to-face with Viper.

"Hey, sexy," he rasped. "What were you doing in there?"

"Oh! Sorry. I didn't know anyone was waiting."

"'S'okay. Want to come in with me?"

I ignored the question and tried to brush past him. He blocked my way, roaming my body with his glassy eyes. I balled my fists, as my adrenaline surged.

"Sure you don't want to give me a hand?" he slurred. "I'll show you why they call me Viper."

In the next instant, he stepped toward me and I wrenched backward.

"Get away from me!"

Erik ran up the hall. "Viper! What are you doing?"

"My bad, my bad," said Viper, holding up both palms in mock surrender. "Just a little misunderstanding." He disappeared into the bathroom, and I cursed under my breath.

Erik looked me up and down with concern. "Sorry about that. He's a handful when he drinks too much."

"A handful? You say that like he's a child. He's a fully grown man."

I stalked off, but stopped short when I reached the living room. Farrah was next to the front door with her purse on her shoulder and her crutches under both arms. Her face was red and her jaw set.

"It's time to go," she said when she saw me.

"What happened?" My mind jumped to the worst possibility. Had Viper assaulted her right before accosting me outside the bathroom?

Her eyes flashed. "That little . . . *juvenile delinquent* drew an obscene picture on my cast. In permanent marker."

I told her what Viper had said to me, and she looked positively murderous. "The nerve of that guy! Are you okay?"

"Yeah. No harm done."

Thorna and Billy wandered in from the dining room. "Snacks are ready," Billy announced.

Thorna grasped the situation faster than he did. "Leaving so soon?"

Erik came up behind me and touched my arm. "You don't have to go. Viper will leave. I already talked to him."

Farrah shook her head. "You know, it's getting late anyway, and we have work tomorrow." Then she put on a smile to ease the awkwardness. "Thank you for teaching us the game! I'd never played before, and I love trying new things."

"Anytime," said Billy. "Come back next week if you'd like."

"Not if Viper is here," I retorted. "Billy, any chance the back door has fewer steps?"

"Unfortunately, no. But we'll make sure Farrah gets down safely."

With Erik on one side and Billy on the other, the two men managed to carry Farrah down the steps and ease her into the car. I placed her crutches in the backseat and settled in behind the wheel. We waved good-bye and took off. As soon as we had cleared the block, we both started talking at once.

"Can you believe—?"

"Of all the—!"

"Ugh," exclaimed Farrah. "Did we even learn anything tonight to make this ordeal worth it?"

"Not about Denise. I almost asked which character she played in the game, but that seemed too tacky."

"As if manners mattered in there."

"Well, besides Viper—who's clearly a creep—everyone else was pretty nice."

"You mean Erik and Billy were nice. Thorna was rather cold. I think you were cramping her style."

"Me? What did I do?"

"Not a thing, besides being beautiful like you always are. You cast quite a spell on Erik the Druid. Or bard or monk, or whatever he was."

I glanced at Farrah in the passenger seat. The country road was dark, so I couldn't see her expression. "Are you serious?" I asked.

"Come on," she said. "You must have noticed how he looked at you. And he was awful touchy-feely, don't you think?"

I thought back over the evening and realized Farrah was right. "Dang. I didn't lead him on, did I? I'm sure I mentioned Wes at least once, if not more."

"If he'd give you a ring, that wouldn't be a problem," muttered Farrah, out of the side of her mouth.

"What?"

"Nothing. Look, don't worry about it. In fact, this could be a good thing. If Erik likes you, it should be easier for you to get more information out of him."

I scoffed. "Let's face it, Farrah. You and I are not detectives. Tonight was a big fail."

"I don't know. Now that I think about it, I'd say we're starting to build a pretty interesting suspect list. In time, it might turn out that tonight was more useful than we think."

I glanced at the cold, clear sky and shook my head. I wished I shared her confidence.

CHAPTER TEN

I had trouble sleeping Tuesday night. By the time I assisted Farrah up to her apartment and helped her color over the graffiti on her cast, it was already past 10:00. When I finally arrived home, Wes was ready for bed. He asked me how the evening turned out, and I gave him the short version—that it was mostly dull until it ended on an obnoxious note with a drunk guy scribbling a lewd drawing on Farrah's cast. I left out the part about Viper making a pass at me in the hallway. I knew it would only anger Wes and, besides, there was nothing to be done about it now.

As I tossed and turned in bed, I regretted my decision not to confide in him. My mind kept replaying the night's events—and imagining all the ways it could have turned out differently. And worse.

The living room telephone rang, making me jump. Wes groaned and rolled over. Two more rings, and the machine picked up. I strained my ears, listening for a message, but there was none. I punched my pillow and snuggled in. The phone rang again.

"Can you turn off the ringer?" Wes mumbled.

"Yeah. Good idea."

Feeling my way in the dark, I padded downstairs and into the living room. As I reached for the phone, it rang a third time. I grabbed the receiver and listened. Crackling, tinny music assaulted my ears. I gasped. "Who is this?"

The music stopped, but the call didn't end. I imagined some weirdo on the other end of the line, and my skin crawled. "Why are you doing this?" I demanded.

I heard a faint, breathy laugh, then a click.

Shaking, I yanked the phone cord from the wall and ran back upstairs as fast as my cold little feet could carry me.

One of the perks of being my own boss was that I could sleep in whenever I wanted. That is, assuming I didn't have any appointments—which, unfortunately, I didn't. I took my time getting dressed Wednesday morning, determined to set a positive tone for the day. After Wes left for work, I went into my altar room and lit a candle.

I took a few deep breaths, as I stared out the window into the backyard. It was a beautiful spring morning. The butter-yellow daffodils and pale pink petals of the flowering dogwood tree made for a happy scene, but they couldn't cut through my underlying sense of worry. I wished I felt more optimistic.

What should I do?

With that simple question, I placed my hands on my heart and closed my eyes. After a moment, a short melancholy verse surfaced in my mind:

Mother Goddess—I'm lost at sea
Forces crashing on all sides of me
I need a beacon, an anchor, a rope
Direction, protection—a sign of hope

All at once, I envisioned a glowing image. Undulating lines shimmered and curved to form a familiar symbol: crossed arms, representing feminine and masculine energies, with a loop on the top evoking the rising sun. It was the Egyptian ankh, an ancient symbol of life, fertility, and power. According to legend, the ankh was a key to hidden knowledge and a gift bestowed by the gods—the gift of eternal life. It was also a sign of protection. It was just the thing I needed to remind me of my own inner strength.

I opened my eyes, extinguished the candle, and headed to the bathroom. I rummaged in my makeup bag for a brown eyeliner pencil, then I faced the mirror and lifted my shirt. With a steady hand, I drew the symbol in the center, lower part of my chest. Then I stepped back to admire the effect. *Perfect.*

Smiling, I lowered my shirt and finished getting ready for work. It gave me a certain thrill of power to carry the secret emblem so close to my heart. As I gathered my things and walked to work, I felt more energized than I had in a long time. I entered my office building ready to face the day.

I unlocked the door, picked up the mail from the floor beneath the letter slot, and opened the blinds to let in some light. It was quiet as usual, with no messages to answer and no meetings to attend. But I didn't let it bother me. For the next hour, I worked the phone, calling every contact I could think of. It was time for some serious networking.

I had just gotten off the phone with the chair of

the service committee at the local bar association, when there was a knock at the door. It was such an unfamiliar sound, I wasn't sure at first what it was. Then I heard a deep, resonant voice.

"Is this a place of business or a closet?"

I hopped up and poked my head into the waiting room. "Crenshaw!"

"I wasn't sure if I should knock or enter unannounced. You don't have a receptionist?"

"No, it's just me. How are you? Can I get you anything? Coffee?"

He raised his eyebrows slightly, then nodded. "All right. I'm doing well, thank you. And you?"

"I'm great." I set about making coffee, as Crenshaw took a seat and gave the office an appraising look. He was dressed in a gray Italian suit, with a silk paisley tie and coordinating pocket square. When he leaned back and crossed his long legs, I was momentarily distracted by the gleam from his highly polished black oxfords. They were almost as shiny as the silver watch glinting on his wrist. I handed him a cup of coffee and perched in the adjacent chair. "What brings you here, Crenshaw? I know how busy you are."

"Can't a man pop in and say hello to his former partner?"

"Sure. But you've never done it before." In truth, I knew he was put out with me when I left the firm. He shouldn't have taken it personally, but I had the sense he felt I'd betrayed him.

He pursed his lips. "I ran into Everett Macy in front of the courthouse this morning."

"Oh."

"I asked him if he'd met with you yet. And do you know what he said?"

"I haven't the foggiest."

"He said he preferred not to trust his personal affairs with someone who seems frivolous and disreputable."

"Ouch."

"Frivolous and disreputable," he repeated. "Naturally, I jumped to your defense. I said, 'That doesn't sound like the Keli Milanni I know.'"

"That was nice of you."

"That's when he told me about a newspaper article he'd read. Do you know the one I mean?"

I shifted uncomfortably. "Yes. I saw it."

"I saw it, too, after I looked it up. And I was *appalled*. Aren't you appalled?"

"Yeah, I can't say I liked it. This whole situation has been very unpleasant."

"It's more than unpleasant. It's outrageous. I presume you'll demand a retraction, if you haven't already."

"What good would that do? My name is already out there."

"I'm not talking about the *release* of your name. I'm talking about the *tarnishing* of your name. The article practically called you a witch. You must write a letter threatening to sue the *Daily Beat* for libel, if they don't publish an immediate retraction. Those journalism students need to learn what happens when they engage in sloppy tabloid-style reporting."

I looked away. "I don't know if that's really necessary. It was such a stupid, little article."

Crenshaw frowned. "Are you serious? You've already lost business because of that 'stupid, little article.' Not only that, but now Mr. Macy thinks I make referrals to unsavory characters. This reflects poorly on me, too, you know."

I almost laughed. Leave it to Crenshaw to bring the issue back to himself.

He fell silent, possibly realizing how selfish he sounded. He took a sip of coffee and looked around again. After a moment, he set down his cup. "Was it worth it, Milanni?"

"What do you mean?"

"Leaving the firm. Are you happier now?"

I considered the question, then nodded. "Yeah. I'm still finding my feet, but I'm enjoying my freedom. Going solo brings a whole new set of challenges, but I think it will be worth it in the end."

"Being called a nut isn't going to help," he said drily. "Do you really want potential clients to think you fancy yourself a broom-riding sorceress?"

"The article didn't say that," I objected.

"It lumped you in with the murder victim's friends. And the implications about *them* couldn't have been clearer."

"Come on. It wasn't really that bad." I stood and took my cup to the table in the corner. "Besides, Wicca is a legitimate religion. Not all modern witches are . . . nutty."

"What are you saying?"

I turned to face him. "I'm saying . . . maybe the article wasn't entirely untruthful."

"You mean, you really were a friend of the murder victim?"

"No. I didn't know her at all. That much was false."

"Then, what—" He broke off as the door swung open. Startled, we turned as one. *I should probably keep that door locked*, I realized. The pop-ins were always so jarring.

"Is this a bad time? I don't want to interrupt an important lawyer meeting." It was Billy, wearing his electronics store uniform and holding a bouquet of flowers. He looked like an awkward teenager on his first date.

Speaking of Denise's friends. "Come on in, Billy. What can I do for you?"

He glanced nervously at Crenshaw. "I wanted to apologize about last night."

Crenshaw's expressive eyebrows shot sky-high. He quickly recovered and made a prim bow. "I need to go. Think about what I said, Milanni."

When Crenshaw was gone, I took the flowers from Billy and invited him to have a seat.

"I can't stay long. I just feel so bad about how the evening ended last night. Erik told me what Viper did to you. I'm so, so sorry."

"It's not your fault, Billy." I wanted to ask him why he remained friends with such a troublemaker, but that seemed a bit rude. As if reading my mind, he offered an explanation.

"Viper and I have been best friends since we were little kids. We've stuck by each other through a lot of things. You know how it is. When you have a bond with someone like that, you can't just cut them out of your life when they behave badly. He's like family."

Billy's use of the word *bond* triggered something in my memory. I recalled the "pact" Denise had talked about on the Witches' Web. I decided to take a chance. "Was Denise like family, too?"

"Denise?"

"I know you were all friends in high school. Julie

told me, remember? And I haven't heard anything about Denise's actual family."

"Oh, right. Yeah, Denise was an only child and her parents weren't married. Her father took off when she was little, and her mom passed away a few years ago. She has some cousins someplace, but I don't think they were close." He paused, but I waited him out. He shrugged and continued. "I knew Denise in elementary school. We became closer in high school when a group of us got interested in Paganism."

I sat down in one of the waiting room chairs, hoping he'd follow my lead. "I became interested in Paganism in high school, too," I said affably. "For me, it started in middle school when some friends and I got a hold of some videos and books and decided to play around with magic." I chuckled at the memory. "Part of the allure, I'm sure, was the exotic style of it all."

Billy mustered up a small smile, but quickly let it drop. I wondered why he seemed so uncomfortable. "It was all in good fun when we started out," I continued. "We raised energy and tested our psychic abilities. Hauled out the Ouija board at slumber parties, like a lot of kids. Of course, we had to concoct a spell to curse the school bullies."

"That's dangerous, you know," said Billy, his expression earnest. "Kids shouldn't mess around with things they don't understand."

"Sounds like the tag line for a movie," I said, trying to lighten his mood. He looked like he was about to bolt from the room.

"It might not work like in the movies, but magic is real. I thought you knew that."

"I do. But most kids don't have the ability to cause

any real damage through magic. Anyway, my friends were more interested in attraction spells than curses."

Billy edged toward the door, clearly trying to leave but being too polite to interrupt me. So, I kept talking. "The commercial spell books we bought were definitely more style than substance. But I couldn't deny the charge I felt when working with nature. I wasn't sure if my friends really felt the same. So, once I got more serious about Wicca as a spiritual path, it became more private for me. My friends found other hobbies, and I continued my studies in secret."

Billy relaxed a little and nodded. "I know a lot of Pagans have to keep it secret, but that was never an issue for me. My family didn't have a problem with my interest in Druidry—I guess it seemed like a natural extension of my passion for sci-fi and fantasy."

"That's cool. Fynn Hollow, as a whole, must be a remarkably accepting community."

"We have our share of Fundamentalist bible thumpers, but they mostly leave us alone. I think we're viewed as just another part of the artsy, hippie trail around the region."

"That makes sense. Denise was an artist, right?"

"Yeah. Well, I need to get to work. Again, I'm sorry about last night. Viper is sorry, too. He's just not very good at expressing himself."

I stood up and reached out to shake Billy's hand. "Thank you. But I don't think self-expression is Viper's main problem. Did he get along with Denise?"

Caught off guard by the question, Billy stammered in reply. "Did he get along—? Yeah, sure. I mean, they had some disagreements. Some differences of opinion. But nothing serious. Nothing that would— anyway, I gotta go. Sorry."

I opened the door for him. "Good-bye, Billy. Thanks for stopping by."

When he was gone, I went to my computer to pull up the Witches' Web again. *Differences of opinion, huh? Like whether or not it's okay to break a pact?*

Just what kind of pact had these three made?

CHAPTER ELEVEN

I spent the next few hours on the Internet, exploring the Witches' Web and researching the pantheon of Norse gods. I had been pretty sure before, but now I was entirely convinced about the identity of Denise's online friends. *BalderBoy* had to be Billy. Balder was a beloved Norse god of purity and light, known for his generosity and all-around goodness. And Balder-Boy's comments sounded like the virtuous, ultra-nice voice of Billy.

DredShaman, on the other hand, posted a lot about marijuana and other psychotropic substances—in a careless, lazy manner that sounded exactly like Viper. I could totally picture Viper making threatening comments about the consequences of breaking a blood oath. Even more troubling, though, was the callous way he talked about Denise's death. Hidden behind the anonymity of his screen name, he'd had no shame in saying her death brought about the end to one of his "problems." *Despicable.*

But what did it all prove?

I shut down my computer and decided to call it a day. As I walked home from work, enjoying the late-afternoon sun on my shoulders and back, I contemplated my next move. Part of me wanted to tip off Deputy Langham about the conversations on the Witches' Web. But the other part felt I'd be selling out my fellow Wiccans. The Witches' Web was their space to be themselves, and Langham didn't strike me as a very open-minded person. Besides, I didn't fully trust him.

My cell phone rang, so I paused on the side of the path to answer it. When I saw the name, I couldn't help smiling. It was someone I had been thinking about lately and had even thought about calling. Was it coincidence that he called me first? I rather thought it was the work of the Goddess.

"Detective Rhinehardt! Hello!"

"Hi, Keli. How are you?"

"I'm doing well. What can I do for you?"

Perhaps I shouldn't have been so cheerful, considering all my past encounters with Adrian Rhinehardt had involved dead bodies. He was a top officer and the sole homicide detective for the Edindale Police. Yet, in spite of all the grim circumstances, not to mention the detective's generally somber, impassive demeanor, I'd always liked the guy. Behind the gruff exterior was a fair and kindhearted man. I wished he were the one handling the Fynn Hollow murder investigation.

"Keli, this is an unofficial call, but I'll get right to the point. You've been helpful to the police force in the past, and I've always found you to be a credible, upstanding individual."

"Thank you, sir."

"That's why I wanted to let you know about a phone call we received on our tip line this morning. The tipster claimed to have seen you early on Saturday morning, around eight-twenty or eight-thirty, at the gas station on Old County Road, out near Rural Route 17. This person thought the police would be interested in the information, given the time of day and the fact that 17 leads out to Fynn Hollow."

"I see." This wasn't at all the kind of conversation I'd hoped for. "I suppose this person saw my name in the *Daily Beat* in connection with the Fynn Hollow murder."

"It's possible. The sheriff has gone on record saying the homicide occurred shortly before nine A.M."

"Well, I wasn't heading to Fynn Hollow at that hour on Saturday morning. I was on my way to Briar Creek. River Road is near that gas station, too."

The detective paused, as if that wasn't what he expected me to say. "So, you *were* on the outskirts of town early Saturday morning. Anybody see you out at Briar Creek?"

"Not that I know of."

"Too bad."

"So what if I was getting gas on the edge of town?" I said reasonably. "That doesn't prove anything. I could have been going anywhere. The fact is, I drove out to Briar Creek, as I often do, for an early-morning hike. You believe me, don't you?"

"It doesn't matter what I believe. I have nothing to do with the Fynn Hollow case. However, I am obliged to hand over this tip to the county. I'm just giving you a heads-up, that's all. Of course, I'm sure you probably already told the sheriff about your whereabouts Saturday morning, so this won't be news to them."

"I've answered all their questions," I said, feeling petulant. "I have nothing to hide."

"That's good."

I thanked him for calling and hung up. With slow steps, I continued my walk home, in a far less optimistic mood. The wind shifted, bringing a cold breeze in from the north. I shivered.

It was true that I had answered all of Langham's questions. But he hadn't asked me where I was before I'd met Erik. At least not yet. He'd asked Mila that question. It was only a matter of time before he circled back to me.

I had to do something. I couldn't just sit back and wait for things to happen. I was itching to take action. As I approached the Fieldstone Park fountain, I pulled out my phone again. At this point, all I could really do was to keep asking questions. I decided to take Farrah's advice and try to get more information out of Erik. Luckily, he had given me his number when he emailed me about lunch the other day.

A few seconds later, I had him on the line. "Hello?" he said, sounding slightly rushed.

"Hi, Erik? This is Keli Milanni. Did I catch you at a bad time?"

"Keli! Not at all. I'm at Thorna's house attempting to fix a leaky faucet. But, as I tried to tell her, plumbing is definitely not my forte." He laughed, and said something I couldn't hear—presumably to Thorna. "Hang on. I'm just leaving."

I continued making my way through the park. A moment later, Erik was back. "Okay. I can talk now. How are you? I was afraid I might not hear from you again after what happened last night."

"I'm fine." I hesitated, choosing my words carefully. It seemed apparent Erik wanted to develop some kind of friendship with me. And I *did* like the guy, in a way. But I had to make sure he knew it wasn't more than as a friend. "Viper was really drunk," I said, "but at least he backed off, and no one got hurt. And Billy stopped by my office to apologize, which was nice. But if anything like that ever happens again, you can bet my boyfriend will not be as understanding."

"It will never happen again. I promise. I told Viper if he doesn't grow up, I'm kicking him out of my drum circle. As it is, the council of our Druid Order is going to have a serious talk with him."

"I'm glad to hear it. Look, I know it's not my business, but I can't help wondering—did the reason you and Denise break up have anything to do with Viper?"

"No, it was nothing like that. She was friends with him long before I was. Denise and I argued about a lot of things, but Viper wasn't one of them. Not especially."

"What kinds of things did you argue about?" I asked, trying to keep my tone conversational.

"Stupid stuff, mostly. She ran hot and cold, you know? She was probably bipolar, now that I think about it. One minute she'd be fine, the next minute she'd be snapping at me for no reason. And she would act angry sometimes, when there was absolutely nothing for her to be angry about." He paused.

"It feels wrong talking about her like this, now that she's gone."

"I'm sorry. Do you know if there are any services planned?"

"I think Poppy is planning some kind of memorial. But she's waiting for . . . you know. The killer to be caught."

"That's understandable." I remembered Erik telling me Denise had had a falling-out with Poppy. But if the woman was planning her memorial, they must have been closer than I'd realized. "Have you heard any news on the investigation?"

"No. Luckily, I haven't been harassed by any police officers lately."

"That's good." I slowed my steps as I approached my town house. I wanted to press Erik for more information about Denise, and was just formulating my next question, when I saw something that stopped me in my tracks.

"What is that?" I said.

"What?"

"There's something on my front porch." I edged closer to get a better look and gasped. "Oh, no! It's a dead bird."

"What kind of bird?" asked Erik.

"I don't know. A black bird. I've got to let you go. Talk to you later."

Stepping carefully around the bird, I unlocked the door and went inside. "Wes! Are you home?"

Josie sprang down from the windowsill to see what I was doing. "You haven't been outside today, have you?" I asked her. "Somebody left us a present on the porch. But it doesn't look like you did it. I don't suppose you saw who did it?"

Josie only mewed.

The house was dark, so I checked our usual spot for leaving notes in the kitchen. Sure enough, there was one from Wes: *Jimi asked me to cover a shift at the Loose tonight. Be home late.* In addition to his work at the *Edindale Gazette*, Wes was a part-time bartender at the Loose Rock, a casual nightclub on the other side of Fieldstone Park.

With a sigh, I found some disposable gloves under the kitchen sink, some old newspaper, and a plastic shopping bag. Then I went back outside to wrap up the bird and look around. The neighborhood was quiet. The St. Johns, the older couple who lived on one side of me with their frisky little dog, had left this morning for their long-awaited anniversary cruise— pet-friendly, of course. The young family on the other side hadn't come home from work yet. I glanced at the front of my town house. The door was made of wood, not glass, and the front windows were to the side of the porch. I'd never had a problem with birds flying into the window, but if they did, they'd land in the bushes—not on the welcome mat.

After disposing of the bird, I came inside and put-tered around the house, my mind churning. What did this mean? Some people might not think twice about finding a dead bird, but not witches. We know that an encounter with a bird—dead or alive—is usu-ally an omen.

I recalled Erik saying he'd been finding dead birds in front of his house. He thought it was a sign of Denise's hex. Suddenly, I thought of something else I had in common with Erik: a string of bad luck. I had clients canceling, cops on my back, prank calls—and now a dead bird.

Was I cursed, too?

Josie rubbed against my leg and purred. I laughed. "You're right, Josie. I'm being silly. I need to stop feeling sorry for myself. More action and less fretting."

I grabbed my phone and shot off a text to Farrah.

How ya doin'? Can I bring you anything?

A few seconds later, I received her reply. I'm cool. I have a *man* stopping by soon. Hot date at home. Fill ya in later.

I sighed, as I tossed my phone back into my purse. So much for that. I looked over at Josie who stared at me with narrowed eyes.

"Okay, okay. I'll get your dinner."

As I opened a can of cat food, my mind returned to the dead bird. There were no marks of a predator. Someone had placed it on my doorstep. I didn't know who or why, but I felt sure it had to be connected to the people in Fynn Hollow. I needed to learn more about them.

I checked the time. Julie usually left the law office at 5:00, so I couldn't catch her there. But I had her number in my address book. I dialed and waited. When she picked up, she sounded exceptionally pleased to hear from me. In fact, she sounded giddy. I checked the time. *Ah. Happy hour.*

"Of course I can chat!" she said, in answer to my question. "Why don't you join us at the Loose? Your man is here, you know. Fighting off the ladies!"

"I don't doubt it. I'll be there in a few."

I freshened up and changed into jeans, a scoop-neck dusty rose sweater, and a necklace Wes had given me as a Yule gift. It was a lovely diamond-accented crescent moon. My lucky charm.

I decided to walk, even though, as I admonished myself, I was going to the nightclub for information, not booze. On the other hand, maybe a nice, stiff drink was just what I needed, considering the week I'd had. And it was only Wednesday.

"There she is!" shouted Julie, as soon as I entered the club. "The rebel attorney!"

I waved at her, then moved toward the bar to say hi to Wes. He beamed in surprise, but was distracted when a waitress handed him a stack of drink orders. I blew him a kiss and made my way to Julie's table toward the back.

She introduced me to her friends, all legal secretaries or receptionists like herself. They were a peppy group of bright-eyed twentysomethings, who appeared well on their way to putting the *happy* in happy hour. *Ah, to be so innocent.*

"Why did you call me a rebel?" I asked Julie. "Just because I'm not wearing a suit?"

"'Cause you gave up your partner position! You made it, then let it all go to strike out on your own, like the Lone Ranger or something. Who does that?"

"Only the brave," said one of the young women.

"Or the crazy," I countered with a smile.

A waitress stopped at our table and set a drink in front of me. "Courtesy of the bartender," she said.

I glanced over at Wes, who tossed me an exaggerated wink. Laughing, I raised my glass in thanks and took a sip. Just as I suspected, it was one of my old favorites: rum and Coke, with a wedge of lime.

Julie grabbed my arm. "Do a shot with us, Keli! Becca got a promotion, so we're celebrating."

"That's awesome! Congrats, Becca. But no to the shot. I'm good."

"Well, the night's still young. Ooh, root beer barrels! Just like in college." She slid a shot glass in front of me in spite of my refusal. I realized I better get a move on with my questions, before the table got too wild for conversation.

"Anyone else here from Fynn Hollow?" I asked.

"No, just me," said Julie. "Oh, yeah, you said you have more questions about Denise Crowley. I don't know what else I can tell you. I hardly ever saw her after high school. She was kind of a funky, different kind of person. But interesting. And self-confident. She seemed like she always stayed true to herself."

Once again, I found myself wishing I'd had a chance to know Denise when she was alive. I always admired people who were true to themselves.

"Oh!" said Julie, grabbing my arm again. "You know who I *did* see recently? Poppy Sheahan. She was hanging up flyers on a bulletin board at the university. I saw her on my way to the law library to pick up a book Crenshaw ordered."

"Crenshaw sent you on an errand?"

Julie shrugged. "You sound like Beverly. But I didn't mind. It's good to get out of the office now and then. Anyway, I recognized Poppy from halfway across the quad. She has the same bright hair and loud, colorful style she always did. I was gonna say hello and, you know, give her my condolences. But she left before I got there."

"Too bad. Any idea what the flyers were for?"

"Yeah, I was curious, too. They were for an art festival coming up this Saturday. It's happening at Fieldstone Park."

"The Earth Day Art Festival? I heard about that. So, Poppy's involved with the festival?"

"I guess so." Julie turned to her friends. "Who's hungry? Should we order some food?"

Just then, Becca looked over my shoulder toward the door and drew in her breath. "Uh-oh. They're coming for you, Julie."

I followed her gaze and nearly spilled my drink. It was Deputy Langham, in full uniform, complete with a Smokey the Bear–style hat and big silver badge. His eagle eyes swept the room, and I quickly turned away and slouched in my seat. *What is he doing here?*

Julie and her friends giggled, but I couldn't join in. I dared another peek and saw Langham speaking with the waitress. She pointed at Wes, who was rattling a cocktail shaker with his back to the door. Langham nodded and moseyed up to the bar, looking anything but casual. He removed his hat and settled onto a stool near the end, where he had a perfect view of anyone entering or exiting through the front door. *Like a sentinel,* I thought.

When the waitress stopped at our table with the next round of shots, I motioned her closer. "What does the cop want?" I asked.

"He wants to chat with Wes. But he said he's not in a hurry. He'll wait for Wes to take a break."

Terrific. He probably wanted to grill Wes about my whereabouts on Saturday. And he came here instead of the house to catch Wes off guard and prevent him from conferring with me. I just knew it.

"Want another rum and Coke?" asked the waitress.

"No, thanks," I said glumly.

After she took food orders from Julie and the others, I watched her disappear through the swinging doors to the kitchen. I knew there was a service door in there that led to the alley behind the bar. A back-door escape seemed awfully appealing right about now.

I squeezed the lime into the remains of my drink as I pondered what to do. I didn't know why I was so jittery. So what if Langham saw me? He wouldn't decide to interrogate me right here and now. Would he?

Julie leaned over and slid a shot glass in front of me. It was filled to the rim. "Come on. For old times' sake. It's not the same without you at the firm. Crenshaw sulked for a week after you left."

"How could you tell?"

Julie cackled. "Good point! He's always kind of a sourpuss, isn't he?"

I spared another glance toward Langham and saw he was now sipping a cola. Then the door opened again, and I nearly fell out of my chair. It was Viper, in tight jeans, leather jacket, and permanent scowl. He sauntered right past Langham and slid into a booth as if he owned the place.

Boy, for somebody who can't drive, he sure gets around. All at once, my mind conjured an unpleasant scenario. What if Viper saw me and came over to apologize for his uncivilized behavior? Stranger things had happened. And then, what if Langham saw us together? It would totally undermine my insistence that I wasn't friends with the Fynn Hollow crew.

Julie scraped her chair back and stood up. "Gotta visit the little girl's room." She swayed on her feet and grabbed my shoulder for balance. "Whoa! Got up too fast. Hey, what's this? You sly dog, Keli! Did you get a tattoo?"

"What? No!" I slapped my hand to my chest, closing the gap Julie had accidentally looked down.

Evidently, my sigil wasn't as low on my chest as I'd thought. "You're seeing things."

Julie wagged her finger at me and giggled. "Don't worry. I won't tell."

As she stumbled off, I shook my head. With my hand still pressed to my heart, I breathed in the energy of the ankh. Then I peered across the bar at Langham, who was as immovable as an iron fixture, and Viper, who scanned the room as if he was looking for somebody. It was getting way too crowded in here. In one quick motion, I tossed back the root beer–flavored shot. Making a face, I darted for the kitchen door. And I didn't stop until I was safely at home.

CHAPTER TWELVE

The next morning, instead of going into work, I hopped into my car and headed for Fynn Hollow. I hoped to chat with Thorna and gather more intel on Denise and her friends. In particular, I wanted to learn more about the midnight callers Denise used to receive. Truth be told, I was also avoiding my office. Not only did I have no clients, but I was also afraid Langham might decide to drop in on me.

When Wes had come home from the bar, he told me he'd made Langham wait for more than an hour. By the time they finally spoke, the deputy had consumed four sodas and was practically dancing before he excused himself to go to the bathroom. Wes thought that was hilarious. He was even more pleased with himself for providing my airtight alibi. He'd guaranteed Langham I was at home, snug as a bug in bed with Wes, right up until the time I left for Moonstone Treasures.

Unfortunately, Wes didn't know about my call with Detective Rhinehardt, and I didn't have the heart to tell him. More likely than not, Langham already knew I was seen out on Old County Road at the crack of dawn last Saturday. Even if Wes had made an honest mistake about the time, my credibility—and his—had just slipped another couple of notches in Langham's eyes.

I put all that out of my mind as I cruised into Fynn Hollow and retraced the route Erik and I had taken to Denise's house. Thorna's house was easy to find, since it was right next door. Her bungalow was similar in size and style to Denise's place, though plainer, with slate-gray siding and black shutters. As I walked up the cobblestone path to her front door, a flock of crows erupted from a nearby tree, cawing madly as they took flight. I glanced over at Denise's house, dark and quiet. The wind chimes hung forlornly on the porch, limp in the still air.

I rang Thorna's doorbell and waited. Her house was dark, too. I should have known she wouldn't be home. After all, it was a weekday morning, a time when most people were at their jobs. I wondered where she worked and if there was any chance I could track her down.

Back in my car, I drove past Denise's house and around the block. I also wondered where Erik lived. He'd said it was within walking distance of Denise's place. But there was hardly anyone around. I saw one gardener pruning hedges and one woman pushing a baby carriage, and that was it.

I turned onto the main drag and circled the tiny downtown. As a bedroom community, most of Fynn Hollow's residents commuted to Edindale or Coralville for work. I passed a few shops, offices, and restaurants, but nothing looked very promising. I imagined the town was probably more bustling in the summertime.

I crossed the railroad tracks and passed by a bowling alley, a shuttered factory, and a mechanic's garage. An old Camaro parked in front of the garage caught my eye. Where had I seen that car before? As if in answer, Viper came out of the garage, wearing stained coveralls and a ball cap. An oily rag dangled from his back pocket. He looked up as I passed by and our eyes locked. If I hadn't been caught off guard, I might have waved, or even stopped. Instead, I hit the gas pedal and sped away.

What a chicken! I chided myself.

After a few more minutes of aimless driving, I returned to Thorna's house. This time I was in luck. There was a car in the driveway. For the second time, I went up to her door and rang the bell. She answered right away, but appeared startled to see me. I couldn't blame her.

"Hi," I said. "Sorry to drop in like this. I wondered if I could talk to you for a minute."

"Um, okay. Come on in." She stood back and ushered me inside. "I'm on my lunch break from work, but I'm in no hurry to go back. I couldn't have picked a more boring job."

"Oh?" I asked pleasantly, as I followed her to her small but clean kitchen. I sat at the table and watched as she bustled about, taking two glasses from a cabinet and filling them with tap water.

"Yeah. I'm an administrative assistant for an insurance salesman, and it's the same thing every day: answer the phone, process claims, mail out sales materials. Scintillating stuff."

"Been doing it long?"

"Too long. I shouldn't complain, though. At least it's a job, right?"

She pulled a prepared diet meal from the freezer and slit the plastic with a fork. "Want one? I have more."

"That's okay. I'm really sorry to interrupt your lunch. I just keep thinking about Denise and wanted to talk with someone who knew her. How are you holding up?"

"I'm managing. It's a bit freaky living so close to a murder scene, but I'm not afraid, if that's what you mean. It was clearly a targeted thing. Denise courted danger."

"What do you mean?"

"I mean she was careless. She stirred up dark energies without taking adequate precautions. I don't know how much you know about witchcraft, but it's not all fluffy bunny candles and crystals. There's real power out there."

"Hmm," I said noncommittally. "But it wasn't a dark spirit that killed Denise. It was a human being acting of their own free will. I assume."

Thorna lifted one shoulder. "Well, Denise wasn't exactly discerning about the humans she let into her life either."

"Are you talking about her customers? The other day you mentioned she often had visitors late at night."

She snickered. "Yeah. Men mostly. A lot of different men. And they didn't leave with their purchases, if you get my drift."

It took me a second to catch on. "Oh! You mean . . ."

She shrugged again. "A girl's got to make a living, I guess."

Thorna took her meal from the microwave and sat

down across from me. She peeled back the plastic,
releasing steam into the air, and stirred the food—
some unidentifiable meat-based stew, from what I
could tell. As I watched her, I began to wonder how
well Thorna had really known Denise. She seemed to
do an awful lot of speculating.

"At least Billy seems nice," I ventured. "I understand he and Denise were school friends."

"Yeah, Billy's a sweetheart. A little naïve, but he
can't help it."

"How did you first meet Billy? Was it through
Denise?"

"Gosh, I don't even remember. This is a small
town and an even smaller Pagan community. I probably met him at some event or gathering."

"Same with Viper?"

She snorted. "Yeah, unfortunately. He's a piece
of work. You gotta watch that one. But I guess you
found that out the other night."

"I guess I did. What's his deal anyway? Is he just a
harmless stoner? Or is he real trouble?"

"Oh, he's trouble all right. But it's usually trouble
he brings upon himself." She took a bite of her food
and chewed thoughtfully. "He thinks he's a ladies'
man. Actually, he does get a lot of women. Don't ask
me how. Maybe it's through magic. Frankly, I don't
see the appeal."

"I'm with you there."

Thorna gave me a sly look. "Denise wasn't. I don't
know what she saw in him. Whatever it was, she saw a
lot of it."

"Was Viper one of her late-night visitors?"

"Mm-hmm. Daytime, night-time. Anytime Erik
wasn't around."

"You mean this was while she was dating Erik?" I don't know why, but this surprised me.

"Oh, yeah. Poor guy. He had no idea."

"Well, they did break up. Maybe that was why."

"Could be. At least, partly."

"From what I can tell, Erik seems like a pretty decent guy. Of course, I haven't known him long. But he invited me to the Beltane Festival next week. Are you going?"

"Of course; wouldn't miss it. It's a great party. You should go." She finished off her stew and wiped her mouth. "Erik *is* a decent guy. He's nice to everybody. I sometimes wonder if he's jinxed, though."

"Jinxed? You mean Denise's curse?"

"I don't know if she really cursed him. I wouldn't put it past her. But Erik had bad luck even before he broke it off with Denise. In fact, maybe *she* picked up some of his bad vibes. People who get close to Erik tend to have their own bad luck—like Viper getting arrested, Billy never keeping a girlfriend. And Denise getting killed. That's what I mean by jinxed."

I was speechless. I had never met anyone so superstitious before—and I was a Witch! I believed in a lot of unconventional ideas, but this seemed a little too far-fetched.

Thorna tossed her plastic meal tray in the garbage. "Don't worry. I'm sure you're safe. Anyway, Erik's bad luck hasn't rubbed off on me yet—knock on wood." She rapped on the table. "I'm sure you don't have anything to worry about."

Right. I'd be sure, too, if it weren't for my own little string of bad luck. But I didn't believe in jinxes. Did I?

* * *

When I returned to Edindale, I stopped by the drugstore for some toiletries and makeup. Then I swung by my office as a matter of course, even though I didn't have much work to do. After watering my plants and dusting the waiting room, I took the opportunity to file and polish my nails. It would figure that the moment my nails were wet the phone would ring. I used the eraser end of a pencil to hit the speaker button.

"Hello! Keli Milanni here."

"Keli, this is Carol Peters. There's something I need to tell you."

"Would you like to come by my office?"

"No, I don't have time. But this has been bothering me, and I realized I need to tell you everything."

"Go ahead, Carol. I'm listening."

"Well, you know my ex-husband is trying to portray me as being irresponsible, et cetera, because I'm Wiccan. And his new wife is telling everybody who will listen that I'm exposing the children to inappropriate things. It's all total B.S. I know you know this. But then I started to think about all these examples they could use. Like, I woke the kids up in the middle of the night so they could see the eclipse—which they loved. But could that be seen as bad parenting? And I've taken them out of school early on nice days, so we could go to the park and enjoy nature. I only did that a couple times, and their attendance is really good otherwise." She was speaking quickly, and I could tell she was nervous.

"Carol, you didn't do anything wrong. Besides, I'm sure non-Wiccan parents have done the same thing."

"There's one other thing. Last summer I took the kids to Wicca-Fest up north. I told their dad we were visiting friends, which was sort of true. Don't get me wrong. The festival is kid-friendly. Some of the ceremonies can be a little intense—a few people get real into it and wail and writhe, the whole bit. But we steered clear of that sort of thing. And one of the circles does allow participants to go skyclad, if they choose, but that section was for adults only. Anyway, the kids had a great time. They thought some of the costumes were funny. But now I'm looking at everything through a judge's eyes, and I'm worried about how this might look."

I thought about my answer before speaking. Carol was right that her ex-husband could make a big deal of the fact that she took their children to a religious event without his knowledge. However, he always knew she was Wiccan, and it wasn't until recently that it had become a problem for him. "At this point, I don't think there's anything to worry about. If he finds out about Wicca-Fest and tries to make an issue of it, I'll argue there was no harm done. It's really not much different than taking your children to a music festival or a Renaissance Faire, which is something lots of people do."

"That's true. Okay, I feel better. By the way, he doesn't know this either, but I'm taking the kids to the Beltane Festival next weekend. I had to stretch the truth a little to get him to switch weekends with me, but only because his wife is so repressed. Anyway, the kids have been looking forward to it for months."

"I've heard it's a fun event."

"For sure. Maybe we'll see you there!"

After ringing off with Carol, I blew on my nails and considered her predicament. How sad that she had to hide such an important part of her life. Of course, I hid aspects of my life, too, but I didn't let it bother me. At least not too much.

There were no more calls or messages. For the next hour, I did little more than stare at the walls. *That's it,* I decided, as I shouldered my purse once more. I'd been putting it off long enough. I needed to perform an abundance spell. *Otherwise I won't even have these walls to stare at for much longer.*

Besides, there couldn't be a more auspicious time for a prosperity ritual. It was springtime during a waxing moon, following the new moon in Taurus. And it was a Thursday, Jupiter's day, which corresponds with financial matters and success. On top of that, Beltane was coming up. As a holiday that celebrates abundance, growth, and increase, Beltane presented a prime opportunity to think about what I wanted to attract more of in my own life.

As soon as I got home, I gathered the supplies I would need for the sympathetic magic I had in mind. I would perform a ceremony that symbolically represented what I wanted to create in my daily life. In this case, I would plant some literal seeds, tend to them, and watch them grow—just as my business would grow and flourish. I hoped.

With both neighbors away from home, and the back of my yard shielded by a wooden fence and tall trees, I felt comfortable working a little magic outdoors. First, I did some tidying up, sweeping the walkway and filling the birdbath. Then I selected a sunny patch near my vegetable garden and marked out a circle, about six feet in diameter. Taking four flat stones from the border around the patio, I placed them at each cardinal direction to use as candle holders. I carefully placed and lit the candles—green

for money and new growth, naturally—and silently
called the spirits of the elements at each direction.
Once the circle was cast, I faced north, the direction associated with earth energies, and invoked the Roman
deity, Ops, Goddess of Plenty, and her husband, Saturn.
Together, they inspired visions of sparkling wealth,
gifts of largesse, bountiful crops, and joyous feasts.

Filled with the energy of abundance, I took up
a stick and poked small holes in the earth, making a
circle within the circle. In each hole, I buried a small
offering and recited a corresponding rhyme:

> *Cinnamon and clove will dreams ignite*
> *Powdered root for blessings bright*
> *A crystal quartz clears blocks where stuck*
> *Copper coins bring riches and luck*

In the center of the circles, I made three more
holes and placed a single sunflower seed in each one.
As I sprinkled them with soil and a splash of water, I
voiced my intention. "I plant these seeds of hope for
my success and prosperity."

Finally, I stuck three whimsical glass-and-metal
garden stakes in the ground and chanted my new
mantra:

> *People to serve*
> *Business to grow*
> *Clients to help*
> *Abundance to flow*

I awoke the next day to sunlight streaming
through my bedroom window. Now that I was my
own boss, I'd stopped setting an alarm clock. But

getting up was no problem. I had a good feeling about today.

After a quick shower, I took my morning brew out to the garden and sat in a lawn chair for a few moments of contemplation. A big part of magical working is what the witch brings to the spell. In other words, her mind-set. For my spell to work, I had to believe it would.

I repeated to myself the words I'd uttered the night before: "People to serve, business to grow. Clients to help, abundance to flow." I held the sentiment in my mind as I dressed in a lightweight pants suit and slipped on jade-and-gold jewelry: a pair of delicate drop earrings and a ring on the index finger of my right hand. I continued to replay the mantra in my mind during my walk to work. By the time I arrived to my building, I'd said it so many times I wasn't one bit surprised to find a man waiting for me outside my office door.

His appearance, however, *was* a little surprising. He had long, curly black hair that draped over his burly shoulders, and he was clad all in black, from his long, beltless trench coat to his clunky buckled boots. Perhaps most striking, though, was the amount of hardware he sported, which included skull rings on every finger, spiked leather cuffs on each wrist, and multiple earrings studding the length of both ears. I couldn't decide if he'd fit in better with a motorcycle gang or a steampunk club. Then I saw the silver pentacle, hanging like a medallion around his neck.

"Hello," I said politely. "Can I help you?"

At that moment, steps sounded behind me, and I turned to see Annie patter up the hallway.

"Good morning, neighbor!" she called. "How are

you this lovely—" She stopped short when she caught sight of the imposing stranger.

"Good morning, ladies," he said. "I hope I'm in the right place. I'm looking for the Witch Lawyer."

Annie wrinkled her brow. "I'm sorry. Did you say 'witch lawyer'?"

He nodded as he reached into his jacket pocket. "I don't use the title myself. I'm a necromancer. But it's not too far off. Let's see." He squinted at the paper he retrieved from his pocket. "Yes. I'm looking for a gal by the name of Miss Keli Milanni, Lawyer to the Witches." He looked at me expectantly. So did Annie.

I swallowed, then raised my hand slowly, like a timid student who wanted to hide under her school desk.

"That would be me."

CHAPTER THIRTEEN

Sometimes the Goddess has a wicked sense of humor. In my experience, manifestation spells don't usually produce such immediate results. They have to simmer for a bit, while the cosmic gears shift and the stars move into alignment. Yet, if I've learned anything in my years as a witch, it's that life is full of mystery and wonder. During my interview with the necromancer, my phone rang no less than eight times, and two other potential clients came knocking on my door.

Of course, none of the other prospects were quite as interesting as the necromancer, aka Arlen Prince. He was a polite, talkative guy, if somewhat intense. Though I was familiar with the practice of necromancy, or divination through communication with the dead, I was still fascinated to hear about Arlen's technique. And he was eager to share. As he explained, he's an animal necromancer. He collects animal bones, feathers, shells, and other physical items found in the wild and uses them to commune with animal spirits. Oftentimes, before using bones in magical work, he must clean and purify them in a ritual that serves both practical and spiritual purposes. Unfortunately, some of his neighbors caught wind of the practice and were none too happy. They thought he was engaging in animal sacrifice and reported him to the authorities.

"I don't sacrifice animals," he told me. "I leave offerings for animal spirits, but that's totally different."

"Was that clear to the county officials?" I asked.

"Yeah, that much was. But they still didn't like the whole thing. I could tell. They were just looking for something to charge me with. They pawed through my collections looking for parts from endangered species." He shook with indignation. "In the end, they gave me a ticket for engaging in taxidermy without a permit."

"Taxidermy? Do you do that as well?"

"Not really. I do mount antlers for hunters sometimes, as a side business. But I work on a barter basis—they give me some of the meat. I didn't think that should require a license."

He showed me a copy of the citation, which indicated his hearing date was on Monday—three days away.

"I have to tell you, this isn't exactly my area of expertise. You might be better off finding an attorney more familiar with the county administrative hearing process."

"No." He shook his head adamantly. "It has to be you. My friend Carol gave me your name, and the bones confirmed it."

"I see. Well, I'm willing to research the law and represent you at the hearing. Why don't we start there and see where that takes us?"

"Perfect."

While Arlen was my most unique visitor that day,

the one who came by in the afternoon was the most exciting for me. He'd called first and was delighted I could see him so soon. So was I. Neal Jameson was a prominent restaurateur, hotelier, and philanthropist with loads of money and influence. I'd met him last fall at the benefit masquerade ball he'd held at his country estate. I was actually a little surprised he'd called. He was my former boss's client.

"Lovely to see you again, Keli," he said, as I invited him into my office. A spry, trim man in a tailored navy blazer paired with white trousers fit for the poshest of yacht clubs, he exuded a sparkling, easygoing manner. I appreciated the fact that he didn't bat an eye at my modest workplace.

"It's lovely to see you as well. Though I have to admit I was a little surprised to receive your call."

"Of course, of course. Beverly usually handles my legal matters. However, she has a conflict of interest in this case. I know I would have been in capable hands with one of the other attorneys at the firm. But when I learned you'd opened your own practice, I knew at once that this was the way to go. The fewer people who know about my plans, the better."

"Well, it's only me here. I can assure you, our conversation is one hundred percent confidential."

"Perfect. That's what I like to hear. You see, I have a little surprise planned for a dear friend of mine. I'm going to purchase her childhood home and land, a twenty-acre property called Red Gate Hollow. It will be a gift for her, a dream come true. In fact, she's been wanting to buy the property herself. She'll insist on giving me a fair price, which is why I absolutely must get the best price possible."

I nodded. So far, it sounded like a standard real

estate negotiation. The goal is always to get the best price possible.

"There's only one small catch. The land is currently owned by Gretta Harrison. As you know, the Harrisons are longtime clients of the Olsen law firm, which is the conflict I mentioned. But the real problem is that Gretta and I have a history, if you will. If she knows how badly I want the property, the price will quadruple. So, we must play our hand close to the vest."

"I understand."

"I knew you would. This is really important to me . . . and to my friend—I hope she'll also be my business partner. You see, the land currently contains an established apple orchard that has been transitioning to organic growing methods for the past three years. It's very close to meeting the requirements for USDA certification. I would love to use those apples in my restaurants."

"Organic apple pie? That sounds wonderful."

"Yes, indeed. And . . . that's not all. The property abuts another farm owned by one of my suppliers. It's also being certified organic, and it's downwind of Red Gate Hollow. So, you see, I need to have control over Red Gate to ensure it never reverts to conventional methods, thus threatening the purity of my supplier's produce. You understand?"

"Yes. That makes perfect sense."

"Wonderful. This is a rare opportunity all around. Of course, I'm not the only interested buyer. So, we have to act fast. And, again, discretion is of the utmost importance. We mustn't appear overly eager."

"Do you have a Realtor you're working with?"

"Oh, I never work with Realtors. It's not necessary.

I'd like you to submit an offer on my behalf, the sooner, the better."

"Certainly. I'll perform a title search and make sure it's clear. I can also find the fair market value and let you know as you decide on your offer. I can have the information by Monday."

"Very good." He stood and shook my hand. "The truth is, I must have that property and will pay any price. But the seller doesn't need to know that."

"Of course."

It was after dark when I arrived home after work, almost like the old days when I used to spend long hours at the firm. Wes had dinner already made and waiting on the stovetop. I inhaled the delicious aroma of linguini with tomato sauce and fresh asparagus as I entered the kitchen. As he filled our plates, I couldn't resist encircling his waist and kissing the back of his neck—which had a slightly distracting effect on both of us and led to a slight delay in the actual eating of the dinner.

I was in quite a good mood when we finally sat down to our warmed-up meal. Not only did I have a satisfyingly busy day at work, but I'd also had a blissfully free interlude from Deputy Langham. Wes and I clinked wineglasses and shared the highlights of our day. Afterward, we were in the midst of clearing the table when the house phone rang. I froze, immediately on alert again.

"I'll get it," said Wes, who was closer anyway.

As I corked the wine bottle, I listened to Wes say "hello." A moment later, he called out, "It's for you. Some guy."

I traded him the wine bottle for the phone receiver and said a tentative "hello."

"Hey, Keli! This is Erik. Do you have a minute?"

"Erik! Hi. Why are you calling me at this number?"

"This is your phone, isn't it?"

"Yeah, but it's not my cell."

"Oh. Right. I accidentally erased your number from my phone and had to look you up. This is the number I found. Listen, I have some news."

"Good news?"

"It could be. It's sort of a good news-bad news situation right now."

I glanced at Wes, who was eyeing me suspiciously. I mouthed the words "*It's okay*," and settled onto the sofa with my legs curled beneath me. Josie appeared and hopped onto my lap.

"Go on," I said to Erik.

"A buddy of mine from the Order is seeing this gal, Soleil, who was a client of Denise's."

"Soleil? That's a pretty name."

"Yeah, that's her craft name, but she pretty much goes by it all the time. Anyway, Soleil has been all upset these past few days, understandably. She went to the cops and asked them if they've examined Denise's appointment book. Soleil figured if Denise had an appointment Saturday morning, it would be written in that book."

"That sounds logical."

"For sure. I'd forgotten about that datebook, until my buddy mentioned it. Then I remembered. It's an unusual book, bound in leather and embossed with fancy designs. And it has a lock, like a diary. Denise was real protective of her clients. So, the good part is that you and I won't be in that appointment book, which means we should be off the hook in the investigation."

"That's great! That's fantastic news. Maybe that's why I haven't heard from Langham lately. As of Wednesday night, he was still interested in me enough to track down my boyfriend and grill him about me."

"Well, now for the bad news. The datebook seems to be missing."

"What? How do you know?"

"'Cause Langham was just here asking me about it. He wondered if I'd seen it when we found Denise."

"Dang. I guess he'll be asking me the same question."

"Probably. I don't remember seeing it that day. I'd love to go look for it, though."

"What, in her house? You shouldn't go back there, at least not without the police. If you think you know where it might be, you should let the cops know."

"I know. You're right. I told them it would probably be in her workroom, but I'm sure they've scoured the place."

We were each silent for a moment, and my mind returned to the success of my abundance spell the night before. "Hey, Erik, let me ask you something. Have you thought about casting a spell to bring forth answers about what happened to Denise?"

"Sure, I've thought about it. I lit a candle for her and tried to send her a blessing of peace. I even set aside the money I owed her and decided to dedicate it to something in her name. I'm just not sure what yet."

"That's really nice, Erik. I think that sounds lovely. But I think there are other things we might try in the meantime."

For the next hour or so, Erik and I compared notes about spells and rituals we'd conducted, especially around protection, banishment, and drawing energy for specific purposes. I told him about past cases where I'd used magic to find lost objects and clues to puzzling mysteries. He was both intrigued and excited about the possibilities.

A few times during our conversation, I was aware of Wes walking by and giving me questioning looks. I flashed him a small smile each time, to let him know there was nothing to worry about. I wasn't sure he was entirely convinced. When I finally hung up and joined him upstairs, he appeared very put out. "Finally off the phone?" he huffed.

"What's the big deal?" I asked, as I slipped on my pajamas.

"Nothing. You just seemed awful chummy with the guy. He's the one whose girlfriend was murdered, right?"

"Ex-girlfriend. So?"

"So, I just think you should be careful, that's all. What do you really know about this guy, except that he's friends with the creep who defaced Farrah's cast?"

"I know a little more than that. He's a nice guy, Wes. I think you'd like him, if you gave him a chance."

"Hmph. Nice or not, I don't trust him."

I kissed Wes good night and turned out the light. In the darkness, I allowed myself a small smile. If I wasn't mistaken, it sounded like Wes was a tiny bit jealous of Erik. Of course, it was completely unfounded.

As I lay in bed, I thought about my client meetings earlier in the day, and recalled the first time I'd met

Neal Jameson at his masquerade party. That was quite an experience. Literally everyone at the party was in a mask.

Suddenly, I recalled the vision at my altar the night Denise was killed. In it, she was surrounded by masked men and women. Everyone around her was hiding something.

Perhaps I shouldn't be so quick to trust Erik after all.

Chapter Fourteen

I spent the first part of my Saturday doing title research online. I was going to do everything in my power to get answers for Neal Jameson faster than he could imagine. If I could help him get a good price, and a fast closing, on the property he wanted, it would be a real boon for my new business. As soon as I completed the research and typed up my notes, I shot off a secure email to Mr. Jameson. Then I joined Wes in the backyard where he was taking pictures of insects. I asked if he'd like to go to the art fair with me and he agreed.

He was unusually quiet on our walk to the park, but I didn't think much of it. I was absorbed in my own thoughts. When we passed through the balloon-festooned archway that marked the entrance to the fair, I paused and took in the lay of the land. Rows of white pop-up canopy tents lined sections of the road-way intersecting a wide lawn. The vendors seemed to be roughly organized by medium, though the wide variety of displays created a kaleidoscope effect. Silk scarves fluttered near tie-dyed shirts, while glazed

ceramics gleamed beside boldly modern canvas art.
Strains of bluegrass music filled the air from some-
where beyond a line of brightly painted food trucks.
I scanned the area for the crafts section.

"I want to see if Fern Lopez is here," I said. "She
usually sells her beadwork at events like this."

"Okay. I'm gonna check out the photography
booths."

"Oh, you don't want to—?"

Wes took off across the lawn before I could finish
the sentence.

"Alrighty, then," I said to myself. I had thought we
would stick together, but it didn't matter. I imagined
Wes wanted to support his fellow photographers, and
possibly even decide if he should rent his own table
next year.

I headed to a line of vendors selling assorted crafts
and handmade jewelry. It didn't take long to spot the
woman I sought. Fern Lopez was unmistakable with
her long, brown braid and Southwest-style shawl. She
had been a friend of Aunt Josephine back in their
commune-living hippie days, and Fern still lived
close to the land on her homestead in the country.
But she wasn't exactly a free-spirited poster child for
peace and love. From the first time I'd met her, she
struck me as more of a suspicious-minded cynic,
always distrustful of "the man." I was pleased when
she'd finally warmed up to me over the past year. She
even smiled when she saw me approach her table.
That had to be a first.

"It's nice to see you, Keli. I wondered if I might
run into you today."

"It's great to see you, too. What a perfect day for
a fair."

We chatted pleasantly for a few minutes, and I admired her latest bead creations. Then I brought up the topic foremost on my mind.

"I suppose you heard about the murder in Fynn Hollow."

"Mm-hmm."

"Do you know anyone who lives there?"

"I know a couple people. I didn't know the victim, though. She was a young woman, I believe. It's sad."

"Yes. Very sad. What are folks saying about the murder, if you don't mind me asking? Have you heard any theories?"

She pressed her lips together and nodded slowly. I wasn't entirely sure how it was that Fern always had the inside scoop on happenings far and wide, though I had a vague idea. I knew she was part of an underground network of environmentalists called the Sisterhood. Perhaps someday she'd let me in on her secrets. On the other hand, maybe I was better off not knowing.

"The prevailing theory seems most likely," she said. "This one was domestic."

"Domestic? But Denise lived alone."

"I mean it was personal, somebody close to her. There's no conspiracy or cover-up of something larger here."

"Oh. Right." Fern had always been quick to suspect corruption and collusion, so I was glad to hear her acknowledge that wasn't the case this time. Not that I ever thought it was.

"From what I gather," she continued, "all evidence indicates the killer was known to the victim. It was probably somebody she trusted. Besides, when it comes to intentional poisonings, it's almost always a family member, isn't it?"

"I suppose so. Such a shame."

I bought a colorful bead bracelet from Fern and moved on down the sidewalk. Even though I'd already come to the same conclusion she had, I was still troubled by what she'd said. I couldn't say why exactly. Maybe it was because domestic disputes usually involved a husband or boyfriend. Or ex-boyfriend.

As I made my way to the center of the fair, the milling crowds became thicker. And no wonder—it really was a gorgeous spring day. I kept an eye out for the other person I was hoping to see, Denise's friend Poppy. In the meantime, I enjoyed looking at the wide variety of artwork, from charcoal, acrylic, and watercolor, to etchings and prints. I wondered if Denise would have displayed her paintings here, though I didn't notice any empty tables.

I paused to study an unusual collage that seemed to consist of bits of flower parts glued to fabric and magazine pages, when my ears picked up a familiar sound. It was a high-pitched girlish laugh that reminded me of Poppy's wail outside Denise's house. I peered around an easel to the line of vendors one row over. Sure enough, there she was, looking considerably happier than I'd seen her before. Her high ponytail was tied in a bright yellow ribbon, and her short pale green chiffon dress called to mind a butterfly. Her cheeks were flushed. As I moved closer, I saw why. She seemed to be enjoying the attentions of a guy at her table. My view was partially blocked by the dawdling pedestrians, but I saw enough to witness the guy raise his shirt, revealing narrow hips and a nicely toned torso.

Hey, wait a minute.

I knew that torso. And those hips. Very well. That guy was Wes!

I pushed my way through the crowd and rushed up to the table in time to see Poppy crouch down and touch my boyfriend's bare skin. She traced the edges of the dragon tattoo inked along Wes's side and lower back. I cleared my throat.

Wes looked up and dropped his shirt. "Hey, babe. Check this out." He draped his arm casually around my waist and pointed at the framed photos posted all around Poppy's table. "She specializes in photographing tattoos. Aren't they cool?"

"Yeah. Cool."

I couldn't help noticing a marked change in Poppy's demeanor. The second Wes had pulled me close to him, her smile dropped off her face. She gave me a stony glare and said nothing.

I glanced at her photos again. They actually were pretty interesting. The portraits were rich in color and detail, while also showcasing their subjects in a way that was strangely moving. I supposed she might be considered her own kind of tattoo artist. As Wes studied one of the photos, I gathered he had no idea who she was. I'd never told him the names of Denise's friends, other than Erik.

Putting on my friendliest smile, I said, "You're Poppy Sheahan, aren't you?"

She nodded curtly and pointed at the banner above her table. It prominently displayed her name.

Undaunted, I kept up the winsome attitude. "You probably don't remember me. I'm Keli Milanni. I'm a friend of Erik Grayson." As soon as the words left my mouth, I realized I was perpetuating the very thing I kept denying.

Oh, well. At this point, maybe we really are friends.

Poppy wasn't impressed. Worse, at the mention of Erik's name, I'd felt Wes stiffen beside me. He dropped his arm and backed up a step.

"And Julie Barnes," I went on, belatedly remembering our other mutual acquaintance. "I know Julie, too. Anyway, I just wanted to say I'm really sorry about Denise. I'm sorry for your loss."

Poppy turned her back on me. I looked toward Wes, but he was no help. He'd drifted away and was now looking at the photo displays at the next table.

I inched closer to Poppy and spoke to her back. "I was wondering if I could ask you a few questions. How was Denise acting in the days before her death? Did she say anything about any conflicts she was having?"

Poppy whirled around. Her eyes brimmed and her lower lip trembled. "I don't have to answer to you," she spat. "I've already spoken to the police."

"Oh. Okay. I'm sorry."

She'd already turned away again, so I retreated, feeling like a heel. I caught up with Wes two tables down.

"I'm ready to go home," I said. "What do you say?"

"Actually, the *Gazette* has a table here somewhere. They're trying to get new subscribers with a raffle or something. I should stop by and say hi. I'll see you at home."

He took off, leaving me alone.

Fine.

I left the fair and walked home at a brisk pace. As I left the park, I decided I should change into running shoes and head over to the rail trail. Maybe I could outrun my frustrations. But when I turned the corner onto my street, I had a sudden change of plans. There was a cop car in front of my house. One look at the overgrown Boy Scout standing at my door told me all I needed to know. It was Langham, and he looked impatient.

Dang it.

I knew I couldn't avoid him forever, but I could sure try. With my eyes on the deputy, I walked backward a few steps, then turned and trotted back to the park. *No need to go home just yet. It is such a beautiful day, after all.*

This time I bypassed the fair and walked alongside the playground. Kids chased each other, shrieking with joyful abandon. One little tyke whooped as he slid down the slide, while another little girl soared in the air on a swing, pumping her legs and tilting her face up to the sun. I slowed my steps and smiled.

I wish—

My phone buzzed, interrupting my thoughts. The display informed me it was the Edindale County Sheriff's Department. It had to be Langham. I let the call go to voice mail.

Why is he wasting his time with me? Does he truly have no better leads?

I exited the park and kept walking until I ended up at the Cozy Café. It was well after the lunch rush, so I had the place to myself. I ordered a cup of tea and shot off a text to Farrah: **How ya doin? Need some company?**

A minute later, she sent her reply: **I'm good. Just wrapping my cast in plastic for a much-needed, if somewhat awkward, bubble bath. Chat later?**

You bet.

I withdrew a notebook from my purse and opened it to a clean page. As I sipped my tea, I filled the

page with doodles and tried to sort out my thoughts.
Before long, the spirals, stars, and flowers became
names and words:

Denise: Artsy, moody, interesting, reckless.

I paused. Was she really all those things? I only
knew what people had told me. I added a question
mark after the list, then moved to the next line and
wrote another name:

*Erik: Ex-boyfriend. Still cared for her, but she was angry
with him. Because of money?*

I tapped my pen on the table, as I called to mind
Erik's friendly, guileless face. Would a woman have
cursed him simply because he owed her money? Or
was there more to the story?

Moving on, I thought of Denise's other friends.

*Viper: High school friend . . . and sometime lover?
Sketchy with a criminal record.*

Then I remembered something. Viper was in jail
on Saturday morning. Billy had to bail him out,
which was why Erik was stranded in Edindale that
day. I wished I knew for sure what time Denise had
been killed. The timing was important, not only for
my own alibi, but for everyone else's.

*Billy: Childhood/high school friend. Loyal. Somewhat
nervous, especially when Denise's name comes up.*

*Poppy: Best friend since high school; also artsy. Close
enough to plan D's memorial, but they'd had a falling-out.
Called D a fraud. Also claimed she tried to visit D earlier
Sat. morning.*

It was too bad Poppy wouldn't talk to me. Was it
because she was too distraught at the loss of her
friend? *She sure didn't seem distraught when she was flirt-
ing with my boyfriend,* I thought uncharitably.

I outlined the question marks scattered all over

the page and thought of another thread tying all these people together: witchcraft. Given the manner of Denise's death and all the talk about Denise dabbling with dark magic, I couldn't ignore that aspect of the case.

Without thinking, I grabbed my phone and dialed Erik's number. He sounded pleased to hear from me.

"I was just thinking of you, Keli!"

"You were?"

"Must have been a premonition you were about to call. What's up?"

"I was wondering if you could tell me more about Denise's witchcraft. How long had she considered herself a witch?"

"Oh, I don't know. Since high school, I think."

"Was she in a circle or coven? Was she part of your Druidic Order?"

"No, she wasn't a Druid. I'd say she was mostly solitary, except she would join in group rituals sometimes. And I think she might have had a circle in the past. Billy would know better."

"How long had you been seeing her? I'm just curious."

"About two years, off and on."

"Do you happen to have anything that belonged to her? Maybe something she made?"

"Yeah, I think so. I have some little cards and pictures someplace. What do you have in mind? A summoning spell? Do you want to come over and see what I have?"

For some reason, the question startled me. I hadn't really thought this through. "Uh, no. I can't today. Maybe another time. I'm not exactly sure what I have in mind, to be honest."

"No, it's a great idea. I'll see what I can find and let you know."

After we said good-bye, I hung my head and ran my fingers through my hair. *What am I doing?*

My phone buzzed. It was a text from Wes. **Where are you?**

I told him I was at the Cozy Café, and he sent a two-word reply: **Stay there.**

I ordered another cup of tea and read through my scribbled notes. Something was missing. Actually, a lot of somethings. My broad generalizations about Denise and her friends lacked any kind of detail. That bugged me.

The café door opened and Wes stepped inside. My breath caught at the sight of him. With his wind-swept dark hair, perfectly fitted jeans, and faded black T-shirt, not to mention the tribal tattoos encir-cling his arms, he was the picture of a model rock star. But it was the intensity in his dark eyes and the set of his jaw that made me lean back a little. He slid into the seat opposite me and put his elbows on the table.

"Hey," I said, my voice coming out in a rasp. I cleared my throat. "What's up?"

He reached into his pocket and pulled out a small, white box. He set it on the table in front of me.

I widened my eyes, as my heart skipped a beat. "What's this?"

"It's a gift. Open it."

I lifted the lid, then frowned in confusion. What-ever it was, it wasn't a ring. With my thumb and forefinger, I picked up the object to have a closer look. It seemed to be a miniature collage of seeds, crystals, and feathery herbs encased in a glass covering. I flipped it over to see a gray backing and understood. It was a refrigerator magnet.

I started to laugh. I figured it must have been sold by the same artist who'd made the mixed media three-dimensional creation I'd checked out at the fair. "I love it," I said.

"It seemed like something you'd like. Plus, the title of the series is 'Peace Offering.'"

"Is that what this is? A peace offering?"

He nodded and took my hands. "I'm sorry I've been kind of a jerk lately."

"You haven't been a jerk. Maybe a little distant . . ."

I trailed off, and he nodded. "After you left the fair, I walked around, people-watching. I saw lots of couples, young and old, and suddenly it hit me. It was like an epiphany. I realized I was doing it again."

I waited for him to explain, though I had a feeling I knew what he meant. It had been an issue we'd worked through more than once over the course of our relationship. And each time it brought us a little closer.

"It's that old, nasty beast," he went on. "Jealousy. Rearing its ugly head."

"There's nothing to be jealous of," I said.

"I know. It's just that you seem to have a connection with that Erik guy, and it kind of bothered me at first. I guess it brought up all my old feelings of insecurity and self-doubt. But then I thought about that whole scene earlier with the tattoo photographer, and I realized how that could have been misconstrued."

"Well, yeah. She was definitely into you, but I can hardly blame her." I smiled.

"But that's just it. You can bond with someone over shared interests without it having to be something romantic. Anyway, we trust each other, right? I don't want you to think I don't trust you."

"Absolutely. I trust you, too." I still wasn't convinced Poppy didn't have ulterior motives in her chat with Wes, but that was beside the point now. All that really mattered was our commitment to each other.

The café door opened again. I glanced over and cringed. It was Langham, surveying the restaurant like he was lord of the manor. "How did he find me here?"

Wes looked over his shoulder. "He probably saw my car out front. Why? What's the big deal?"

Before I could answer, Langham spotted us and strolled over. He didn't bother with petty formalities, such as saying hello. "You didn't return my call," he said.

"You called?" I shot a perplexed look at my phone, as if I didn't fully understand how it worked. Instead of responding, Langham pulled up a chair.

"I called to warn you."

"Warn me? About what?'

"About Erik Grayson. He's been lying to you. He's not who he says he is."

CHAPTER FIFTEEN

The more I thought about it, the more I doubted Deputy Langham's supposedly benevolent intentions in warning me about Erik. I stewed about it all evening and into Sunday morning, replaying the conversation in my mind.

Langham had claimed he was looking out for my best interests, trying to prevent me from being duped by an imposter. He said he believed that I, a respectable attorney, wouldn't want to become involved with someone unethical—and possibly dangerous. But his description of Erik didn't ring true for me. From the moment Langham dropped his little bombshell, I thought there must be some kind of mistake. Perhaps it was the gleam in the deputy's eyes, and the way he watched sharply for my reaction, when he said Erik wasn't who he said he was.

"What do you mean?" I'd asked. "Who is he, then?"

"His real name is Frederick Grayson. But he's used a number of other aliases."

"So . . . Erik is short for Frederick?"

"Just listen. Mr. Grayson showed up in Fynn Hollow five years ago, with no prior connections here. He came from Chicago, where he'd gone to pharmacy school. Only, back then he was using the name 'Merlin Grey.'"

Wes snickered. "Merlin?"

Langham ignored him and continued. "Grayson got in trouble for using a false name, and his pharmacist license was suspended for six months. After the suspension, he came down here and eventually got a job at Ellerby Pharma. But a year ago, his license expired, and he failed to renew it. That means he engaged in unlicensed pharmacy work for almost a year before he was let go from the job."

"Is that it?" asked Wes. "It sounds like a paperwork problem to me."

Langham practically sneered at Wes. "Obtaining a professional license under an assumed name is a lot more serious than 'a paperwork problem.' Acting as a pharmacy professional without a license is also a lot more serious than 'a paperwork problem.' It's fraud."

I recalled the information I'd read about Erik's former employer online. "As I understand it, Erik was downsized out of his company. He wasn't fired."

Langham gave me a pitying look, as if I just didn't get it. "If his use of false names doesn't bother you, maybe this will." He reached into an inside pocket and pulled out a folded piece of paper, which he opened and handed to me. It was a printout of an email from Denise to Poppy, sent a week before Denise's death. I guessed Poppy must have brought it to the police.

Wes moved to my side of the table, so we could read the message together. The gist was that Denise was sending Poppy a link to an art gallery here in Edindale and encouraging her friend to submit her portfolio. To me, this proved that Denise and Poppy were still friends in spite of their supposed falling-out. But it was the paragraph at the end that someone, probably Langham, had highlighted:

> *By the way, remember that thing I said was bothering me? I still can't tell you, because there are others involved . . . and someone could go to jail over it. But I want you to know I won't keep silent for much longer. The cards are telling me I should reveal what I know. I'm just waiting for the right time.*

I looked up at Langham, who was watching me closely. He raised his eyebrows as if to say, "See?"

"What does this have to do with Erik?" I asked. The lawyer in me knew this cryptic message didn't prove anything.

"As his girlfriend, Miss Crowley would likely know about all the shenanigans with Erik's license. If she reported his latest infraction to the licensing board, he might have been barred from any future work as a pharmacist. I'm sure he wouldn't have wanted her to 'reveal' that kind of information."

I looked at the message again without replying. After a moment, Langham snatched it up and returned it to his pocket. "Erik Grayson can't be trusted," he said, pushing back from the table. "Think about it. And call me if you remember anything about him you think I ought to know."

After he left, Wes and I discussed the odd encounter and came to the same conclusion: Langham was trying to play me. Why else share a piece of evidence in an ongoing investigation? Plus, what he *didn't* say was just as telling. He failed to mention the fact that someone had seen me out on Old County Road early Saturday morning. Either Detective

Rhinehardt hadn't told Langham about the tip, which seemed unlikely, or else Langham didn't want me to know I was a suspect.

He thought I knew something about the murder, or about Erik, and suspected I was trying to protect Erik. Heck, maybe he even thought Erik and I had plotted together to get rid of Denise. By painting Erik as dishonest, maybe Langham hoped I'd turn on my supposed partner before he could turn on me.

One thing I knew for sure: I was glad Langham hadn't sprung this news on Wes and me prior to our heart-to-heart at the café. Like Wes said, I'm usually a good judge of character. If I thought Erik was innocent, Wes was willing to back me up.

I had a hard time focusing on anything else the rest of the weekend. But there was one thing I'd already committed to that I needed to see through. On Sunday afternoon, I headed to the civic center for another one of my efforts to raise my profile in a positive light. One of the networking calls I had made earlier in the week was to the community director, Chelsea Owen. I had asked her if there were any volunteer opportunities I could take part in, and she jumped on my offer. She needed all the help she could get setting up and staffing a charity bazaar for the local children's hospital.

When I arrived at the civic center, I followed the signs to the gymnasium and found Chelsea buzzing about, clipboard in hand. She directed me to a folding table stacked with cardboard boxes containing donated glassware. My first job was to unpack the boxes and arrange the glassware in a nice display on the table.

As I worked, I glanced around the room to see if I recognized any of the other volunteers. There were a few familiar faces from around town, including a couple of vendors I'd seen at the art fair the day before. Two tables down, much to my delight, was my old friend, the book seller, T.C. Satterly. He was unpacking crates of books, while chatting with another volunteer. I decided I would go say hello as soon as I finished my assigned task.

No sooner had I finished when I heard someone call my name. I looked across the gym and spotted Billy Jones, smiling and waving. I returned the wave. *On second thought, maybe I'll just say "hi" to Billy first.* I weaved my way around boxes, tables, and people toward Billy and paused a few feet away to watch him. He moved in overdrive, unpacking one box and moving to the next like some kind of supercharged automaton. He'd clearly done this before. When I approached, he looked up and grinned, without missing a beat.

"Hey, Keli! I'm glad to see you here. I'm trying to put together game night again this Tuesday, and I'm running short on players. Viper won't be there, and my buddies from work all have excuses. Think you and Farrah can make it again? Now that you know how to play, it will be even more fun."

"Hmm. I'm not sure." The last game wasn't exactly my idea of fun, but I'd never say so to Billy. He was so earnest and sweet. "I'll check with Farrah and let you know."

"Awesome. I know Erik and Thorna would love to have you guys join us again."

"Speaking of Erik, I heard something interesting about him. Is it true he goes by the name Merlin?"

"Oh, yeah. He uses that as a craft name in ceremonies sometimes. Cute, huh? In the past, I think he even used it as a nickname, but then he had a hard time getting employers to take him seriously. The name 'Merlin' doesn't exactly look good on a job application, you know?"

"I guess it depends on the job. You know it's funny, this is the second time I've heard about craft names recently. Erik mentioned a friend called Soleil."

"Oh, sure. I know her. Nice girl."

"Do you have a craft name?"

"No, not really. I never saw the need. I've always been open about my tradition and who I am. But it's not uncommon at all. Some people take on a craft name to protect their true identities and others like to pick a new name just for fun. And some use craft names only during magical workings, while others use the name all the time."

"Like Thorna?" I remembered the newspaper had mentioned her real name when she was quoted following Denise's murder.

"Yeah. She might still go by Vanessa at work, or on official papers. Other than that, she's been Thorna for as long as I've known her."

"I can see how it would be fun to choose your own name." I thought about the screen name I'd chosen for the Witches' Web: *FlightyAphrodite*. It *was* fun coming up with the name. On the other hand, I hoped I hadn't inadvertently doomed myself to take on attributes to match the name, like some kind of flaky alter ego.

"Yeah, I guess so," said Billy. "I think it's healthy to bring a lighthearted attitude to your spiritual practice. But with Thorna, I think there's also a touch of superstition."

"What do you mean?"

"Oh, you know. The whole power-in-a-name kind of thing. Like Isis and the secret name of Ra?"

I shook my head. "Sorry, I don't follow you."

"It's like, some people believe you can use a person's true name as a taglock in a curse. So, they want to protect their real name."

Again with curses. "I understand now. I've heard of hair and nail clippings being used as taglocks, as well as photos, but never a person's name."

Billy shrugged. "To each his own, right? Or her own, as the case may be."

He broke down his empty boxes and heaved them under his arms. "I gotta take these to the recycling bin and see what Chelsea needs me to do next. Let me know about Tuesday."

I made my way back to the other side of the gymnasium and stopped at T.C.'s table. He was sitting in a folding chair, with his hands crossed over his ample midsection. His eyes twinkled when he saw me.

"I knew it," he said.

"Knew what?"

"You're on the case, aren't you?" He dropped his voice to a loud whisper and leaned forward. "I heard your name in connection with the Fynn Hollow murder, and I said to myself: 'That gal's gonna get to the bottom of it.' You always seem to be one step ahead of the cops, just like Miss Marple."

I smiled. "I don't know what you're talking about. I'm a lawyer, not a detective."

"So was Perry Mason. Ha. I saw you chatting with young Billy Jones over there. He's from Fynn Hollow, isn't he?"

"Mm-hmm. You know him?"

"Sure I do. He's got to be the nicest kid you've ever met. I can't think of a single fund-raiser he hasn't had a part in, going back to his school days. We can always count on him to lend a hand."

"I met him only recently, but he does seem nice," I agreed.

T.C. chuckled. "That boy ought to run for office. He's built up enough good will. Gives of his time, as well as his money." T.C. gave me a sly look. "If I were the suspicious type, I might wonder where all the generosity comes from. With anybody else, you'd think they're trying to make up for something."

"Oh, I don't know," I said. "It seems to me he does his family credit—as well as his school and his faith." I almost surprised myself with my subtle plug for Paganism. I wasn't sure how much T.C. knew, but Billy had told me himself that his Druidic beliefs weren't secret.

Glancing at the stack of books on T.C.'s table, my eyes fell upon a familiar cover. It was deep blue with silver lettering for the title: *Old Spells for a New Age*. I picked it up and showed T.C. "Is this one of the books you bought from Erik Grayson?"

"Ah, yes. There was too much writing in that one. I couldn't sell it in the shop, but I thought someone here might get a kick out of it."

I flipped through the pages and saw what T.C. meant. There was underlining throughout and frequent annotations in the margins. It looked like Erik had tried the spells and jotted down his opinions of them. I found myself smiling at his irreverent tone— much of the commentary was sprinkled with phrases like "As if," "Baloney," and "Not even close." Other spells, presumably the successful ones, were marked with big, hand-drawn stars.

But then I paused. Something about the writing bothered me. As I read a few more notes, I realized they didn't actually sound like Erik. In fact, the handwriting was kind of girly. I turned another page and

came upon a heavily marked-up "Attraction Spell."
Someone had changed the words and scrawled a
more personalized version at the top of the page.
When I read the incantation, I knew at once whom
this book had really belonged to.

> *He will come to me*
> *He will be mine*
> *He'll unwind from her clutches*
> *And drink me like wine*
> *He's drawn to me*
> *Like beetle to flame*
> *He's forgotten her*
> *He knows only my name*
>
> *DeeDee Star x Merlin Forever*

I shut the book and tried to hide the tremble in
my hands. "How much do you want for this?"

T.C. looked at me in surprise.

"For a lark," I explained.

Purely a lark.

CHAPTER SIXTEEN

"You are the best lawyer ever! I knew you could do it!"

Arlen the necromancer pumped my hand until I felt my fingers go numb. We had just emerged from the courthouse after an hour-long hearing in which the county officials tried to defend their ticket, and I argued it should be thrown out. Luckily, the hearing officer ultimately sided with me.

"I'm happy it all worked out," I said. "Sometimes you never know with these things."

"Oh, I always knew. But it's still gratifying to see it play out." He tilted his face to the sky and filled his lungs with air. You'd have thought he'd just been released from forty years in prison. Turning to me again, he rubbed his hands together. "I want to do something for you! Come by my place and I'll give you a free reading. The spirit animals can foretell many things. Bring a question and the bones will answer."

For a fleeting moment, I thought about all the questions that had been plaguing me about Denise

Crowley and her mysterious death. But I had to demur. "You've already paid my fee, Arlen. You don't owe me anything."

Besides, I have other methods for divining the future.

He clapped his hand on my shoulder and beamed. "Call me anytime if you change your mind. I'm going to tell everybody I know about you. Thank you again."

With somewhat mixed feelings, I thanked Arlen and watched as he bounded down the courthouse steps. Though he'd worn a suit for the occasion, he still struck an unusual figure with his below-the-shoulders, black-as-night hair and all the excess of skull jewelry. Truly, I was happy to help him and grateful for the work. But did I really want to become known as "the witches' lawyer?"

I pushed the thought out of my mind, as I followed him down the steps and headed across the square in the direction of my office. I was halfway across the courthouse lawn when my cell phone rang. I stood under an oak tree to retrieve it from my purse.

"Keli Milanni," I said, by way of greeting.

The torrent on the other end of the line hit me with a force so great I staggered. I dropped my purse and reached to the tree trunk for support.

"I trusted you!" yelled the angry voice. "I put my faith in you! And this is how you repay me?"

"What—?" It took me a minute to realize the voice belonged to Neal Jameson. He was so livid, his voice shook.

"I could not have been clearer about the need for discretion. I thought you understood that! And yet you still told someone. I don't know who you blabbed to, but apparently you don't know the meaning of the word *discretion*—or *confidentiality*."

"I don't know what you're talking about!" I exclaimed.

"Oh, really? Well, check the newspaper! This is exactly what I took great pains to avoid. Now you've ruined everything, you incompetent—" He broke off, as if trying to get control of himself. "Consider yourself fired. And on notice. I *will* be suing you for malpractice. You can count on it."

The abrupt silence told me he'd hung up. I stared at my phone, utterly paralyzed. Tears stung my eyes, but I couldn't move to wipe them away. My chest was so tight, I had trouble breathing. *What had just happened?* After the high of the successful hearing, I now felt I'd been hurled into a bottomless well. Or maybe it did have a bottom, because I felt I'd landed with a thud and now huddled in the cold, pitiful darkness.

It was probably only a minute or two before I became aware of people walking nearby. Murmured voices mixed with twittering birdsong to pull me back into the present. With a concentrated effort, I pressed both palms into the tree trunk and forced myself to take in a slow, deep inhale.

Mother Earth, restore me.
Mighty Oak, give me strength.

Almost immediately, I felt a whoosh of energy rush through my hands, up my arms, and into my heart. I closed my eyes and sent my love and gratitude back into the tree, in a symbiotic exchange of energetic light and power.

"Are you okay, miss?"

Opening my eyes, I turned to see a young man dressed in nice slacks and an Oxford shirt. I figured him for a courthouse intern. Mustering up a smile, I reached for my purse, which was still on the ground. "Yes, thanks. I felt light-headed for a minute, but I'm okay now. Guess I shouldn't have skipped breakfast."

His expression betrayed a mix of confusion and relief. "Yeah. Okay."

I smiled again and took off, picking up speed as I went. When I reached my office, I hurried inside, logged onto my computer, and pulled up the website for the *Edindale Gazette*. The article I sought wasn't the top story, but it didn't take long to find. The headline said it all: BIDDING WAR FOR RED GATE HOLLOW? BUSINESS OWNER NEAL JAMESON PURPORTEDLY 'VERY INTERESTED.' I groaned. "Yep," I said to myself. "It's as bad as he said."

After reading and rereading the article, I stood up and paced my office. What could I do? Now that I was past my initial shock and distress, I was able to think calmly about the whole situation. I knew I hadn't breathed a word of Neal's intentions to anyone, not a single soul. Therefore, he must have been the one who let it slip. Surely he would come around and see the truth. He had absolutely no basis for a malpractice lawsuit—let alone cause for the rude way he'd spoken to me. In fact, the more I thought about it, the more I imagined I'd soon receive another phone call from the man. Once he came to his senses, I was sure he'd want to apologize—profusely. And I, being the gracious, high-minded person I was, would generously accept his apology.

I smiled ruefully at my fanciful daydreams. Misunderstanding or not, the whole thing was still very unfortunate. And it definitely cast a pall on the day. This was totally not in alignment with the newfound sense of abundance I was starting to create. But I didn't have time to dwell on it. I had other work to do. Plus, I had to be at the university radio station by 4:00 P.M. for another one of my efforts to drum up positive publicity.

A few blessedly uneventful hours later, I walked over to the lush campus of South-Central Illinois University and made my way to the redbrick building that housed the college radio station. In addition to playing underground rock, avant-garde jazz, indie folk, and other anti-pop musical genres, the station hosted a number of talk-radio podcasts. One show, called "Ask An Expert," drew in a broad array of listeners, from students exploring their career options to community members with questions for the experts. It was the latter group I hoped to impress most.

Of course, when I'd reached out to my contact at the university to pitch myself for a spot on the radio show, I had yet to be named in the college paper's salacious murder story. I was a little nervous when I entered the building and headed to the Media Communications Department. I knocked on the door and crossed my fingers.

A young woman, presumably a student, answered the door and led me past walls of CDs, vinyl records, and music posters to the office of the program director. Two casually dressed men hopped up from their task chairs to shake my hand. They introduced themselves as Julien, the show's producer, and Todd, the host. Both men appeared to be around my age, in their early thirties. Julien was tall and soft-spoken, while Todd, prematurely balding and ruddy-cheeked, was more gregarious. They both went out of their way to put me at ease. If they were aware of the article, they didn't say so.

After several minutes of chitchat, Todd took me to the small on-air studio and invited me to have a seat across from him at the radio desk. We could see Julien through a glass wall, where he tested his equipment and prepared to accept incoming calls. After a minute, he gave us a thumbs-up sign.

"Have you ever done radio?" Todd asked, as he handed me a pair of headphones.

"No. This is the first time."

"No sweat. Just relax and keep it conversational. We have some regular callers we can usually count on to keep things moving. If there are any lulls, I'll ask you one of the basic questions you provided."

"Sounds good."

He swiveled a large microphone toward my face and asked me some test questions as he adjusted the sound levels. Then, before I knew it, he was counting down to showtime. A lighted red sign on the desk before me flashed on to warn MIC LIVE.

Upbeat music played through the headphones. As the music faded, Todd launched into his introduction. "Good evening and welcome to WEDN's Ask-An-Expert call-in show, where every Monday local professionals answer questions that affect *your* everyday lives. I'm your host, Todd Wardelle, and today I'm pleased to welcome Edindale attorney Keli Milanni. A graduate of the SCIU School of Law, Keli was an associate, and then a partner, at the venerable firm Olsen, Sykes, and Rafferty for eight years before hanging out her own shingle. She recently opened her own law practice, where she

handles a wide variety of legal concerns for her
clients, including family law issues, real estate matters, and trusts and estates.

"We'd like to remind our listeners that the answers
today are informational only and do not constitute
legal advice, a solicitation for legal business, or in any
way the creation of an attorney-client relationship.
Welcome to the show, Keli."

"Thank you for having me, Todd."

The interview started out well. Todd asked me a
few softball openers that allowed me to showcase my
legal expertise. I was feeling pretty good about the
whole experience. Then he opened the phone line
for questions.

The first call seemed promising at first. The caller
was a third-year law student who hoped to open his
own solo practice. I was gearing up to offer some helpful tips when he made an abrupt switch in direction.

"In my criminal justice course, we're following the
Fynn Hollow murder investigation, and we were
wondering why the county took over the case. Is it because the investigation isn't confined to the limits of
the village?"

"Um, I couldn't say for sure. I believe Fynn Hollow
has a small police force."

"Why hasn't the medical examiner released the
autopsy report? Is there some question about the cause
of death?"

"I don't know that either. I'm not involved—that
is, criminal law is not my specialty. After law school, I
went straight into private practice with a focus on
family law."

"Thanks for the call," Todd interjected. "Let's go

on to the next one. Sheryl from Craneville, you're on the air. What's your question for our expert today?"

"Yes, thank you. I'm concerned about my mother-in-law, who lives in a nursing home. She can't get around very well and I'm afraid she's starting to lose her memory."

"I'm sorry to hear that," I said, as I mentally prepared myself for a question about powers of attorney or elder rights.

"Is it true that the murder in Fynn Hollow was a ritual killing?"

"I beg your pardon?" I glanced up at Todd, who shot a stern look at Julien in the booth. Julien appeared to be as surprised as we were.

"The murder victim was a witch, wasn't she?" Sheryl continued. "When you found her body, was there writing on it? Were there black candles and runic symbols?"

"Okay, caller," said Todd, speaking over Sheryl's voice. "I'm afraid we have to stay on topic. Keli, I have a question for you. I have a friend who knows he should prepare a will, but he never got around to it. What should he bring with him to his first meeting with a lawyer?"

"That's a very good question, Todd," I said, as I dabbed the sweat beading on my forehead. "There are a number of documents that can help your attorney prepare an estate plan for you." I proceeded to rattle off a list of items, while Todd and Julien exchanged significant looks. When I finished, Todd cleared his throat.

"Excellent. That's really good to know," he said. "Well, the phones are all lit up, so let's take another call. Hello to Dee from . . . Summerland? I don't believe I've heard of that town. Is it in Edin County?"

"Keli Milanni knows where it is." The low voice on the line sounded strange and disembodied, almost like a robot in an echo chamber. Clearly disguised, it was impossible to tell if the voice belonged to a man or a woman. I immediately felt my skin crawl. Summerland wasn't a town in Edin County. It was the name most Wiccans ascribed to the afterlife.

"What's your question for our expert?" Todd asked.

"My question for Keli Milanni, the *expert* Keli Milanni, is this: How is it working out for you, Keli Milanni?"

"I'm sorry—you mean my new law practice? It's been great—"

"That's not what I mean, Keli Milanni. I mean the curse. How is the curse working?"

I glanced at Todd, but he had removed his headphones and turned to retrieve a water bottle from a table behind him. Julien waved his arms in the booth, then helplessly shook his head.

"Live by the curse, die by the curse, Keli Milanni. You better stop playing with fire. If you don't, then what happened to the 'Witch of Fynn Hollow' will happen to you."

Todd replaced his headphones in time to hear the call disconnect. "Thanks for that. Next caller? Pete from Fynn Hollow, you're on the air."

I walked home from the university, grateful for the darkness. I wished it could swallow me whole. I was so flustered after the creepy call, I had trouble answering what few legitimate questions came in afterward. It was just as well that most people wanted to talk about the murder—it forced Todd to cut the show short. He filled the remaining minutes by playing "I Fought the Law," by the Clash. It was his attempt at humor, I guessed.

Julien apologized before I left, but I was so embarrassed it didn't matter. I said a hasty good-bye and bolted. I should have known it was a mistake to go ahead with the live radio show. The timing was terrible.

I took a well-lit path home, but it was still dark in the shadows. The clouds overhead blotted the stars and moon. As I left the main thoroughfare and entered a quiet, residential street, the words of the creepy caller came back to me: *How is the curse working out for you?*

What was that supposed to mean? Was the implication that *I* had cast a curse? And how about that name—"Dee" from Summerland. Was I supposed to believe it was Denise Crowley placing a phone call from beyond the grave? *As if.*

Suddenly I remembered the spell book I'd bought from T.C. at the charity bazaar. I hadn't had a chance to pore over it any further, but I was positive it had belonged to Denise. At first it seemed disconcerting that Erik would sell a book that had belonged to his ex-girlfriend—especially when the sale money was meant to repay his debt to her. But then I realized she surely must have given it to him. It was probably a book she didn't want anymore. After all, half the spells apparently hadn't worked out for her. I snickered to myself as I recalled the funny comments she'd written in the margins.

Yeah, I thought. The Denise I was getting to know—in a manner of speaking—had a playful, almost sassy way about her. With her whimsical style and quirky friends, she didn't strike me as someone who would say things like "Live by the curse, die by the curse."

On the other hand, there were other clues that pointed to a very troubled individual. People talked about how moody and unstable Denise could be. And something seemed to be weighing on her in her last days.

I stopped in my tracks as a thought occurred to me. What if Denise had been getting creepy, anonymous phone calls, too? Could someone have been harassing her? Threatening her to "stop playing with fire"? Stalky incidents like that would be enough to set a person on edge. I should know.

Then I had another disturbing thought. As I tried to figure out what had happened to Denise, was I walking in her footsteps? Would I retrace her steps all the way to the same grisly end, like something out of a bad horror movie?

I shuddered—and jogged the rest of the way home.

CHAPTER SEVENTEEN

I couldn't bring myself to go into the office on Tuesday. Actually, I might have gone in, except the one client on my schedule had called to cancel. Again. Why had my abundance spell stopped working?

Wes left for work, so I cleaned up the kitchen, then headed to the backyard. It was a chilly morning, so I pulled on a long-sleeved flannel top with old blue jeans. First, I tended the flower bed, pulling weeds, planting bulbs, and deadheading daffodils. Then I moved to the vegetable garden and sowed a row of spinach and one of lettuce. Once that was finished, I rested on the hoe and contemplated the spot where I'd planted the sunflower seeds. It appeared untouched, just a bare patch of soil beneath the glass-and-metal garden stakes. Of course it was too soon to see any sprouts, but I knew the magic was working underground. I supposed I ought to be patient—and not just for the sunflowers.

It was hard. This whole curse business was really getting to me. I couldn't shake a feeling of foreboding. I felt as if a black cloud hovered over me.

The instant I thought it, a breeze rattled nearby

branches and rolling clouds darkened the sky. I looked up and laughed. Signs from the Goddess never ceased to amaze me. "All right, I get it! My thoughts are creating my reality. Is that what this is?"

But that wasn't all. I wasn't fully in control here. Outside forces were messing with my life, and I didn't like it. I didn't like it one bit.

Well, what good is being a witch, if I can't take charge of my own life?

I went back to the flower bed and cut three white tulips. Then I put away my garden tools and went inside. I arranged the tulips in a mason jar with some water and took them to my altar room. Josie followed me and bounded onto the spare bed, where she settled serenely among the multitude of decorative pillows scattered on the white and blue quilt. *What a pretty picture.* Chuckling, I grabbed my phone and snapped a photo.

"If only I had your sense of calm, Miss Kitty."

I turned to the altar and dusted off the candles and figurines. Then I placed the tulips in a prominent place in the sunlight and thought about the flowers' meaning. Tulips were well-known to symbolize perfect love. It seemed an apt choice to elevate my mood. *Love conquers evil, right?* Leaning down, I inhaled the delicate scent of the flowers. I wasn't sure why I'd selected three. "One for me," I murmured. "One for Wes. And one . . . to represent our union?"

We had been a couple for more than two years now. In fact, it would be three years this summer. Yet we rarely talked about the future. On the contrary, Wes frequently commented about how great our relationship is and how lucky we are—as if he's perfectly content with the status quo. Why mess with a good thing?

I reached for my favorite deck of tarot cards from a nearby shelf and held them between my hands. *What does the future hold?* I could ask the cards. More accurately, I could use the cards to ask the Goddess. I could ask her for a sign.

Or I could just ask Wes.

I heard a stir behind me and turned to see Josie jump off the bed. Apparently, she had developed a curiosity about the shopping bag on the floor by the door. She batted the paper handle, making it crinkle. I watched for a moment, until I remembered what was in the bag. It was the oracle deck Mila had given me: the Tarot of the Valkyries.

"Are you trying to tell me something, Josie?" I put away my cards and retrieved the deck from the bag. Then I settled myself on top of the bed.

I opened the box, removed the cards, and spread them out before me. The illustrations were beautiful. I admired the vivid colors and the artist's attention to detail. While I didn't have a particularly strong connection with Norse mythology, I appreciated the symbolism and decided I wouldn't mind learning more.

Josie nudged her way onto my lap. "Girl, you're everywhere today. What's the deal?"

After duly scratching her head and neck, I reached over her to gather the cards into a stack and turn them over one by one. The *Seer,* the *Elf,* the *Troll.* The god *Odin,* the Goddess *Frigg,* their son, *Balder.*

I remembered *BalderBoy* from the Witches' Web. He had to be Billy. In his messages, he came across as nervous, but kindhearted.

I turned over another card and found myself face-to-face with the Viking card. It was the one in Denise's hand when she died.

I studied the card closely. Take away the beard and

the flowing mane, and he reminded me a little bit of Erik, especially with the blond hair and blue eyes. But in the fantasy tabletop game, Billy was the one who played the Viking. In fact, Billy seemed to have a strong connection with the whole Norse pantheon. The game was his, after all.

My eyes slid to the stylized *V* in the corner of the card. V for . . . Viper?

Was this card a message at all? Or was it nothing more than an accident? Something Denise clutched onto as she fell to the floor.

What had happened that morning? I conjured the scene in my mind's eye. Denise had invited someone into her home—and, beyond that, into her personal workroom. Therefore, it was most likely not a stranger. It must have been a friend or client. Denise was fully dressed, not in her pajamas, so perhaps she was expecting the person. Based on the cups the police had found in the sink, Denise had made tea for two. And this person—the killer—knew there would be tea. They came prepared to put a hefty amount of belladonna into Denise's cup. Did the person slip it in when Denise's back was turned? Or did the killer—

I stopped myself at the word. The term *killer* called to mind a vicious-looking villain or a crazed maniac. But to Denise, the killer—her visitor—probably appeared normal. Maybe the visitor offered to make the tea. They could have even brought the tea, claiming it was a special herbal blend.

I suddenly recalled Viper's interest in psychedelic substances. I could just picture him with a devilish grin, holding up a baggie of some illicit plant—like ayahuasca or magic mushrooms. "Lookie what I have," he'd say. "Want to have some fun?"

I shook away the image and forced myself to stick with the facts. What else did I know?

Denise and her friend, or at least acquaintance, sat across from each other at Denise's divinatory table. Denise offered to read the visitor's cards—or perhaps that was the ostensible purpose for the visit. If only Denise's appointment book would turn up. If it was a scheduled reading, the client's name would be in the book. Of course, I realized it was likely that the killer took the book. That, in itself, would be another indication the visitor must have known Denise pretty well—well enough to know about the appointment book in the first place. I hadn't heard anything about Denise's cell phone or computer. I assumed the police had searched them, and they didn't provide anything useful . . . unless there were messages between Denise and Erik, which strengthened the cops' interest in Erik. And, by extension, me.

Josie mewed, and I scratched her beneath her chin. "Right. Back to the tainted tea." Obviously, it wasn't an accidental poisoning, because only Denise ingested the belladonna. And the so-called visitor washed out the cups before leaving. Then, there was the whole business with the bleach and ammonia. The killer must have covered their mouth and nose, dumped the chemicals, and fled. But why? To make Denise's death appear like an accident? Maybe the killer figured the cops wouldn't order an autopsy for a tragic cleaning mistake. And they weren't supposed to find traces of belladonna. Maybe the killer wasn't able to thoroughly wash the cups and put them away as planned, because he or she heard someone at the door. As Poppy stood on the doorstep ringing the bell, the killer could have been sneaking out the back door. I shuddered at the thought.

But why belladonna anyway? I supposed it wasn't exactly an obscure plant. I was pretty sure it had been used as a murder weapon before, at least in movies and novels. In theory, anyone could grow it. From what I'd read, there were medicinal uses for the plant, in small doses. As a pharmacist, Erik would know that. But the cops had found the raw stuff. It would seem that someone had harvested it in their own backyard or greenhouse, dried it, and then decided to use it to murder Denise.

Who would do such a thing? What would motivate someone to such an extreme—and extremely sick— action?

Someone who didn't like Denise, that was for sure. Or someone who had a lot to lose by her continued existence.

I thought back to Viper's online comment to Billy that their "problem" was solved with Denise's death. Then there was the thing that was "bothering" Denise that she mentioned in her email to Poppy.

I moved Josie aside and stood up from the bed. I had a notion to Google these characters again, starting with Poppy. I knew so little about her. I picked up my smartphone and opened a browser. When I entered her name in the search field, the first thing that came up was an announcement for an art show. Her photographs were scheduled to be displayed at a gallery here in Edindale—tonight. For a second, I considered showing up. It could be a good opportunity to smooth over my blundering questions at the art fair and ask her about Denise in a more delicate way. But then I reconsidered. Maybe it would be cruel to accost her at her own art opening. She already didn't seem to like me much.

However, there was one person I was pretty sure

she *did* like. Maybe I could enlist Wes to go to the opening. He could probably slip in some questions, while genuinely admiring her work.

I turned back to the bed and gathered up the oracle cards. As I put them away, I looked at the Viking card once more.

Meow. Josie nudged me playfully.

"Yeah. I agree. This card has to mean something. But what?"

Whatever it was, the place for answers wasn't here, hidden away in my altar room. It was in Fynn Hollow. That much I knew for sure.

I grabbed my phone again and pulled up Erik's name in my list of contacts. I touched the name, then pulled back. I called Farrah instead.

"Hey, girl," she answered. "What's up?"

"How would you feel about going to 'game night' again? I've been promised that Viper won't be there."

"Um."

"I know it was a snooze. But I thought this time we could do some actual detective work. I have more questions for Erik."

"I would go with you, snoozefest or not. But I actually have a date tonight."

"Really? You're going out?"

"I'm not completely lame, you know."

"Never."

"But the date is here. Sorry, honey. You should go anyway."

"Yeah, I might. So, who's your date? Is it Randall?" For a while, Farrah had dated one of my old partners at the law firm. I thought they'd gotten along really well.

"Randall? Nice guy, but way too busy. I told him to

call me when he can stay out later than nine o'clock. Anyway, call me tomorrow. 'Kay?"

"Yeah, okay."

I hung up and looked at Josie. "I guess I'm on my own tonight. Oh, well. I'm sure I'll be fine." What could happen in a roomful of gamers?

Except that one of them might be a murderer.

Maybe I should find someone else to come along.

It was nearly dusk when I arrived at Billy's place—alone. I had called Catrina, thinking she might be up for the adventure, and she had said yes. But then she bailed at the last minute . . . something about a friend visiting from out of town. *Thanks, Catrina.* By that time, I was already all geared up and ready to go, wearing every lucky charm and protection amulet I owned. After a short meditation and a quick grounding exercise, I decided to go anyway. I felt pretty good when I climbed his front steps and knocked.

This time, there was no big welcome like before. When Billy answered and saw me by myself, his face fell. "Farrah couldn't make it?"

"She had other plans."

I followed him into the living room, where Erik and Thorna sat on a sofa watching TV. Erik flipped off the set and stood up. "Hey, Keli. It's good to see you again. But I don't know if game night is happening now."

"Oh? Why not?"

"We're two short," Thorna explained. "And Billy is *very* clear on the rules. You must have exactly six to play." She rolled her eyes.

"The guys from work already bailed," said Billy glumly. "And Viper was busy, too."

Busy? I hoped that was just Billy's polite way of saying Viper wasn't invited. I wouldn't have come if I knew there was even a chance of Viper being here. I was in no hurry to repeat what had happened the last time.

"Wait a minute," said Billy, brightening. "I thought of somebody else I can call. There's still hope." He pulled out his cell phone and punched in some numbers as he walked to the kitchen.

"Yes, let's hope," said Thorna drily. "If you'll excuse me for a minute, I'm just gonna visit the powder room."

Erik dropped back onto the couch, and I sat in an adjacent rocker. "So, just wondering," I began. "Do you work with tarot cards much?"

"Not a lot. I did for a time, when I was younger. I'm more into runes now for prophecy work."

"I was thinking about Denise and the cards on her table when we found her. It looked like she was giving a reading for someone."

He nodded somberly. "Yeah, I've been thinking about that, too. I mean, she pulled cards for herself all the time. But she also had people come by and pay her for readings sometimes."

He tapped his chin thoughtfully, then suddenly sat up straight. "I've got it! I know where Denise's appointment book might be."

"Really? That's great! I have Langham's number in my phone. We should call him right away." I reached for my purse to dig out my phone.

He put his hand on my arm to stop me. "No, we can't do that."

"Why not?"

"This place I'm thinking of . . . it's secret. It would be better for me to find the book and give it to the police myself." He grabbed my hand and gave me a little tug toward the door. "Come on. It's not far from here. If we hurry, we can make it before dark."

"Um, by car?"

"Nah, we can walk. That's one of the benefits of living in a small town. No need to bother with a car. Besides, a car can't get back there anyway."

Back there?

We were already halfway out the door when Billy came into the living room, with Thorna at his heels. "Are you guys leaving?" he asked.

"Sorry, buddy," said Erik. "There's something we have to do."

"Bye," I called over my shoulder, as Erik pulled me along after him. When we reached the sidewalk, I extricated my hand from his. Glancing up at Billy's house, I noticed Thorna standing in the doorway. She had a worried expression on her face. I wondered if I should be worried, too.

"Why don't we ask Billy and Thorna to come along?" I suggested. "The more people who look, the better, right?"

"Not necessarily," said Erik. "To tell you the truth, I'm kind of worried about whose name we're going to find in the book."

He started off down the sidewalk, and I had to trot to keep up with him. "What do you mean?"

"Just a feeling. Never mind."

As we passed my car on the street and rounded the corner, it occurred to me that I was breaking a promise to myself. Based on past experience, I had vowed never again to let myself be alone with a murder suspect. The truth was, I still felt comfortable with Erik. But I was no dummy. I wouldn't have stuck with him if not for the fact that we were out in the open and headed toward downtown Fynn Hollow. Though it wasn't exactly broad daylight, there was still a fair amount of light in the western sky.

A few minutes later, we approached a low-slung gray building next to a half-full parking lot. A sign out front said FYNN HOLLOW HIGH SCHOOL. Instead of going inside, Erik skirted the building and led us past the practice fields in back. Groups of kids played soccer or ran around a track, while others hung out on the bleachers to watch and enjoy the evening. I was mystified.

"What are we doing here?"

"You'll see."

And a minute later I did see. Erik kept walking, until we were beyond the school grounds and nearing a tree-covered bluff.

I slowed my steps, as the whistles and shouts from the high school faded in the distance. Oblivious to my hesitation, Erik hiked up the bluff and disappeared into the trees.

I took a deep breath and pressed my hand to my chest. "Goddess, guide me," I whispered. Then I trudged up the hillside, following Erik's lead. When I reached the top, I looked around. The forest continued, but there was a cleared area here, with boulders and logs arranged like seats around the remnants of a fire pit. Beer cans and cigarette butts littered the ground. It was obviously a well-used teen hangout. A few yards away, Erik was poking around in the bushes. Why he thought Denise's appointment book would be up here, I had no idea.

As if reading my mind, he looked up and grinned. "I'm trying to find a footpath. It's hidden, but I know it's around here someplace."

"Um, okay."

We spread out and looked together, picking our way through the brambles. To my surprise, I found the trail. It was narrow at first, but soon opened up and wound upward. I kept Erik in my sights, as he hurried up the trail. Finally, we came upon another clearing at what must have been the highest point of the bluff. At the peak was a tall flat-roofed steel structure that resembled a free-standing tree house. Four flights of exterior stairs switch-backed to a small cabin at the top.

"It's a fire lookout tower," Erik explained. "It hasn't been used for any official purpose in years, but Denise used to come up here to get away. She'd come out here to do 'sky magic,' as she called it."

I turned away from the tower and let my eyes roam across the vista beyond the bluffs. The sunset made pink, orange, and purple streaks across the sky, as the hills of Shawnee National Forest melted into velvety shadows below. "It's beautiful."

Erik strolled over to stand next to me. "I know. That's partly why I wanted to hurry up and get here—so we could watch the sun set." He draped his arm casually over my shoulders, and I immediately pulled away.

"Erik—"

"Plus," he said, cutting me off, "I don't know if there's a light up there. Probably not." He walked over to the tower and looked up. "You think the view is spectacular now. Just wait 'til we see it from up there." He grabbed the handrail and placed his foot on the bottom step.

"Are you sure it's safe? It's going to be dark soon, and some of those steps look rusty. Maybe it would be better to come back tomorrow."

"I'm too anxious to wait. But you do have a point.

I don't want to put you in any danger. Why don't you wait for me down here? I won't be long."

Before I could argue, he was scrambling up the steps. "Erik, you shouldn't put yourself in danger either!"

"I'm fine," he called over his shoulder. "Besides, you can catch me if I fall." I heard him laugh, as he ascended out of sight.

Hugging my arms against the growing chill, I turned to watch the sun sink below the horizon while I waited for him to return. Before I knew it, I was standing in the gloom. I checked the time on my phone and saw that it was after 8:00. I thought of Wes, gamely gathering information for me at Poppy's art opening. I hoped at least he was having a good time.

I heard a rustle on the side of the bluff. A small animal probably. What was taking Erik so long? I was growing impatient. I paced to the base of the tower and strained my neck to see into the cabin above. I was a poor judge of distance, but I guessed the height was anywhere from forty to sixty feet in the air. It appeared dark up there.

I checked the time again. Erik had been gone for more than ten minutes. As I replaced my phone in my purse, I noticed my small, silver flashlight tucked between my wallet and a packet of tissues. I'd forgotten I had it; otherwise, I would have lent it to Erik.

Another minute passed, and I couldn't take it anymore. I clicked on the flashlight and shined it on the bottom few steps. *Maybe I should just go up partway.*

Halfway up the stairs I called Erik's name. "Is everything okay up there?"

He didn't answer. I sighed and continued climbing the stairs, carefully placing my feet on each step. When I reached the top, a little out of breath, I saw that the door was ajar and the lock busted—probably years ago by the looks of it. I peeked inside. It was dim, but not completely dark. A yellow pillar candle flickered on a ledge, revealing a spare one-room cabin, about seven-feet square, with glass windows on each wall. I saw an ancient-looking cot on one side of the room, and a built-in desk on another. I imagined the desk had probably once held communication equipment, back in the days when a keen-eyed watcher was the best hope for early detection of forest fires. In the center of the room was a square metal table and two canvas folding chairs. Erik sat at the table with his head bowed. He was crying.

"Erik?"

He looked up and wiped his eyes. "Hey."

"Are you okay?"

"Yeah. Sorry. I just got . . . overwhelmed. This place is filled with her energy. Can you feel it?"

I sat down across from him. I did feel something. It was a palpable sense of loneliness, and it seemed to be emanating from Erik. I reached into my purse and handed him a tissue.

"Did you find the appointment book?" I asked.

"No. But she did leave a few other things, like the candle and some stones. I also found this on the floor." He held up a piece of paper and passed it to me across the table. I shined my flashlight on the paper to examine it. It was frayed on the edge, as if ripped from a spiral notebook, and it was covered in scribbled writing with lots of strike-outs and doodles in the margin. I had no doubt about what it was: a homemade magic spell.

"This is Denise's handwriting, isn't it?"

Even before he nodded, I knew the answer. The writing on the paper matched the writing in the book

I'd bought from T.C. The author's poetic style was the same, too. My skin prickled with goose bumps, as I read the words out loud.

> *"You will leave from here.*
> *You'll go far away.*
> *Disappear from my life,*
> *Like nightfall shrouds the day.*
>
> *You're not wanted here.*
> *No longer say my name.*
> *The connection is severed—*
> *I'll never play your game.*
>
> *I banish you. I banish you. I banish you."*

I looked up and met Erik's eyes. He bit his lip.

"Who is this about?"

He shook his head. "I have no idea."

"Are you sure?"

He raked his hands through his hair. "I swear. I wish I knew. Whoever it was—this isn't good. Denise was afraid of somebody."

I continued to eye Erik, trying to get a read on him. I thought he was telling the truth, but I couldn't be sure.

"Erik, forgive me for asking, but when you and Denise split up, who ended the relationship? Was it mutual, or—"

"She did. She kicked me to the curb."

"Oh!" I was a little startled by his honesty.

"She accused me of cheating on her—which I wasn't! I told her so, but I don't know if she believed me. She said I wasn't good for her anyway. She called me a freeloader and a slacker. Said I was bad luck." He flinched at the memory. "It was a low point."

"So, this banishing spell," I said, pointing at the paper. "You don't think it's about you?"

He furrowed his brow. "Nah, it wasn't like that. She kicked me out of her house, but not out of her life. Two days after we broke up, she called me and asked me to come over. She wanted my help installing a motion light."

"Hmm. I wonder when she wrote this." I rubbed the paper between my thumb and forefinger. "It doesn't seem very dusty or dirty."

Erik stared out the window at the rising moon. Suddenly, he gasped. "Of course!"

"What? You know who Denise wanted to banish?"

"No. But I know how we can find out."

"How?"

"We can ask Denise."

CHAPTER EIGHTEEN

I stood at the west-facing window of the lookout tower and gazed out over the dark forest below. Clouds had moved in, blocking the moon and stars. Every now and then a pinpoint of light flickered on and off, and I realized it must be headlights on a winding road in the distance. This sign of civilization might have been comforting for some, but not for me. I was alone in a deserted cabin sixty feet in the sky, with a man I barely knew. And he had just suggested we contact the spirit of his angry ex-lover.

"Okay," he said. "I'm ready."

For the past several minutes, Erik had set about consecrating the space around the table, chanting in a language I guessed to be Gaelic or Welsh. This was his idea—and his loved one—so I let him take the lead.

As I sat across from him at the table once more, I marveled at the setup he'd managed with so few supplies. With a piece of charcoal he'd picked up off the floor, he had drawn a large pentagram on the table-top, augmented with a few rocks and twigs. He set the candle at the base of the five-pointed star and placed the notebook paper in the center. On top of the paper was something else he'd surprised me with: a gold ring with a large, round Tiger's Eye. Erik had found it when he was searching his house for items that had belonged to Denise. He'd stuck it in his pocket, intending to show it to me at Billy's place tonight.

"I think you should wear it," he said.

"I beg your pardon?"

"It's too small for any of my fingers. I think we'll have a better chance of connecting with her if you wear the ring."

I swallowed, but held out my right hand and allowed Erik to slide the band on my ring finger. It was a perfect fit.

"This is weird," I said. "I'm not sure if this is really a good idea."

"It's fine. Trust me. We might not get a better chance." He held out both hands, palms up. "Let's do this."

I had to admit, this did seem like the perfect opportunity to summon Denise's spirit. If we could actually learn something about her death, it would all be worth it. Still, as I reached for Erik's hands, I hesitated.

"What's wrong? You're not afraid, are you?"

"No. It's just . . ." I tried to smile. "Just so we're clear, I'm in a happily committed relationship with my boyfriend. No mixed signals, right?"

"Yeah, of course."

"Alrighty, then." I placed my hands in his. They were rough and warm. He squeezed gently, as he sat up tall and took a deep breath. Again using a language I didn't understand, he murmured what sounded like an invocation. I closed my eyes and allowed myself to be swept up in the moment.

> *Máthair Earth*
> *Athair Am*
> *Cumhacht ársa*
> *Bí linn.*

> *Dhá cheann amháin*
> *Le Chéile*
> *Mar atá sa Dúlra.*

Erik paused, then spoke again, this time translating his words:

> *Teacht anois, Cailín réalta*
> *Teacht anois, Denise*
> *Come now, Star girl*
> *Come now, Denise*

> *Téigh tríd an veil*
> *Labhair linn ó bhás*
> *Pass through the veil*
> *Speak to us from death.*

For my part, I tried to focus on the lighter side of Denise's personality—her whimsical artistry and sense of humor. But I had trouble concentrating. Dark images kept invading my thoughts: dead birds, black clouds, poisonous plants. And then, unbidden, I saw Denise's twisted body on the floor of her workroom.

A chill coursed through my veins. I felt woozy, as Erik repeated the final lines of his incantation like a broken record: "*Labhair linn ó bhás. Speak to us from death.*"

Suddenly, the table trembled beneath our hands. Was it my body that caused the shaking? Or Erik's? The temperature in the cabin dropped, and I shivered from the cold. Paradoxically, my fingers burned beneath the touch of Denise's ring. My dizziness intensified, so I opened my eyes. Erik appeared to be in a trance, his lips moving soundlessly. To steady my nerves, I focused on the candle. Wax dripped down the side and pooled on the table, as the flame danced and flickered.

What are we doing? This didn't feel right. The last time I'd summoned a spirit, it was done in a conscious, peaceful manner, within a loving, protective circle of women. This felt off. The energy in the air felt turbulent and angry—a white-hot, blinding anger.

As I stared at the flame, I realized, too late, that it was drowning in the melted wax. The candle sputtered and went out, leaving us in the dark.

The windows rattled, and I jumped. With the increasing clouds, the wind had picked up. In the back of my mind, I wondered if wind gusts were causing the tower to sway. That might explain my dizziness.

A choking sound from Erik made me forget about the wind. He spoke in a strangled whisper. "No! Dee, no. Don't. Dee!"

I tried to pull my hands away. I wanted to turn on my flashlight and end this party. But Erik wouldn't let me go. In fact, the more I struggled, the harder he gripped. His fingers squeezed mine until Denise's ring cut into my finger. I screamed in pain.

That broke the spell.

With a gasp, Erik released me. I stood quickly, knocking my chair over, as I wrenched the ring from my finger and tossed it on the table. I brought my hand to my lips and tasted blood.

I couldn't see a thing, but I heard Erik push back from the table and make his way toward me. "I'm sorry," he whispered. "I'm so sorry."

He wrapped his arms around me in a hug, and we stood that way, enveloped in darkness, for what felt like a very long time.

The rest of the evening passed in a blur. Erik and I said very little as we descended the tower stairs and scrambled down the bluff. Once we reached the high school, I flicked off my flashlight to conserve the battery. The town was quiet and desolate. We didn't pass a single person or vehicle on our way back to Billy's house. When we reached my car, Erik stood by while I found my keys and unlocked the door. Then he mumbled something about calling me later and shuffled down the street.

On the drive back to Edindale, I turned the radio up and let rock music fill my senses. I didn't want to think. I was too confused. I would analyze the night's events later, when I had more energy.

At home, I let myself inside and headed for the stairs. My only thought was to crawl into bed and curl up under the safety of my blankets. But Wes came out of the kitchen and stopped me.

"Hey, babe. I was about to call you. I just got home myself."

"Really? What time is it?" I tilted my face up to meet his kiss. He smelled like wine and a hint of perfume.

"Eleven. Come and sit with me. I have a lot to tell you."

"Okay," I said reluctantly. "I'm pretty tired, though."

He pulled me over to the sofa. "Another boring game night? Can I get you a glass of wine?"

"Actually . . ." I trailed off, trying to find words. I wasn't going to lie to Wes, but I didn't know where to begin. "Do we have whiskey?"

He laughed. "I think so. I'll go check."

"Just a smidge, please."

"Ice?"

"No. I'm already too cold."

He returned with a tumbler of whiskey and grabbed a blanket from the recliner. As he draped the blanket over my legs, he peered at my face. "Are you feeling okay?"

"Yeah. I am now. We, uh, didn't end up playing the game. Instead, Erik and I . . . we had a sort of séance. It was kind of weird."

"You're kidding. You tried to contact the dead woman?"

I took a sip of the whiskey. It burned my throat and made my stomach feel warm. "You know what? I don't feel like talking about it right now. How was the art opening?"

He brightened and settled on the sofa beside me. "Really good. Not a lot of people came out, just a few of Poppy's friends and a couple members of the town art council. Poppy was really grateful I came."

I'll bet. I smirked but let him continue.

"I had a nice long chat with the gallery owner. He wants to set up a showing of my work sometime this summer."

"Wes, that's great!"

"Yeah, it should be cool. I might get involved with the art council, too."

"That sounds exciting." He looked so pleased and cute, I spontaneously leaned over to kiss him again. And again I caught a whiff of perfume, floral and slightly musky. I narrowed my eyes. "Did Poppy ask to photograph your tattoos?"

"What?" He quirked his eyebrows, but then chuckled. "As a matter of fact, she did. I didn't make her any promises, but I had to keep things friendly. You're not worried, are you?"

I made a face, then smiled. "No. I know how hard it is to resist your charms. And you were on a mission after all. Did you learn anything about Denise?"

"I'm getting to that. So, after everybody else left, Poppy and I were still talking shop. Bruce, the gallery owner, lives above the place. He said to stay as long as we liked. So, we sat in the back room and finished off the wine and cheese."

"How romantic," I said, with not a little sarcasm.

"Oh, it was," he teased. "Especially when I kept bringing up your name."

"Now, why'd you do that? That's no way to loosen a girl's tongue."

"You mean you *wanted* me to seduce her?" he asked, in mock seriousness.

I swat his arm. "Go on."

"So, as we were having our perfectly platonic discussion of the photography business, we commiserated about how hard it is to make ends meet as an artist. I mentioned my side jobs—and also how much it helped reduce expenses when you and I moved in together."

"Smooth."

"I thought so. I asked how she managed, and I found out it's a big sore spot for her."

"What? Money?"

"Yeah. She said she got so desperate a couple months ago, she even asked her friend for a money spell."

"You mean Denise?"

"Yep. That's when I mentioned you again. I said you're Wiccan, and I asked Poppy if she was, too. She's not."

"She's not a witch? She said that?"

"In so many words. She said she's open-minded and willing to try anything—"

"I'm not sure I like the sound of that," I interrupted.

Wes put his fingers to my lips. "Hush. She said her best friend was a witch, so she knew all about it, but she's not really a believer. Still, she could never understand how Denise was able to live so well. They came up together, with similar backgrounds, both artists from a small town. They each had to take on part-time jobs after high school to supplement what little they could earn selling art. Yet somehow Denise always had money. She bought a house and a car on her own. She always had spending money. And then she quit her part-time job to focus on art and tarot readings."

"Did Poppy have any idea where Denise got the money? Supposedly people would come to her house at all hours to . . . buy things."

"Poppy was suspicious. She thought Denise might be cheating her customers. You know, charging lots of money for bogus psychic work."

"It seems like there are other ways to make illicit money, especially in a small town."

"At one point, Poppy asked Denise for a money spell. She figured if it worked for Denise, it might work for her. Of course, it didn't. That only made Poppy more bitter."

"So, that's why she called her a fraud that day in front of Denise's house."

"I guess. Poppy's still pretty broken up over the whole thing. She said the last time she saw Denise, they'd fought pretty hard. I gathered Poppy made some nasty accusations, and Denise said she never wanted to see her again."

The words from Denise's banishing spell surfaced in my mind: *Disappear from my life . . . The connection is severed.* Could she have been trying to exile her own best friend?

"So, Poppy was pretty upset, huh?"

"Yeah. What's even worse is that Poppy went to Denise's house to try to patch things up the morning Denise was killed. When Denise didn't answer the door, Poppy thought Denise was ignoring her. Now she wonders if she could have saved Denise, you know, if she wouldn't have just walked away."

"Wow. What an awful thought to carry around."

"Yeah. I tried to comfort her, poor thing."

I could see it now. Crocodile tears and a sympathetic hug from a tall, dark, and sexy photographer. I finished off my whiskey. Considering my interesting night, I had no right to complain.

Besides, Wes and I trusted each other—even if it seemed that trust was increasingly put to the test.

CHAPTER NINETEEN

I *really* didn't want to go into work on Wednesday morning. I still felt depleted from the long night in Fynn Hollow, and the even later night chilling out with Wes. Plus, I still hadn't received an apology call from Neal Jameson. I was starting to fear he would really follow through on his threat to sue me for malpractice.

Nevertheless, I couldn't play hooky today—I had an appointment with Carol Peters. I needed her to review and sign the affidavit I would file along with our motion to dismiss the custody challenge. After working on her case for the past week, I felt pretty confident about our odds of prevailing. When she came in to sign the papers, I tried to reassure her, but she was still nervous. She fidgeted in the chair across from my desk, swinging her crossed foot and tugging at the cuffs on her waitress uniform.

"You don't know my ex," she said. "He's been very vindictive lately. Oh, and get this! Somehow he found out I took the kids to Wicca-Fest last summer and that I planned to take them to the Beltane Festival this weekend."

"He found out both of those things? How?"

"That's a good question. I tried to play it cool and told him these events weren't secret. I may have insinuated I thought he'd already known about the trip last summer—and he seemed a little unsure himself. But now he refuses to switch weekends with me, so the kids can't go to the Beltane Festival. I probably won't go now either. I'd feel bad being there without them."

"I'm sorry, Carol. Do you want me to add something in our motion about your right to take the children to Pagan events?"

"No, let's not push our luck. My priority right now is to maintain custody."

"Understood."

After she signed the papers and left, I sat at my desk and stared out the window. The only thing to see was the brick wall on the other side of the alley, but my thoughts were turned inward. My mind flickered to the scene in the lookout tower the night before. I was a little disappointed I didn't have a vision, as I sometimes did when meditating or seeking magical guidance. Perhaps I was too uncomfortable. From what I could tell, Erik had seen something. He didn't tell me what it was, but I knew he was troubled. I wondered if it really was Denise's spirit causing the unsteady energy in that cabin. If so, she was not only a restless spirit, she was also an angry one.

I picked up my phone and shot off a text to Farrah: How was your date? I have a lot to share. Call when you can.

I waited a minute, expecting her to respond. When she didn't, I set my phone down and glanced at the custody papers on my desk. I still felt a nagging sense

I was missing something important. Something more than the unsolved murder.

I stood up and walked in a loop around my small office as my mind churned. It was what Carol had told me—that was what bothered me. How did her ex-husband happen to find out about two separate things Carol had shared with me just the week before? One of the things hadn't even happened yet—it was only her intention to take the children to the Beltane Festival. Of course, she could have told others besides me. But what a coincidence that this was my second client to have a secret revealed after telling it to me.

For a split second, the word *curse* popped into my mind again. I dismissed it at once. This didn't feel like a curse. If anything, it felt more sinister.

As I circled my office once more, I found myself face-to-face with the small fairy figurine I'd set on my shelf the other day. Perched on her log with her delicate gossamer wings and mischievous, twinkling eyes, she added a touch of lighthearted joyfulness to the room. I still didn't know who had sent her to me.

All of a sudden, I was seized with a dreadful suspicion. I drew a sharp breath, which caught in my throat like a gag. I snatched up the figurine. As I held it under my desk lamp, I grabbed a nail file and went to work prying open the fairy's log—with particular focus on a carved knot in the front. Before long, I found the thing I hardly dared believe I would actually find: a tiny camera, shiny and spherical, like a robot's eye. For days, this thing had been pointing at me! It had been situated behind the knot in the fairy's log—which I had conveniently placed right across from my desk, where it could record me and all my client meetings. The thought made my blood boil.

Who was watching me?

Shaking with fury and fear, I scanned my office for the heaviest thing I could find. If I'd had a hammer, I would have used it. My eyes fell upon the plants behind my desk. Without a second thought, I tossed the camera on the carpeted floor, lifted the heaviest ceramic planter, and brought it down upon the device with all my might. It took only a couple tries before the camera was smashed to bits. Glass, plastic, and tiny wires mingled with dirt and leaves on the carpet. I stamped it with my feet for good measure.

Why was no one answering their phone? I left messages for Wes, Farrah, and Detective Rhinehardt, and no one was calling me back. With my earlier surge of adrenaline, I'd burst out of my office and run up and down the corridors of my building looking for someone to talk to. Annie's office was dark, as were most of the other offices. On the second floor, I followed sounds of life to a therapist's office with its lights on, but a sign on the door said IN SESSION: DO NOT DISTURB. I found myself missing my old colleagues at the law firm.

Back in my own office, I stared at the mess on the carpet. I longed to vacuum it up, but I didn't want to get rid of vital evidence—at least what was left of it. I was already regretting my hasty decision to smash the thing to smithereens.

Finally, Wes texted me back. He said he was in a photo shoot and would call me later. Then Detective Rhinehardt called. He was sympathetic, but not very encouraging. He advised me to come down to the police station and fill out a report.

Before I left, I used my phone camera to snap some photos of the fairy figurine and the broken camera pieces on the floor. Unfortunately, I had already thrown away the envelope and packaging materials the fairy had been wrapped in.

I locked the door behind me and exited the building. As I walked down the sidewalk, I tried to make sense of it all. The problem was, it made no sense. I felt like I was working with mismatched pieces from multiple sets of jigsaw puzzles. There was no way to make them fit together.

When I reached the corner and waited for the light to change, I was startled by the sound of flapping wings. I looked up and saw a large black crow swoop down and land on a nearby utility wire. It seemed to be staring at me, its beady eyes intense and inscrutable. It reminded me of the way Josie sometimes looked at me.

Making a split-second decision, I turned left instead of right and headed away from the police station. I suddenly had a burning desire to talk with Mila.

A few minutes later, I pushed open the door of Moonstone Treasures and was greeted by the delicate sounds of flute and harp and the heady scent of fresh peonies. Catrina stood at the checkout counter arranging flowers in a vase—or attempting to arrange them. As I approached, I noticed the surface of the counter was littered with pink petals. Catrina's pierced lower lip curled in a frustrated snarl.

"Mila makes this look so easy! I don't know why I can't do it."

"Can I help?" I asked.

"Gladly." She slid the vase away from her as if it were poisonous.

"Looks like you have too many leaves," I commented, as I began stripping the stems. "Where *is* Mila? In the back?"

"Yeah, she's with a client. They should be done soon. What's new with you?"

I shook my head. "Where to begin? I saw a single black crow on my way here. That's usually a bad sign."

"Is it? Crows and ravens are good omens for me. They can be warnings, but in a helpful way. They can also serve as guides."

I thought about this. "You're right. I guess I'm in a negative frame of mind right now. Somebody's been stalking me. I'm kind of freaked out right now."

"You could have fooled me." Catrina peered at my face. "I mean, your aura's a little murky, but you hide your nerves well. Then again, you always seem to have your guard up."

"Thanks—I think."

"How do you know you're being stalked? Is somebody following you?"

I told Catrina about the prank phone calls, including the radio show caller, as well as the dead bird on my porch. "Then I found this." I showed her the pictures I'd taken of the figurine and the smashed recording device. "It was a tiny video camera, hidden in an anonymous gift. And here I thought someone was being kind."

"A nanny cam? It must have been connected to a Wi-Fi system," Catrina mused. "So they could watch you through a computer without having to change a tape like with older security cameras."

"I guess." I shuddered. "I'm so creeped out. I

almost feel jinxed, to be honest. I don't know what to do."

"I don't recognize the fairy." She handed me back my phone. "But I know what I'd do. I'd fight back."

"How? I don't know who's doing this."

Catrina glanced at the purple curtain covering the entrance to the back room, then leaned forward and lowered her voice. "Sometimes you have to fight fire with fire. Know what I mean?"

"I'm not sure."

"Hang on." She turned around and unlocked the glass cabinet behind the counter and selected an amber-colored vial. With another glance at the curtain, she handed it to me. "Mila wouldn't approve."

"What is this?" I asked.

"It's a potion booster. What you need to do is cast a reflection hex. Now, I know you're good at writing your own spells, but here's one you might want to try." She took a piece of Moonstone Treasures' stationery, jotted some words, and folded the paper. "Take this home and try it tonight. All you need is a black candle and any protection herbs. Mix the herbs with the potion booster and use them to anoint the candle. Then light the candle, focus your energy, and say those words. I did it once, and it worked for me."

"Thanks, Trina." I slipped the paper and the vial into my purse. "I'm getting to the point where I'm willing to try anything."

"Have you made a witch bottle yet?"

At that moment the curtain parted and Mila emerged with a pretty middle-aged woman in jeans and a long sweater. They were chatting and laughing, as they walked to the front door. Mila hugged the woman good-bye, then joined Catrina and me.

"What's this I hear about a witch bottle?"

"Keli has been hexed," said Catrina.

"I don't know that for sure. But somebody *has* been messing with me. And spying on me."

"*Spying* on you?" Mila furrowed her brow, her expression the picture of motherly concern.

I told her about the camera and showed her the pictures on my phone. "The creep apparently intends to damage my reputation and my business. They exposed information that was shared with me in confidence, causing me to lose at least one important client." I didn't want to mention Jameson's threat to sue me for malpractice. Somehow I feared that voicing it might make it more likely to happen.

"She's had bad luck, too," Catrina added. "Like being mixed up in the Fynn Hollow murder investigation."

"Thanks for reminding me."

"I'm not sure if a witch bottle is the best way to go here," said Mila, looking from me to Catrina. "It's a tad dark."

"I've heard of witch bottles, but I've never made one. It's really old magic, isn't it? Based on folklore?"

"Yes," said Mila. "They were used hundreds of years ago in Europe, and later in the eastern United States. The ironic thing about them is that they were an *anti*-witchcraft tool, back when witches were feared and condemned for being evil."

"It's still a powerful way to combat dark magic," insisted Catrina. "They can be used for both protection and deflection."

"They can be powerful, yes. As with all spells, your own beliefs, intention, and energy are what determine the effectiveness of the magic. You should just be careful if your intention is to mirror the negativity rather than capture or convert it. Trying to send the darkness back to the perpetrator has some tricky ramifications, both ethically and karmically."

I glanced at Catrina who studiously avoided my eyes. What Mila said applied equally to the reflection spell she had just given me.

"I might make one for protection purposes," I said. "Do you have a glass bottle I can buy?"

"I'll get one for you," Catrina volunteered. She slipped into the back room.

"You know what to put in it?" Mila asked.

I nodded. "Anything sharp and dangerous, right? Bent nails, tacks, broken glass."

Catrina returned with a bottle. "You're talking about what goes in one? Don't forget to include a piece of mirror if you want to add a reflection component. A shard from an old makeup compact works well."

Mila shook her head but kept silent.

"Then you'll need to add a liquid." Catrina grinned, and I knew where she was going with this. "Wiccans usually use consecrated wine or salt water. But you know what they used to use in the old days?"

"All right, Catrina," said Mila, holding up her hand.

"Their own urine!" Catrina laughed. "Can you imagine? And sometimes other bodily fluids, too."

"That's enough, Catrina," said Mila.

"Um, yeah," I said, as I reached for my wallet. "I won't be peeing in the bottle. I might be desperate, but I'm not *that* desperate."

CHAPTER TWENTY

From Moonstone Treasures, I popped into Callie's Health Food Store and Juice Bar for a quick snack. I'd felt calm enough in the presence of Mila and Catrina, but now I was on edge again. I lingered on the sidewalk in front of the store, munching on a protein bar and trying to decide what to do next. Farrah still hadn't responded to my calls and texts. I tried her again. As I listened to the phone ring, and then to her perky outgoing message, I felt a growing uneasiness in the pit of my stomach. It wasn't like Farrah not to send a quick reply, even if to say she's busy and will call later.

Where is she?

I tossed the last two bites of the snack bar into a nearby trash bin and headed back toward my office. The more I thought about Farrah, stuck in her apartment with a broken leg and unable to drive, the more my worry increased. I walked faster and faster until I was jogging down the sidewalk, my boot heels clicking loudly on the pavement. When I reached my

building, I went straight to my car and took off for
Farrah's apartment.

As I pulled into the lot behind her apartment
building, I automatically looked toward her assigned
parking spot. Farrah's sporty Jeep was exactly where
it should be. Far from cheering me, it only spurred
me onward. I raced inside, punched the elevator
button, and bit my lip as I rode up to the top floor.
At Farrah's, I rang the bell several times, then started
pounding with my clenched fist.

"Farrah! Are you in there? Open the door!"

A door opened, but it wasn't hers. Her neighbor,
a wide-eyed older woman in a caftan, stuck her head
out cautiously. "Everything okay?"

"Have you seen Farrah lately? Her car is downstairs, but she's not answering her phone."

"Oh, she's not back yet? I saw her leave last night,
just as I was getting home."

"She left? When? How?"

"Yes, it was around nine o'clock. She was with a
young man. One of those 'bad boy' types some girls
go for. You know, not bad-looking, but a little rough
around the edges. They got in an old car—one of
those classic types, a Camaro, I think. It made a lot of
noise. I remember thinking they must be in a hurry."

Viper. It had to be. Never mind that he supposedly
didn't have a driver's license. I already knew he was
one to flout the law. But what was Farrah doing
with Viper?

"How did she seem?" I asked. "Did she seem worried or scared?"

"I don't think so. Let's see." The woman stared
down the hallway, as she tried to remember. "I was on
the other side of the parking lot, so I didn't see her

closely. I think she had on those big sunglasses she wears. And I did notice she was sort of leaning on the man—because of her leg, I imagine."

"She was leaning on him? What about her crutches?"

"I saw just one crutch. Either she was holding on to him, or he was holding her." The neighbor looked at me curiously. "I saw them for only a few seconds, but nothing struck me as out of the ordinary. Why are you so worried?"

I shook my head, then turned and tried Farrah's doorknob. Naturally, it was locked. "Did you happen to see which way the Camaro went?"

"No, sorry. Ed might have, though."

"Who's Ed?"

"He's the super. His apartment is on the ground floor near the parking lot. He was on his patio grilling out last night. I remember thinking he was having a late supper."

"Thanks."

I took off down the hall and waited for the elevator once more. I didn't know what else Ed the super would be able to tell me, but at least this gave me something to do. Otherwise, I was at a loss. Why in the world would Farrah be with Viper? How did he even know where she lived? Whatever was going on, I had a really bad feeling about it.

Once on the first floor, I headed for the last apartment before the back exit. A nameplate on the door said SUPERINTENDENT. Before I could knock, the door opened and a man stepped out carrying a stepladder.

"Excuse me. Ed?"

He set down the ladder. "Yes, ma'am. Can I help you?"

Speaking quickly, I introduced myself and explained that I was trying to track down Farrah. I knew I must sound borderline hysterical, but frankly I didn't care. "I don't think she left with this guy voluntarily. Did you hear them talking at all, or see which way the car went?"

His expression betrayed a mixture of amusement and disbelief. "Now, now, let's not get carried away. I did see your friend, and she looked perfectly fine to me. She had on nice jeans and a pretty top with—" He paused and waved his fingers in front of his chest. "Buttons. And she had her hair up in one of those big ponytails. She looked good."

"Did you talk to her?"

"Nah. They were in a rush. But she's always coming or going with some guy or another. All different types. She has a wide variety of tastes." He grinned, and I felt like punching him. His powers of observation were woefully skewed.

"Which way did the Camaro turn?" I asked, biting back what I really wanted to say.

"I don't know, but I bet the skid marks are still out there. They peeled out with tires squealing. Showoff." He chuckled.

"Thanks, Ed." I pushed through the exit door and ran out to the parking lot to look for tire tracks. *Like a true detective,* I thought grimly. Farrah should be at my side looking for clues.

The late-afternoon sun cast an orange glow on the border shrubs and wrought-iron fence along the perimeter of the small parking lot. Residents would be coming home from work soon, but for now the place was quiet. With my gaze trained on the ground, I headed for the driveway leading out of the lot.

A glint of bright pink caught my eye. Like a forgotten plastic Easter egg, it poked out of the muddy grass near the curb. And it looked familiar. When I got closer, I saw it was a cell phone in a hot pink case. I picked it up and turned it over. The small snow bunny sticker in the corner clinched it. This was Farrah's phone—the one I'd been calling all day.

With heart thudding, I pulled out my own phone to call 9-1-1. There was no doubt in my mind. *Sunglasses at night. Cell phone on the ground. Unable to walk on her own. Viper hauling her to his car and peeling out in a hurry.* Farrah had been kidnapped. Viper must have drugged her and kidnapped her. My hand shook as I fumbled with my phone.

I almost dropped it when it rang.

"Hello!" I panted, way past caring for decorum.

"Keli? It's Erik. I thought we should talk about last night. I hope you're not—"

"Erik! Oh, thank Goddess. I need you to call Viper right away. He has Farrah! He took her last night, and I don't know where they went, and they're not back yet. She dropped her phone, so I can't reach her. I was about to call the police."

"Whoa. Slow down. What are you talking about?"

I took a deep breath. Still speaking quickly, but hopefully more coherently, I explained what I feared.

Erik was silent for half a second. "Hang tight, Keli. I'll call Viper and call you right back. Don't involve the cops yet. I'm sure there's nothing to worry about."

I continued to investigate the grounds while waiting for Erik to get back to me. Sure enough, there were skid marks on the street. Evidently, the speeding car turned left out of the parking lot. Where they went from there . . . was impossible to tell.

When Erik called back, I crossed my fingers as I answered. "What did he say?" I asked.

"Uh, he didn't answer. But that's not unusual. I called the garage, too, and he wasn't there. I'm on my way to his house now."

"I'm calling the police."

"No, wait! I just remembered. What day is this? Yeah, I know where he probably is. There's this old honky-tonk dive out on Old County Road a few miles outside of Fynn Hollow. Once a month this Southern rock band comes through for a three-night run. They rehearse on Wednesdays and perform Thursday through Saturday. Viper sits in with them on percussion. And he likes to bring girls along, you know?"

"But yesterday was Tuesday. Where did they go last night?"

"Who knows? Maybe his place . . . which I'm at now, and his car isn't here. But I'm sure he's at that bar. It's called the Dusty Road Saloon. They might not be open yet, but Viper goes in early with the band. I'll drive out there now and call you as soon as I find him."

"Thanks, Erik, but I'm not waiting. I'll drive out there myself."

"Oh, of course. I understand. How about if I meet you there?"

"No, that's okay. Why don't you keep trying to reach Viper on the phone? And don't worry about me. I won't be going alone."

I would bring a man along, but it wouldn't be Erik. He wasn't the one I wanted at my side.

* * *

Wes knew how to find the Dusty Road Saloon. He'd grown up in Edindale and spent his youth working at his grandpa's farm outside of town and fishing the nearby lakes. As a teen he'd cruised the winding country roads, sometimes for fun and sometimes to track down his younger brother, who had a tendency to find trouble.

"Rob used to come out here sometimes," Wes said, as he pulled his car into the gravel parking lot. "Before he got hooked on gambling and spent all his time at the riverboat casino. He'd come out here to drink cheap beer and ride the mechanical bull. Frankly, I never saw the appeal."

I stared at the huge metal pole barn with flashing beer signs in the windows and had to agree. From the outside anyway, it didn't look very appealing to me. Nor did it fit my image of a saloon—except, perhaps, for the rusty spittoon squatting beside the entrance.

Wes stopped the car in front of the entrance, but I didn't get out. According to the sign on the door, the place wouldn't open for another half hour yet. The only vehicle in the parking lot was a muddy pickup truck that, from the looks of it, might have been there five minutes or five years.

"Let's drive around back."

As we circled the building, my senses began to tingle and I knew—even before spotting the Camaro—that Farrah was here. We found Viper's car parked between a white panel van and dusty black sedan. Wes shut off his engine, and we hurried up the short ramp to the back door. I pushed it open and stepped inside, with Wes close behind me.

It was like a different world. Whereas the outside

of the building was plain and utilitarian, the inside featured warm wood paneling, soft lighting, and vibrant music. On a corner stage, a four-piece band stomped their feet and picked out raucous fiddle music. Abruptly, the music stopped, and I feared for a moment that we were the cause. Then it started up again, and I realized they were only rehearsing.

Wes and I stood against a wall and surveyed the place. Viper and Farrah were nowhere to be seen. I was about ready to interrupt the musicians when a stout man with a ponytail and bandanna emerged through a swinging door. He carried a carton of beer mugs over to the bar counter. Wes approached him and spoke a few words, one bartender to another. I saw the guy nod and point to another dark corner of the building.

"There's an apartment upstairs," said Wes, when he returned. "Mack said we can find our friends there."

"Then let's find them," I said.

At the top of the stairs was a loft spanning the width of the barn. We walked past an office to a closed door at the end. Instead of knocking, I reached for the knob and turned. It was unlocked.

Wes and I looked at each other. He nodded, and I pushed the door open. Moving silently, we stepped inside. I wasn't sure what we'd find, but I was counting on the element of surprise to work in our favor.

We found ourselves in a small, cluttered living room. To the left was an adjoining kitchen and straight ahead was a narrow hallway. We heard noises coming from a room at the end of the hall. Gliding silently down the hall, I realized it was the sound of a television, some sitcom with a laugh track. Then

there was a lull in the noise, and I heard a voice—
Viper's raspy drone. My heart jumped in my chest.

From the edge of the doorway, we peered inside.
In a glance, I saw a large-screen TV, newspapers and
magazines strewn about, dirty dishes, beer bottles,
and, to our right, a sagging, rust-colored sofa—with
Farrah, sprawled across it. Her eyes were closed, and
Viper was leaning over her.

I gasped involuntarily. Wes charged. In one swift
movement, he grabbed Viper by the collar and jerked
him backward. Viper let out a startled, strangled cry,
and Farrah's eyes popped open. She sat up straight,
her hands flying to her mouth.

In that instant, it occurred to me that things might
not be quite what they seemed. I parted my lips to
tell Wes to hold up for a minute. But it was too late.
He swung his clenched fist and socked Viper in the
jaw, causing the younger guy to lose his balance and
fall to his knees. With a pathetic whimper, Viper covered his head with his arms. Wes looked down at him
with contempt—and a degree of surprise. I was sure
he expected Viper to put up a fight.

"Is Farrah okay?" he asked, without taking his eyes
off Viper.

"Yeah," I said. By this time, Farrah had swung her
legs to the floor and was reaching for her purse. She
pulled out a lipstick and compact, and began touch-
ing up her makeup, as if she didn't have a care in the
world. "She's fine."

Farrah looked up at me expectantly, amusement
twinkling in her eyes. I handed her her cell phone.

"So, there it is! I've been looking for that."

"I take it you weren't kidnapped then?"

"Um, no. I wasn't kidnapped." She snapped the
compact shut, then heaved herself off the sofa.

"We've just been hanging out, but I should probably get home now. Can I catch a ride with you guys?"

Now that he realized he wasn't still under attack, Viper stood up and rubbed his jaw. "What the hell, man?"

Wes appeared confused, the poor thing. His eyes slid from me to Farrah, then over to Viper. "Sorry," he mumbled. "Misunderstanding, I guess."

Farrah plucked her single crutch from the table where it leaned, then turned and gave me a coy look. "My, my, Keli. That man of yours is quite the hero, isn't he?" She hobbled over to Wes and patted his arm. "Think you could channel some of that strength into helping me down the stairs?"

He nodded and eagerly obliged. I could tell he wanted nothing more than to get the heck out of there and put this embarrassing incident behind us. I picked up Farrah's purse and followed close behind.

As we made our way toward the exit, Farrah called cheery good-byes to all the band members, by name. Grinning broadly, they all tipped their cowboy hats and waved. Mack lifted a bottle to her. "Y'all come back now."

She laughed and blew him a kiss. "You know I will! Thanks for everything, big guy!"

I didn't know whether to hug her or shake her. I knew one thing, though. She had a lot of explaining to do.

CHAPTER TWENTY-ONE

Wes dropped off Farrah and me at her apartment building, then headed to the Loose. He was scheduled to work the late shift, which was just as well. I could tell he'd had about all he could take of Farrah's ditzy, giggly excuses. She kept insisting Viper was a sweetheart once you got to know him, which Wes clearly found hard to believe. Frankly, I wasn't buying it either. As soon as we were settled on her sofa with a late dinner of hummus-and-cucumber sandwiches with white wine, I let her have it.

"How long are you going to make me wait?" I demanded.

"What do you mean?"

"Come on, Farrah. You can drop the act now. I really thought you were in danger!"

"I'm sorry. I was going to call you today, but I couldn't find my phone. Obviously. But you knew I had a date last night."

"With Viper? *He* was your date? Wait a minute. The other night when you said you had a guy coming over, was that Viper, too?"

She dropped her gaze and winced guiltily. "Yeah."

"How in the world did this come about? I thought you didn't like him. You must have had an ulterior motive. Am I right?"

She held up her hands in surrender, sloshing wine from her glass in the process. "All right, all right. I'll tell you. Of course, I was going to tell you anyway, but I didn't expect it to come out like this."

"I'm listening." I handed her a napkin, and she dabbed at the spilled wine. By this point, my earlier fear and subsequent irritation had worn off. I decided to help her out. "You were playing detective, weren't you?"

"I just wanted to help. When the opportunity presented itself, I couldn't pass it up."

"He called you?"

"Yeah. He apologized for being an ass, and said he felt really bad. He asked me what he could do to make it up to me. Without thinking, I blurted that he could bring me dinner and roses. And he said, 'Done.'"

"So, you gave him your address."

"See, this is why I didn't tell you before! You were cozying up to Erik the Druid to get information. I figured I could do the same."

"I haven't been 'cozying up' with Erik! Anyway, he's nothing like Viper."

"Listen, I was never in any danger. He was a perfect gentleman. Anyway, I had my windows open when he was here, and I could have hollered if I needed help. I have neighbors who watch out for each other all around me."

"Are you sure about that? None of them seemed too concerned when you stumbled out of here on a strange guy's arm. Where was your other crutch? And why the sunglasses?"

"Huh? I don't know. We were being silly, I guess. And I might have partaken in a hit of a certain kind of cigarette, which made my eyes red."

"Farrah!"

"Stop judging me! I'm a grown woman, and I knew what I was doing."

We fell silent and glared at one another. Then her words sank in, and I realized I might have been laying it on a little thick. As it turned out, she apparently was never in any real danger.

"I'm not judging you," I finally said. "I just worry, that's all. A woman was killed, and we still don't know who did it."

"Well, it wasn't Viper. He was picked up by the cops that morning and was stuck in jail until Billy came and bailed him out."

"What time was he arrested?"

"Between nine-thirty and ten o'clock."

"Last I heard, they think the murder happened earlier in the morning. It might have already happened by nine o'clock."

Farrah looked away, and I realized nothing good would come from arguing. I reached for the wine bottle and refilled both of our glasses. After a hearty sip, I smacked my lips. "I, uh, had an interesting night last night."

She raised her eyebrows. "Oh?"

"Yeah. The game was cancelled, so Erik decided to show me this place where Denise used to go to be alone and perform spells." I recounted my evening in the fire tower, sparing no detail. When I'd finished, Farrah wagged her finger at me.

"And you were worried about me! At least I was

never really alone with Viper. There were always people within shouting distance."

"All right. So, we're both . . . risk-takers." I was going to say something less flattering, but it seemed a little rude.

"Or we both have a well-honed sense of women's intuition," she suggested.

I decided to let that one go. "Hey, you never told me. Did you learn anything useful from Viper?"

She pursed her lips. "Not so much. He was rather serene about Denise's death. He said it was unfortunate she went the way she did, but we all have to go eventually. He said she'd learned all the lessons she was meant to learn in this lifetime, and she'll come back as a more evolved being in the next."

"He really said that? I didn't take him for a mystic."

"You should have heard him, Kel. Once he got started—whew! I felt like I was listening to a yogi or something. And it wasn't all hot air. He *really* believes magic is for real."

I frowned at that. "*I* believe magic is real, you know."

"Yeah, I know. But this was different somehow. It's like he thinks he's a magician or something. He said the only reason he was arrested the other day was because he forgot to put up his 'psychic shields.' Usually, he's untouchable."

"Untouchable? That sounds a little cocky."

"Totally. He claimed he can cast a spell and have anything he wants. He said he's known it for years, ever since high school. I think he wanted me to dare him to prove it."

"But you didn't?"

"To tell you the truth, it was a little scary." I gave her a sharp look, and she shook her head. "I wasn't afraid of *him*," she said quickly. "It's just that he was really intense. His confidence was almost unnerving. In fact, when he was talking, I couldn't help thinking of the snake in *The Jungle Book*. It's like he has this hypnotic quality, you know?"

"Are you sure that wasn't a result of the 'special cigarette' you smoked?"

She threw her napkin at me. "Stop being a little Miss Keli Two-shoes."

"Ha ha." I set my glass aside and sat back. "By the way, something else happened today. With all the excitement of tracking you down, I put it out of my mind." I told her about finding the hidden camera in my office.

"Are you kidding me? That's so creepy!"

"You're telling me."

"You don't think it has something to do with the murder, do you? I mean, unless the killer wants to know if you're on to them. But it seems hard to believe."

"Yeah, I've been thinking about that. The woman in my office building who brought the package to me said she'd been holding on to it for a couple of days. So, it was probably mailed before the murder happened."

"Gosh, Keli. Maybe you're the one who needs to put up some psychic defenses."

I tried to laugh—hearing Farrah use witchy language was kind of funny. But instead I shivered.

I tried to stay at Farrah's place until I knew Wes would be home from work, but I couldn't do it. Though we chatted some more and watched a little television, I found myself struggling to keep my eyes open. When she dozed off in her recliner and started snoring, I knew it was time to go.

I pulled my boots on and gathered up my purse.

"Call me tomorrow, partner," she said sleepily.

"Don't go losing your phone again," I said, as I switched off her lamp.

All her neighbors must have been sleeping, too. The apartment complex was hushed and dim as I let myself out. I drove home on quiet, desolate streets, lost in thought. Why had I flipped out today over the fanciful idea that Farrah had been kidnapped? It must have been because of all the weird things happening lately, all the violations to my peace of mind. I was wound so tightly, it was probably inevitable that I would snap.

I yawned as I pulled up in front of my town house. Maybe I'd skip going into the office tomorrow. What I needed was a vacation. I'd love nothing more than to pack my bags and hit the open road with Wes. We could head west to Nebraska and visit my family, then veer north and go all the way out to Washington to see Wes's brother. We'd be gone for weeks. There's nothing like travel to clear the mind and put life's worries in their proper perspective.

If only Deputy Langham hadn't ordered me not to leave the county.

Thinking of the dogged officer made me want to escape all the more. I drove past my house to the end of the block and circled around to the narrow alley in back. I usually parked on the street, because it was quicker, but tonight I decided to put the car in the garage. I angled the car inside, cut the engine, and pressed the garage door remote to lower the door behind me. The moment I stepped out of the car, I knew something was wrong. There was an acrid odor in the air that shouldn't have been there.

When I stepped out of the garage into the back-yard, it was unmistakable. Something was burning. I looked first to the St. Johns' empty house, which I was supposed to be keeping an eye on while they were out of town. There was nothing to see there. A fat pine tree blocked the view of my own house. With a mounting sense of dread, I made my way up the stone walkway through my backyard. As soon as I rounded the tree, I froze in horror. Billowing smoke and jagged flames filled my vision. My house was on fire!

The sound of sirens snapped me into action. I couldn't imagine who had called the fire department—all the homes on my block were dark. But I was grate-ful. Now I wouldn't have to waste time calling 9-1-1. My only thought was to rescue Josie.

I lifted my shirt over my mouth and nose and rushed to get a closer look. It was hard to see through the thick smoke, but I was pretty sure the fire was confined to the deck. The house itself wasn't on fire. Yet.

There was no space between the townhomes, so I had to run back to the garage, down the alley, and around the corner to get to the front of the house. The sirens were louder now. The thought crossed my mind that I should stay outside and direct the fire-fighters to the rear, but as they peeled down the street, they already seemed to know where to go. My keys were still in my hand, so I unlocked the door and went inside.

"Josie!" I flipped on the lights and looked around.

The smell of smoke was strong, but it was still outside. "Josie!" I repeated.

Her loud mew came from upstairs. I ran for the staircase and stopped as she appeared at the top of the stairs. "Come here, kitty. Are you okay?"

She mewed again, then started down the stairs, her tail hanging low. I could tell she was nervous. Before she reached the bottom, she surprised me by jumping into my arms. I caught her neatly. "Oh, you poor thing. You must have been so scared."

I stroked her head, as I turned to head for the back door. Before I reached it, there was a pounding on the patio door.

"Coming!" I turned on the outside light, fumbled with the latch, and slid open the glass doors. I found myself face-to-face with a tall, burly fireman, who directed a penetrating gaze at me. I couldn't tell if the expression on his ruddy face betrayed concern or irritation.

"Everybody all right in here?"

"Yes. Just shaken a bit."

"Well, the fire's out now. You the one who called it in?"

"Who, me? No." I looked past him at the mess. The deck was covered in white foam and ash. The patio chairs were blackened, and my potted plants were burnt to a crisp. In the middle of it all was a dented silver garbage can. I looked at the can in some confusion. It should have been at the rear of the yard next to the garage.

The fireman unzipped his reflective, yellow jacket and reached inside for a black notebook. "Mind if I come in for a minute? I'm Captain Blake."

I glanced at the deck again and nodded. Another

firefighter, younger but equally burly, was shining a spotlight on the garbage can, while a third man hauled gear through my yard to a red fire engine idling in the alley. I hoped they hadn't trampled my garden too badly.

Stepping aside, I invited Captain Blake to have a seat at the table in the breakfast nook near the patio doors. Josie squirmed in my arms, so I set her down. She darted away, presumably for one of her many hiding places. I couldn't say I blamed her.

"Name, please."

"Keli Milanni. Can I offer you something to drink, Captain? A glass of water?"

"No, thank you. This your home?" I nodded, and he asked the next question on his list. "Does anyone else live here?"

"Yes. My boyfriend, Wes Callahan." I checked the time and saw it was almost 1:00 A.M. "He should be home any minute now."

"How did the fire start?"

"I have no idea. I just got home a few minutes ago and saw the deck was on fire. I would have called for help, but you were already on your way."

He narrowed his eyes, giving me the uncomfortable feeling he doubted the truth of what I said. It was like being interrogated by Deputy Langham all over again.

"That your car in the garage?"

"Yes, I—"

There was a tap at the door, and the younger firefighter came inside. "Captain, take a look at this. It was in the trash can. It's doused in gasoline, but the flames didn't reach it. Looks like somebody dropped a match on the plants and set the porch on fire before they could burn the contents of the can."

In his gloved hand was a thick, brown leather-bound book. I had never seen it before, but I knew in an instant what it was. Embossed with a spiraling Celtic design and fastened with a copper clasp, it fit Erik's description of Denise's missing datebook.

"Can I look at that?" I asked.

The captain slowly shook his head. "Lieutenant, go get an evidence bag. And call the sheriff's office. I think they're going to want to see this."

CHAPTER TWENTY-TWO

As it happened, Deputy Langham was unavailable to come to my house to retrieve the datebook himself. I took that as a good sign. If I was really his number one suspect, I'd expect him to move heaven and earth to be the one to grill me at the scene. And there was no doubt it *was* a crime scene. As I soon learned, Captain Blake was a fire investigator, and he made no secret of the fact that he believed the fire on my deck was set intentionally. Whether it was arson or the attempted destruction of evidence didn't seem to matter at this point.

The county officer who came in place of Langham was a fresh-faced woman who appeared not much older than me. I watched through the kitchen window as she spoke to the firefighters in the backyard. She didn't seem a bit ruffled at being called into action at 1:00 in the morning. Perhaps she always worked the late shift.

When she tapped lightly on the door and politely introduced herself as Deputy Tricia LaMott, I decided I liked her a lot better than both Langham and Blake. She even accepted my offer of a glass of water.

Wes arrived in the middle of Deputy LaMott's preliminary questions. She listened quietly, as I explained to Wes what had happened. His emotions transitioned quickly from concern to anger. Eyes flashing, he nearly spat out the first name that came to him.

"Vi—"

"It *is* vile," I said, cutting him off. "I can't imagine who would do this."

He caught on quickly. While Viper had plenty of time to get here and start the fire, not to mention ample cause to be angry at Wes and me, we had no proof against him. Besides that, we'd already wrongfully suspected him of one crime today—and Wes's actions could very well be viewed as battery. It might not be the most prudent idea to share that bit of information.

Wes stood behind my chair and rubbed my shoulders, as we answered the deputy's remaining questions. First she obtained some basic information from Wes, including his boss's name at the Loose. Then she returned her attention to me.

"Where were you coming from when you arrived home tonight?" she asked.

"My friend Farrah's apartment. I'm sure she's asleep now, but she can vouch for me." I gave the officer Farrah's contact information.

"Did you try to put out the fire?" she asked.

"No. I have a fire extinguisher in the kitchen, but I didn't have time to get it. As I mentioned, my first thought was the safety of my cat."

She smiled. "I can understand that. I have two fur babies of my own at home."

Returning her smile, I almost asked if she'd like

something to eat. Then she brought out the evidence bag. My smile dropped away, as my mouth went dry.

"Does this look familiar to you?" she asked, placing the bag on the table.

"I have an idea what it might be," I said truthfully. "May I look inside?"

She reached into her pocket for a pair of disposable gloves and handed them to me. "If you wear these, you can take a peek."

I eagerly slipped on the gloves and removed the leather book from the plastic bag. It reeked of gasoline. As I turned the cover and saw Denise's star-encircled name on the first page, I could have sworn I felt a slight charge prickle through my fingertips. Denise must have cast a protection spell on her day planner. The realization gave me pause—and not because I feared I would sprout warts. Rather, I felt it would be a violation of, not only Denise's privacy, but also the privacy of her clients. For that reason, I skipped over the first several pages of the book and turned straight to the page for Saturday, April 17. The day of Denise's demise.

My breath caught as I read the first item on her agenda—though perhaps I shouldn't have been surprised. Printed in bold purple ink were the damning words: *8:45 A.M. Tea with Kelly.*

"Oh, no."

"What does it say?" Wes leaned over my shoulder to get a closer look. "That can't mean you. That's not how you spell your name."

"True. Though a lot of people get it wrong."

"Can I have that back now?" The deputy's voice was polite, but I knew she'd been watching me carefully.

"Yeah." I continued to stare at the writing, then

angled the book toward the light. If I wasn't mistaken, Denise—or someone else—had traced over the original lettering in a darker ink. The name "Kelly," in particular, might have had different letters beneath it. "Can I just take a quick picture of this?"

Wes was way ahead of me. Before the deputy could respond, he whipped out his cell phone, leaned down, and snapped a flash photo of the page in question. I carefully closed the book then and replaced it in the bag. I didn't have to tell Deputy LaMott what this object was. I was sure she already knew.

"Clearly, someone is trying to set me up." I tried to smile, as I handed her the book and removed the gloves. "I'm sure you can see that."

She stood up and shook my hand. "Thank you for your time, Keli. We'll be in touch if we have any follow-up questions." She opened the patio door and exited the way she had come in. Then she paused and turned back. "Given the circumstances, you might want to consider hiring an attorney."

Right.

Once everyone had left, and the backyard was dark and quiet as it should be, Josie came out of hiding and joined Wes and me in the kitchen. She mewed reproachfully.

"Oh, my goodness! Did you miss your dinner today?" I reached for her bowl, and Wes put his hand on my arm to stop me.

"Why don't you go to bed, babe? I'll take care of Josie. You must be beat."

"I should be, but I'm too wired to go to bed. With everything that happened today, my mind is bouncing all over the place."

"Mine too."

While Wes served Josie fresh food and water, I cleaned the kitchen and swept up the dirt and ashes tracked in by the firefighters. I'd tackle the deck in the morning. I was about to head upstairs when the house phone rang. It was such a jarring sound I jumped.

"Who would be calling so late?" asked Wes.

"I have an idea." I jogged over to the phone and pressed the speaker button. "Hello?"

The music started up right away. It was the same tinkling music box melody as before, familiar yet elusive. Wes and I stared at the phone as it played. When the song finished, there was silence.

"What do you want?" I shouted. "What is the point of this?"

Wes narrowed his eyes. "You're nothing but a worthless coward," he said, his voice low and dangerous. "We *will* find out who you are. You can count on it."

I thought I heard a faint snicker, then the line went dead.

Wes grabbed the receiver and dialed *69.

"I tried that before," I told him.

He listened to the same unhelpful message I had and hung up with a scowl. "There's got to be a way to trace it. Maybe we should call the cops."

"Yeah, maybe. But I'm not very optimistic."

"What was that song? Maybe it's a clue."

I had to smile. It was cute, and somehow cheering, to hear Wes talk about "clues." And he gave me an idea. I snapped my fingers. "I still have the song on the answering machine from the other day! Isn't there an app that identifies songs?"

"Yeah, there is. But let me hear it again. It sounded familiar, like I should know it."

"I thought the same thing." I pressed the repeat

button on the device. As the music played, Wes began to hum along.

"Dum dum, da dum, da dum . . . That's it! 'Smoke Gets in Your Eyes.'"

"You're not a half-bad singer," I said. "And I think you're right. I've heard that song somewhere before."

"I'm sure you have. It's probably been covered by dozens of singers over the years. But why . . ." He trailed off and shook his head. "Because where there's smoke, there's fire? Is the song supposed to be a threat?"

"The person who called the radio show mentioned fire, too. Something about not messing with fire. That one was definitely a threat."

"And this stunt tonight is the creep fulfilling the threat? You know, we should look into buying a home security system tomorrow. Or a guard dog."

"If you want to look into home alarms, that's fine with me. And I'm going to work on another kind of home protection, if it's okay with you."

"Of course. You mean, like salt in the doorways and sage incense? That sort of thing?"

"Exactly. I don't know why I haven't done it sooner." I leaned forward and kissed Wes on the lips. He pulled me in for a tight hug.

"Let's go to bed. I have a feeling the mischief is over for the night. And we can make sure there won't be any more calls." He unplugged the phone from the wall.

"You go on up. There's one thing I'd like to go ahead and do tonight."

"You sure it can't wait?"

"My gut tells me no."

"Well, by all means, follow your gut."

As soon as Wes went upstairs, I retrieved the bottle
I'd bought from Moonstone Treasures, then set
about finding the nastiest, sharpest little objects I
could find. It didn't take long. The idea must have
been ruminating in the back of my mind all day.
Wearing gloves for the second time tonight—only
thicker this time—I collected the sinister ingredients:
a razor blade from the bathroom; a needle from my
sewing kit; three rusty nails from a junk container
under the kitchen sink; and six spines from the
cactus in the living room window. Next I went into
the kitchen and filled the bottle with salt water.

"And now for a personal touch," I murmured.
Taking careful aim, I spit into the bottle. Then I
closed it tightly and gave it a vigorous shake. Finally,
I lit a black candle and let the wax drip over the cork,
sealing the bottle and the magic within.

Though I often performed spells at my altar, I
didn't always. I decided not to this time. For one
thing, I didn't want to disturb Wes, who was probably
already drifting off to sleep. For another, this spell
was best performed outside.

I grabbed a jacket from the closet, slipped on my
boots, and stepped out the back door. Captain Blake
had said it was a good thing my deck was made from
flame-resistant composite wood. Otherwise it might
have collapsed, and the fire could have spread to
the house. As it was, all the damage occurred on the
surface of the deck and didn't affect its structural in-
tegrity. Still, I used a flashlight and watched my step
as I tracked through the ashy debris and descended
to the patio.

The bright moon, a waxing gibbous, was four days
shy of full. According to lunar tradition, it was a ripe

time for creating and attracting. Not so much for repelling. But a witch has to do what a witch has to do. Besides, I was creating peace of mind. Or at least trying to.

I walked softly across the dewy lawn to the rear of the yard. The intruder would have entered through the alley gate next to the garage. Under cover of darkness, it would have been easy to creep in unnoticed, especially with the St. Johns and their excitable dog out of town. As for my neighbors on the other side, they were so wrapped up in their work and child-rearing, I rarely saw them at any hour. They hadn't even ventured outside during all the commotion following the fire. And to the rear of the yard, behind the garage, was an alley, which ran along the edge of Fieldstone Park. There was nothing but a wrought-iron fence and acres of parkland on the other side.

Fortunately, ideal conditions for trespassing were also ideal for moonlight magic.

I chose a spot in front of the gate—the threshold to our property. With a spade from the garage, I pried up two stepping stones and began to dig. Once I had a hole about two feet deep, I set the spade aside and took a deep, cleansing breath. Then I closed my eyes, anchored my feet to the ground, and took three more breaths. As I inhaled, I imagined myself drawing energy up from the earth, filling me with a warm, golden glow. It was a simple grounding and centering ritual, but it did the trick. When I opened my eyes, I felt calm and resilient. I held the witch bottle in both hands and brought it toward my heart center, charging it with my own energy. Then I held it to

the sky and invoked the gods of protection with my
whispered words.

> *Syn, Bes, Tara, Athena*
> *Aine, Nut, Brighid, Aegina:*
> *Suffuse this object with your timeless power;*
> *Activate my intention from this hour.*
> *Henceforth, whosoever shall cross this way*
> *With ill intent, the price shall pay.*

I lowered my arms and gazed into the dark pit at
my feet. A twinge of guilt pulled at the back of my
conscience. In my mind, I heard Mila's voice caution-
ing me not to use my magical gifts to inflict harm.

I shook it off. "This is self-defense," I argued, as
much to myself as to Mila.

Kneeling to the ground, I turned the bottle upside
down and wedged it into the hole.

> *May this bottle repel, and wrongdoers flee.*
> *Guard this land well. So mote it be.*

Quickly, I scooped the dirt on top of the bottle
and refilled the hole. Then I replaced the stones. I
would double-check their sturdiness and clean them
off in the daylight. For now, I returned the spade to
the garage and locked it behind me. It was beyond
late, and I was starting to feel it.

Back in the kitchen, I moved to gather up the
things I'd left on the counter, including the black
candle and the small paper bag from Moonstone
Treasures. As my fingers grasped the handle of the
bag, I paused. There was one more thing I could
do tonight.

I reached into the bag and pulled out a small amber vial and a folded piece of paper: Catrina's spell. Silently, I read the words she had written.

Curse return from whence you came
The one who cast gets all the blame
He who dares to block my path
Will feel the force of recoiled wrath
Ash to ash, blood to bone,
Pain to you, who threw the stone.

Hmm. Should I do it? Salt and sage were all well and good, especially to ward off dark spirits and bad juju. But I was dealing with a human antagonist. Not only that, but the unknown person had now crossed into more serious territory. They'd moved beyond creepy phone calls to trespassing and property damage—not to mention trying to frame me for murder. I had left the broken mirror out of the witch bottle, but perhaps I should have included it. The malice this creep directed at me *should* be reflected right back at them.

I opened the vial and held it beneath my nose. It was faintly redolent of coffee, licorice, and some kind of oil. I squinted at the label, which simply said POTION BOOSTER SERUM. FOR EXTERNAL USE ONLY. Remembering Catrina's instructions, I checked my spice cabinet for any herbs associated with protection spells and selected a jar of bay leaves. I took out one leaf and crumbled it in my hand. Then I poured several drops of the potion booster onto the crumbled leaf and mixed it with my palms. As I rubbed the mixture up and down the sides of the black candle, I focused on the purpose of the spell.

Once again, Mila's warning surfaced in my mind. I wiped my hands on a towel and wondered if I should hold off. There was danger, I knew, in sending negative energy blindly out into the universe. Counter-curse or no, anything you projected could come right back to you. But that wasn't the only reason for my hesitation. Deep down, it was the dark nature of the spell. I had always prided myself on being a practitioner of "light magic." To consciously direct negative energy at another person didn't sit well with me. It felt more like revenge than self-defense.

Suddenly, an image of Denise's fallen body flashed in my mind. I couldn't be sure my harasser was her killer, but I had a strong sense they were one and the same. A wave of revulsion washed over me. This sicko was playing games with me and enjoying every minute of it. Anger burned in my heart.

Fingers trembling, I struck a match and lit the candle.

CHAPTER TWENTY-THREE

Something soft tickled my face. Then the tickle turned into a jab. Groaning, I reached out to push it away. It responded by pouncing heavily onto my chest.

"Josie," I grumbled. "What's the big idea?"

I opened my eyes and scooted her off me so I could sit up. Bright sunlight seeped through the edges of the window blinds, telling me it was late even before I turned to peer at the bedside clock.

Yikes! I'd slept away half the morning.

Then I remembered the night before and fell back upon the pillow. No wonder I'd slept in. By the time I'd crawled into bed next to Wes, it must have been nearing dawn. In spite of the late hour, I still probably logged only six hours of sleep.

Josie started swatting at me again, so I decided to get up. I was sure Wes had filled her food bowl before leaving for work, so she wasn't hungry. She just didn't like me staying in bed so long. Apparently, it disrupted her routine.

After a quick shower, I threw on some black yoga pants, a well-worn charcoal T-shirt, and a comfy hoodie. Turning to the bedroom mirror, I was somewhat startled to see how somber I looked dressed all in black. Not that there was anything wrong with that, but I somehow felt a more uplifting color was in order today. I switched to a faded coral T-shirt and headed downstairs to make breakfast.

As the coffee percolated, I checked my work email. I had two messages: one from an old client asking for a copy of his will, and one from my former boss, Beverly. She wrote that she had spoken to Neal Jameson and was surprised, and distressed, to hear about his "recent experience with me." She offered to lend an ear if I wanted someone to talk to.

I had almost succeeded in forgetting about Neal's threat to sue me for malpractice. I didn't want to think about it now. My head had started to pound, which was probably due to caffeine withdrawal and hunger, but might have had something to do with tension and worry as well.

I poured myself a big mug of coffee and a bowl of cold cereal with almond milk, and sat at the table facing the patio doors. As I ate, I stared outside and contemplated the muddled state of the backyard— and how it was a perfect metaphor for the current state of my life. Hidden beneath the surface were seeds of hope right alongside barbed emblems of fear. And on the surface was a muddy, chaotic mess. I sighed.

Will my world ever be normal again?

As if in answer to my question, my cell phone rang. It was Erik.

"You didn't call me back," he said, a note of accusation in his usually genial voice.

"What?"

"Farrah was missing, remember? I know now that you found her with Viper, but only because I tracked him down myself this morning. I figured she was fine all along, but you were so worked up, I'd started to doubt myself."

"I'm sorry. You were right. She was fine."

"Is there something else you want to tell me?"

"Um." I was at a loss. So much had happened recently, I wasn't sure what he was talking about. I also wasn't sure I liked his tone. I didn't owe him anything.

"About Denise's appointment book?"

"Oh! Yeah. How did you hear about that?"

"Someone posted it on the Witches' Web. They said the sheriff's department found it in the garbage at a witch lawyer's house. You're the only witch lawyer I know."

"Wait—Who posted that?"

"I don't know. Everyone's anonymous on there."

"Well, did they also mention that someone set a fire at my house and planted the datebook to frame me?"

"No! Is that true? God, Keli."

"Yes, it's true. They even wrote my name in the book."

He was silent for a moment, as if mulling it over. "Your name was in the book? You didn't know Denise, did you?"

"What? Of course not." Jeez, he could be dense sometimes. "I didn't even know you until, what, twelve days ago?"

"Right. Sorry. It's just weird. I don't understand what's going on."

"It's a mystery," I said drily.

"So, was there anything helpful written in the book?"

"I didn't get to look at it for long, but it was clearly tampered with. I'm sure the police aren't going to be

pounding on my door with a warrant for my arrest."
Even as I said it, I glanced toward the front door. I
actually wasn't sure of anything.

"Maybe we should try to summon Denise again,"
Erik ventured.

"You can if you want to, but I'll pass." I was suddenly feeling irritated at Erik. If it weren't for him,
I wouldn't be in this mess to begin with. "I gotta
go now."

"Yeah, okay. Talk later?"

"Sure." I hung up and shook my head. I knew it
wasn't fair of me to blame Erik, but I couldn't help
it. I also couldn't help feeling he was holding something back. Did he know more about Denise's secrets
than he was letting on?

I got up to refill my coffee cup and grabbed the
notebook from my purse. I wanted to update my
notes with the information I'd learned over the
past few days. Turning to the page where I'd listed
Denise's friends, I once again had the feeling that
these people knew more than they had divulged. At
least to me.

Let's see . . . what have I learned?

Thanks to Wes's chummy chat with Poppy, I now
knew Denise had an unaccountable influx of money
after high school. From what Wes had told me, it
sounded as if Poppy was jealous of her friend's success. Perhaps she even felt a sense of betrayal, because
Denise didn't share her secrets. After all, they were in
similar fields. Why couldn't they have partnered up
and found success together?

On the other hand, if the real source of Denise's
income was something less than reputable, maybe
Denise was protecting Poppy by keeping her in
the dark.

I tapped my pen on the table as I considered the possibilities. Was Denise *really* involved in some illicit enterprise? If she had been mixed up in drug dealing or prostitution, I would think the cops would already know about it. Surely they would have found evidence in Denise's house or been tipped off by an informant. But if that were the case, Deputy Langham probably wouldn't be so interested in Erik and me—and the gossip around town would be about Denise's life of crime, rather than her brand of witchcraft.

Now that I thought about it, the only person who implied Denise was involved in late-night criminal activities was Thorna. And how reliable was she, really? Sure, she lived next door to Denise, but there was no indication they were close. Thorna was at least ten years older than Denise and her friends—not counting Erik. Of course, age is not a barrier to friendship, but Thorna tended to speculate about Denise more than I'd expect from a close friend.

Looking down at my scribble of names, I realized I'd left out Thorna from the initial list. In the interest of thoroughness, I made a new bullet point and wrote:

Thorna: neighbor, fellow witch, suspected Denise of . . . ? Something dark. Seems unusually superstitious.

I thought about the fact that Thorna sometimes joined in Billy's game night get-togethers, even though she obviously didn't love the game. She probably went for the company. Maybe she just wanted to hang out with other witchy people. I could understand that. For as long as I'd been a solitary practitioner, I'd lately come to appreciate the benefits of connecting with like-minded folks.

Back to my list—what more did I know about Billy and Viper? They were Denise's tightest friends in high school, aside from Poppy. An image flashed in my mind of the two guys standing on either side of Denise like the proverbial angel and devil. It made me grin to picture Billy with a halo and wings and Viper with horns and a forked tail. It was kind of true, though. Everyone who knew Billy had only positive things to say. According to Julie and T.C., Billy had been kind and generous ever since high school, if not earlier.

Viper, by contrast, was the consummate trouble-maker. I still couldn't believe Farrah had let him into her home—and then gone away with him in his car. And him without a driver's license. I'd like to think Farrah was savvy enough to know when she was in danger, but she'd been duped by a charming scoundrel before. I shook my head.

Farrah, Farrah, Farrah. You must live a charmed life.

I grabbed my cell phone and shot off a text: **How goes it today? Need anything?**

This time, true to form, she responded right away. **I'm good. Got some business calls to catch up on today.**

It was just as well. I wasn't exactly eager to rehash my night of fire, smoke, and delirious digging. I told her I'd check in with her later, then returned to my notes. Farrah's adventure with Viper actually wasn't for nothing. She had gained some insights into his personality and the depth of his devotion to magic. It was interesting how confident he seemed in his ability to cast a spell and make any wish come true. I believed in magic wholeheartedly, but I knew it wasn't always that simple. Viper apparently thought he could snap his fingers and . . . *poof!* He said he'd known it since high school.

A shaft of sunlight spilled across the table in front of me at the same time something clicked in my brain. *High school.* Something had happened when Denise was in high school, something to do with money. Something that resulted in a secret pact among three friends.

I had an idea about what it was. I grabbed my phone and opened a browser. It took only seconds to find the article I was looking for. *Yes. This could very well be it.* I snapped my notebook shut and stood up. Now I needed to talk with Julie.

It was shortly after 1:00 when I pulled into my old space in the municipal parking lot. Before I left home, I'd changed out of my lounge-around clothes and donned a stylish gray pantsuit. Maybe it was a tad more formal than necessary, but visiting my old law firm felt like returning home for a class reunion. Everyone would be judging me, at least in my mind, and I wanted to make a good impression.

When I stepped off the elevator on the fourth floor and faced those familiar glass doors bearing the firm's name in elegant, flowing script, I felt a slight pang of nostalgia mingled with—what, awkwardness? It was a sense of being out of place, like I'd accidentally walked into the wrong meeting.

Julie and Pammy stood near Julie's reception desk chatting, as they often did after lunch. The moment they turned and saw me, their faces brightened in welcome and pleasure, and my self-consciousness disappeared. It was just like old times.

"Keli!" said Pammy. "So nice to see you! You need to join us for lunch one of these days. We just returned from Gigi's. I told Julie we should have walked there and back—I ate way too much."

Julie waved her hand dismissively. "She had a salad

and a sandwich. It was nothing. So, Keli, what's new with you? Are you still looking into that matter you were asking me about the other night? About what's going on in Fynn Hollow?"

"Actually—"

"I thought I heard a familiar voice." Crenshaw sauntered in from the hallway leading to the attorneys' offices. "How are you, Ms. Milanni?"

From the way he looked at me, with the guardedness one might show a wild cat, it was clear he knew about my recent troubles. Which troubles, I couldn't say. I carried a virtual grab bag of misfortunes.

"I'm well," I said. "Is Beverly around?"

"She's at a lunch meeting," Julie volunteered. "She won't be back for a while. Do you want to leave her a message?"

"You can let her know I dropped by, and tell her I said thanks for her note. But the real reason I'm here is to ask you a few questions."

"About friends of Denise Crowley again?"

Pammy cocked her head. "Isn't that the woman who was murdered in Fynn Hollow?"

"Yeah," said Julie. "I knew her. Didn't I tell you?"

"If you keep playing private investigator," said Crenshaw, looking down his nose at me, "you're going to have to apply for a license."

I ignored him and smiled at Julie. "Thanks for your patience with me. I'd like to talk to you about Denise and two of her friends, Billy and Viper. They were one year ahead of you in school, right?"

"Right. It was a small school, but I didn't really know them well. I didn't hang out with them or anything."

"That's okay. I'd like to focus on what you *do* know about them. For example, you told me Billy was kind and generous, involved in charity fund-raising and the like."

"Yep. That's true."

"Thinking back on it, when was the *first* time he organized a fund drive or raised awareness for a cause in a big way? Does anything stick out in your mind?"

Crenshaw raised an eyebrow and leaned casually against the wall, while Pammy perched on a lobby chair. They both seemed curious about where I was going with my line of questioning. In fact, I did feel like I was questioning a witness in a courtroom. I hoped her answers would lead inexorably to the conclusion I'd already come to.

Julie crinkled her forehead as she thought. "I'd have to say it was probably the walk for Alzheimer's research. We had a school assembly all about it, and Billy was presented with an award because he'd raised so much money."

"And when was that?"

"That was in the spring of my junior year. I remember because I was dating Christian Sperry at the time." She grinned and rolled her eyes. "Those were the days."

"Early spring or late spring? Do you remember?"

"Hmm. It was chilly, so probably March or early April."

"Okay, turning now to Viper, do you remember him as sort of a show-off? Did he flaunt his snake tattoo or his car, things like that?"

"For sure. I think he got the tattoo the day he turned eighteen. His whole attitude was all about drawing attention to himself."

"What was the biggest thing he ever showed off?"

"Probably his car. He drove so fast and loud, you couldn't *not* notice him."

I imagined what Viper must have been like in high school and pictured him much as he was now. He didn't seem as if he'd matured greatly in the intervening eight years. This gave me an idea.

"Do you happen to know if he graduated with his class?"

"If he graduated? You know, now that you mention it, I know for a fact that he *didn't* graduate. It was a big topic for our lunchroom gossip for a few days, because he quit school with only two months left 'til graduation." She shrugged. "He was probably going to flunk out anyway."

Crenshaw couldn't keep quiet any longer. "What are you driving at, Milanni? What is the point of this little excursion down Julie's memory lane?"

"Shh," scolded Pammy. "Don't interrupt. Keli knows what she's doing. Don't you, Keli?"

"Of course I know what I'm doing," I said, with a smile. "Julie, do you recall if Denise had a part-time job when she was in high school?"

Julie nodded slowly. "Yeah, I think she did. There aren't a lot of jobs to go around in Fynn Hollow, especially for high-schoolers. So the younger classes were always paying attention to the jobs the older kids had—so we could snag them as soon as they became available. After school and on Saturdays, Denise worked in an office downtown. It was an insurance office, I think, one of the cushier positions out there—especially in the non-summer months when lifeguarding and lawn mowing isn't an option."

"Or bean walking or detasseling corn," offered Pammy. "That's what we did for money in the summertime when I was growing up."

"So, it must have been noteworthy when Denise quit her office job, right?"

"Yeah, sure," agreed Julie.

"And when was that?"

"Let me guess," said Crenshaw. "In the spring of her junior year?"

"Julie's junior year," I clarified. "Which would be Denise's senior year."

"That's right!" said Julie. "Right around the same time Viper dropped out of school."

"Why are you so interested in that time?" asked Crenshaw.

"Something else happened around that time. Something Julie mentioned the other day."

"I did?" She screwed up her face in confusion.

"Yes. You said it was the last big thing to happen in Fynn Hollow before the murder. The last time Fynn Hollow made the news."

Her eyes grew big. "You mean the armored truck crash and all the money that disappeared? You think Denise and Viper and Billy . . . ?"

I nodded. Pammy blew out an impressed whistle.

"That's a fine bit of deductive reasoning," said Crenshaw. "Do you have any proof?"

"Not yet. This is just a theory. But thanks to Julie, I'm more convinced than ever that those kids took the money."

"What are you going to do now?" asked Pammy.

"That," I said, "is the million-dollar question."

CHAPTER TWENTY-FOUR

I thought about stopping in at my law office, if for no other reason than to pick up the mail and clean up the mess of dirt and camera parts I'd left on the floor. But as I backed out of the municipal parking lot, a plan started to take shape in my mind. I had an idea about what to do next, and it wasn't something I wanted to do in my office. I still didn't feel entirely safe there—or confident I wasn't still being watched.

Instead, I returned home and parked on the street out front. When I entered through the front door, Josie jumped off the couch as if I'd startled her.

"I know," I said, laughing softly. "My schedule is all over the place. Maybe someday I'll keep regular hours again."

I proceeded to my home office and lit the votive candle on my desk. Then I took a deep breath and typed in the same search terms I'd entered into my phone a few hours ago. As before, a dozen headlines instantly appeared on the screen. They were all about the armored truck accident eight years ago. A farmer passing by had spotted the truck in the ditch and called the authorities, but it was already too late. The driver was dead, and all the money was gone.

After skimming the articles earlier, I vaguely recalled hearing about the incident when it had happened. I was in my third year of law school at the time and busy planning my own future. I probably shook my head and clicked my tongue at the news— saddened by the loss of life and appalled by the callousness of someone who would rob an accident scene and not even call an ambulance. Then I'd forgotten all about it.

Now I thought about how it might have occurred. Perhaps the wheels were in motion days before the tragic event.

I could see it in my mind's eye. Three friends who had newly discovered witchcraft, meeting in secret on a bluff behind the high school. Perhaps they fashioned a stone circle around a fire. I imagined them tossing things into a steaming cauldron—bits of herbs, slips of paper with wishes and dreams. And what was one of the first spells a young witch might think to cast? Especially a kid at the cusp of adulthood, possibly from a poor family, and with few prospects for getting rich? A money spell, of course.

A short time later, maybe a day or two, the friends are out driving. It's early in the morning, before dawn. They had probably been out all night. They are going fast. Perhaps the driver is the one who loves cars and illegal substances. He drives recklessly. They round a corner and cross the center line. A truck is coming. It swerves and crashes. They stop, dazed, and stumble to the smoking, mangled truck. The man inside appears to be dead, and the back doors are open, revealing a huge stash of money. The kids take it, believing the universe has delivered the answer to their spell. They make a pact to tell no one.

Over time, each friend reacts differently to the influx of money. Billy, with a guilty conscience that follows him the rest of his life, donates his share to charity. Viper, feeling entitled to the money, blows it on his vices. Denise tries to be responsible: She lives off of her money, supplementing her meager income as an artist, tarot reader, and seller of curses and spells. But she feels guilty, too. She doesn't want to carry the secret anymore. She wants to break the pact. This is a problem for Viper and Billy.

At this point in my ruminations, I hit a wall. What did Billy and Viper do next? Did they threaten Denise? Did they harass her or try to manipulate her to keep her quiet? Or did they do the unthinkable and silence her forever? If it was the latter, then they had another thing coming. As witches should know, after death comes life. And spirits are rarely silent.

I pulled up the Witches' Web and hovered the cursor between two buttons: *sign in* and *sign up*. I clicked *sign up*. For what I had in mind, *FlightyAphrodite* wouldn't do. This plan was too serious for such a frivolous-sounding name. My goal was to scare the boys straight.

At first, I thought of trying to appeal to Billy's conscience and compel a confession that way. But I realized it wouldn't work. If his sense of guilt hadn't prompted him to come forward by now, it probably never would. No, he alleviated his guilt in other ways. His fear of the consequences, legal and social, outweighed any inclination to come clean. Or maybe it was his fear of Viper. Either way, what I had to do was come up with something that would induce a bigger fear. Like a message from an angry ghost.

I had to use a different email address to create the new account, so I used an old one I kept around for marketing emails and assorted newsletters: KeliM@yesmail.com. It wouldn't be visible on the website anyway. For my new username, I typed in *DDStarSpirit*.

Before continuing, I gazed at the candle on my desk and pressed my hand into my chest. *Goddess, be with me. And Denise Crowley, wherever you are, please know I'm doing this for both of us.*

My stomach fluttered nervously, but I forged ahead. Choosing my words carefully, I composed the same message for both *BalderBoy* and *DredShaman*:

Guess who? Did you really think you could get rid of me that easily? Did you think your little problem had gone away? Well, I'm not gone . . . but the pact is dead. Come clean NOW, or else everyone will know what happened that night . . . and your problems will multiply like magic. You have until Beltane.

After rereading the message three times, I finally clicked *send*. For the next five minutes, I stared at the computer screen, clicking *refresh* every few seconds. Then I laughed at myself. There wouldn't be a response that fast. Viper and Billy were probably at work. They wouldn't even see the message until this evening. Until then, I'd have to find something else to occupy myself—besides compulsively refreshing the screen like a crazy woman.

Since I couldn't concentrate on anything mental, I decided to do some much-needed manual labor, starting with the deck. I gathered up the remains of my ruined plants and hauled them out to the compost heap. While in the yard, I checked on the stepping stones I'd removed and replaced the night before, as well as the state of my flowers and vegetable garden following the unexpected influx of firefighters . . . and fire starters. To my relief, nothing appeared damaged or amiss. It was amazing how things could appear so normal on the outside, with no indication of past turmoil—or mysteries buried beneath the surface.

It was kind of like the mask worn by Denise's killer, I realized with a start. Someone was out there leading a seemingly normal life in the outer world, while inside they carried a depraved heart and a hideous secret. I shuddered and returned to clean-up duty. I had to stop thinking that way.

The patio furniture and grill were dirty but salvageable. I dragged them to the side and grabbed a broom from the kitchen. After one sweep of ash and dirt, I realized I should wear a dust mask, so I went inside and came back with a bandanna tied around my face.

As I swept, I tried to envision any lingering dark energy and negativity being sent away with the dust. It was a basic creative visualization technique I'd done many times before. Yet deep down, I knew it wasn't enough. The dark cloud over my life wouldn't lift until the person, or people, behind the trouble were exposed, caught, and locked up.

I was so absorbed in my thoughts, and the rhythmic motion of my sweeping, that I almost missed the blip of color among the gray debris. I reached down and picked it up. It was a piece of purple satin ribbon, thin and flat like the page marker in a datebook— which was exactly what it was. I held it in my palm and felt a strange connection with Denise. I was sure this had been ripped from her beloved datebook— her day planner, where she recorded all her appointments, client notes, and possibly even her goals and dreams. Now it was ruined, just like her life. By her own friends? Or by her own decisions?

With these depressing thoughts, I pocketed the ribbon. Maybe I'd use it in some kind of gift or tribute to Denise when this was all over.

Something touched my shoulder. I yelped and whirled, broom at the ready.

"Whoa! Steady there, partner."

"Wes! You scared the heck out of me!"

"I scared you? You're the one brandishing a big stick. I feel like I'm caught in a holdup—on the Pony Express." Laughter sparkled in his eyes.

I pulled the bandanna off my face and used it to mop my cheeks and forehead. "Very funny."

He took the broom from my hands and finished the job for me. "I think I'll scrub the deck with a little soap and water before bringing stuff back on here," he said.

"Good idea, but it can wait. There's something I have to tell you. Are you done with work for the day?"

"Yeah. Jimi asked if I wanted to bartend tonight, but I said no. The security company I called can't get here until tomorrow. In the meantime, I don't want to leave you here by yourself."

Normally, I'd make a smart remark about being a strong, independent woman. After all, I'd lived by myself for years before Wes moved in. But I wasn't in a playful mood. He could tell. "What's up, babe? Did something happen?"

"I'm a little on edge. Let's go inside."

I grabbed a couple cold bottles of beer from the fridge and curled up on the couch next to Wes. He listened intently as I told him my theory about Denise and her friends taking the money from the armored truck, as well as the bluff I'd posted on the Witches'

Web. When I finished, I expected him to tell me I'd been brash, that it was a risky move. Instead, he seemed doubtful.

"You really think they'll fall for it? It might have been more believable if you claimed to be a witness to the accident, rather than a ghost. You know, like 'I know what you did that summer.'"

I stared at him a moment, then laughed ruefully. "Dang it. I didn't even think of that. But these are witches, remember? I'm sure they believe in ghosts." I started to stand up. "I want to see if they've responded yet."

He put his hand on my leg. "Wait, I've got my laptop right here on the floor." He handed me his computer and looked over my shoulder as I pulled up the website and signed on. There was still no answer to my message.

I reached for my beer and took a swig. Then I refreshed the screen. Not surprisingly, there was still no reply.

"What do you expect them to say exactly?" asked Wes. "Do you think they'll incriminate themselves? Confess to the crime?"

I shook my head. "I don't know. I didn't even specify that they have to respond to me at all. And I shouldn't have given them so much time to turn themselves in. What was I thinking? Maybe I should send another message." I hovered my fingers over the keyboard, but my mind was blank.

A clatter from the kitchen made me jump. Josie streaked out of the room, and Wes hopped up to investigate. "It was just the broom," he called. "I shouldn't have left it leaning on the wall."

I pressed my hand to my chest to still my pattering heart. I felt so vulnerable, like any minute now the cops would bang on the door, or the stalker would ring the phone, or an intruder would try to break in. Finding my beer bottle empty, I set the laptop down and stood up. But on my way to the kitchen, I stopped in the middle of the room. I didn't really want another beer. I didn't know what I wanted.

Wes came up to me and wrapped his arms around me. "Let's get out of here, at least for tonight. We can go stay with my parents. They'd love to have us."

I looked up at him and smiled. "That's a nice idea, but I don't want to worry them. And I don't have it in me to pretend everything's peachy."

"Then we'll go stay in a hotel. We shouldn't have any trouble finding a vacancy on a Thursday night. Or, better yet, how about the Cadwelle Bed and Breakfast? We haven't been back there since they reopened. Unless it holds bad memories for you?"

"Not at all. That's a great idea. In fact . . . let's request the Rose Petal room."

Cadwelle Mansion was a gleaming three-story, Queen Anne–style showplace, complete with lacy, gingerbread trim, elegant wrap-around porch, and an octagonal tower straight from the pages of a fairy tale. It was built at the turn of the century by a wealthy philanthropist-turned-bootlegger, then refurbished and converted to a bed-and-breakfast in recent years. Perched on a hilltop in an old section of Edindale, it was a perfect local getaway.

After checking in and settling into our room, we explored the open areas of the mansion, from the stately dining room and formal parlor, to the cozy library. The door to the basement, with its antique speakeasy and secret tunnel, was locked. It was just as well. That was a scene from another adventure, harrowing for sure, though not without its moments of fun.

We ended up relaxing, hand in hand, on a wicker love seat on the veranda overlooking the vineyard and, farther down, the winding Muddy Rock River. As the sky turned brilliant shades of orange, violet, and pink, I couldn't help thinking how much more at ease I felt with Wes than I had with Erik a few nights ago. Without a word, Wes spontaneously brought my hand to his lips. I sighed contentedly.

"Wes, do you ever—"

"Sure, all the time." He grinned at me like an imp. "Sorry. Do I ever what?"

I smiled in return. "Do you ever . . . think about what it would be like to live in a big, old mansion like this?" I'd save my real question for a better time, after my life had calmed down to a more regular state of craziness. "Is this a dream house for you?"

"Nah. This place is great, but I wouldn't call it my dream house. If I had my choice, I'd probably go for something a little less Victorian, a little more Frank Lloyd Wright. Or, better yet, a big ol' SoHo loft— with lots of natural light and space, maybe an exposed brick wall and sculpted pillars. That would be cool."

I looked up at him in surprise. "You want to move back to New York?"

"I didn't say that. I thought we were just dreaming here. What's your fantasy house?"

"No particular style. I also like lots of light—and warmth. For me the land is more important than the house. I need to be close to nature."

"Then I guess you're living your dream already, huh? There's plenty of nature here in Edindale."

"Yeah, I guess."

We fell silent as another couple strolled by. I fought the urge to check my phone—and lost the fight. I had no messages.

After an interval, Wes asked if I was ready to go upstairs. We made ourselves comfortable in the Rose Petal room, an unabashedly romantic haven decked out in shades of red and pink. This was the place where I'd first told Wes about my Wiccan identity. We had fun reminiscing. Wes took it upon himself to take my mind off murder and mayhem. Quite effectively. We had a lovely time. Then we shut off the lights and kissed good night.

I lay on my back and stared into the darkness, with my eyes wide open. Wes's even breathing told me he was asleep, but my traitorous mind wouldn't let up. What had gone through Billy's and Viper's minds when they read my message? What were they doing now?

More importantly, what should I do?

A faint creaking sounded from the walls. I sat up, straining my ears for further noises. By the pale light of the moon filtering through the gauzy curtains, I could just make out the contours of the bedroom door. I stared fixedly at the brass doorknob, willing it not to turn. All was still. A few minutes later, I lay back down. It was just the creak of an old house. I knew that.

Rolling over, I reached for my phone on the bedside table. Then I stopped myself. *This is nuts. Why am I putting all this pressure on myself?* Crenshaw was right. I wasn't a private investigator, so I should stop acting like one.

That's it, I decided. *Tomorrow I'll go to the police.* Maybe I would call the nice one, Tricia LaMott, first.

Or my old friend, Detective Rhinehardt. Or maybe I'd just bite the bullet and go see Deputy Langham. I would tell him everything, lay all my cards on the table—all my suspicions and conclusions, and all the weird things that had been happening to me.

Having made the decision, I felt as if Atlas had reached down and plucked the weighty world off my shoulders. I yawned and closed my eyes, as I snuggled up next to Wes. At last, I could sleep.

My dreams were jumbled and peculiar, as they tend to be when sleeping in a strange place. It was one of those movielike dreams, where I watched from a place outside of the action. I saw Denise and Erik, living together as a couple, only their home morphed from a cozy cottage to an airy New York loft apartment. They were engaged in a lovers' quarrel. Denise had made a potion and was trying to get Erik to take it, but he didn't want to. Then they argued about their future. One of them wanted to get married and the other didn't.

I awoke before dawn feeling confused and displaced—and, at the same time, quite certain that the dream wasn't really about Erik and Denise at all.

CHAPTER TWENTY-FIVE

When I woke up for the second time, later in the morning, it was to the heavenly smell of hazelnut coffee and blueberry muffins. For a moment I forgot where I was, until my bleary eyes focused on the red rose petals scattered on the bedside table. I sat up and saw Wes pulling breakfast things from a picnic basket and setting them on the bureau. He heard me stir and walked over.

"Morning, sleepyhead. Ready for a cup of coffee? It's a B&B special."

"Yes, please." I took the cup he handed me and inhaled the fragrant steam. "Can we do this every day?"

He chuckled. "It'd be nice, wouldn't it? Not a care in the world."

We sat in the center of the bed, eating our continental breakfast and chatting about the weather and all the fun outings we could plan in the coming months. Then I reached for my phone and handed it to Wes. "Will you check?"

He set down his coffee cup and signed on to the Witches' Web. After a quick scroll, he shook his head. "Nothing, babe."

"Dang it. It's like I never even sent the message."

"On the bright side, you haven't heard from Langham either." He took out his own phone and opened the photo gallery. "I've been studying the picture I took of Denise's appointment book. Something was definitely written beneath the word *Kelly*. I think it was another four- or five-letter name. All the letters are a little blurred except for the *y*. Either it was added to the end of a four-letter name, or the original name already ended in a *y*." He handed me his phone and pointed at the zoomed-in image.

"I see what you mean. I wonder if the police have a forensics investigator who can reveal the writing underneath. I bet there's a way to do it."

"No doubt. Though I'd be surprised if there's a lab here in Edindale with that capability. They'd probably have to send it off to a bigger city."

"I'll ask when I stop by the station." I told Wes about my decision to go to the police. He agreed it was a good idea.

"Want to go now? I can call the *Gazette* and tell them I'll be in late today."

"No, I want to go by the house first and check on Josie. You can drop me off on your way to work. I'll take my own car to the station and check in with you later."

"You sure?"

"Yeah, I'll be fine. Maybe I'll even stop in at my office and pretend to work for a bit." Wes raised his eyebrows at that, so I mustered up a half smile. "Should I make sure I'm home to meet the security company this afternoon?"

"If you want, but I'll be there, too. They're supposed to come around three o'clock."

I was sorry to leave the B&B. It had provided a

nice respite from my multifaceted worries. When we arrived back at our house, Wes came inside for a minute to make sure everything was as it should be. Josie was fine, and nothing was out of place. But the minute Wes left, my anxiety began to seep in. I wandered around the quiet, empty house and wondered if installing a home security system was really the right move. Part of me felt it meant giving in to paranoia, while the other part felt it wouldn't go far enough. After all, a home alarm wouldn't stop anyone from setting fires in the backyard or leaving dead birds in the front.

Then again, maybe the witch bottle had taken care of that little problem.

I took a last look around, then tossed my phone into my purse and grabbed my keys. I was already in the foyer when the doorbell rang.

Who could that be?

I pulled the door open and found myself face-to-face with Billy Jones.

I was so startled, I think my mouth gaped. He rocked back on his heels, hands stuffed casually in his pockets, but his charming dimples were nowhere to be seen. His expression was hard and serious.

"Billy!" I said, when I finally found my voice. "What are you doing here?"

"Hello, *DDStarSpirit.*"

It was like a blow to the stomach, robbing me of my breath. "What?" I squeaked.

"I know it was you. Can we talk?"

He stepped forward, as if he expected me to invite him inside. There was no way that was going to happen. I dodged past him, pulling the door closed behind me.

"I was actually on my way out. Sorry." I trotted down the steps, with Billy close behind.

"Keli, please. I need to know what you're playing at. Why would you pull such a cruel prank?"

That stopped me in my tracks. He thought *I* had played a prank? Now that I thought about it, perhaps my impersonation of Denise's spirit over the Internet wasn't that different from the radio caller who'd done the same thing. Reluctantly, I turned to face him. "Let's go for a walk."

Without waiting for an answer, I headed down the sidewalk toward Fieldstone Park. Billy made an exasperated sound, then fell into step beside me. This was definitely not the response I'd expected to my provocative message. I had a lot of questions for Billy, not least of which was how he'd found me out. Were there hidden cameras in my home, too? Before I could ask, he provided the answer.

"You *did* send that message, right? I'm a website administrator for the Witches' Web. I traced *DDStarSpirit*'s IP address to your house."

I mentally slapped my forehead. Nothing was secret, or sacred, on the Internet. I would have argued that he'd committed an invasion of privacy, but that seemed well beside the point now.

We entered the park and followed the winding concrete path with no particular destination. It was a chilly morning. Several people were out taking advantage of the sunshine, from retirees fulfilling their daily exercise to young mothers pushing baby strollers. I led us away from the noisy playground and toward a cluster of weeping willows that marked the edge of the park pond.

"Okay, you're right. I sent the message. But it wasn't a prank. I was serious about what I wrote."

He stopped and gave me an incredulous look. "Wait. You mean—were you *channeling* Denise?"

I hesitated for half a second, then decided to go with it. "Maybe I was. I've seen her in my dreams and visions."

He shook his head in frustration. "We had a pact. We agreed. There's no point in breaking it now. We can't undo what happened. We can't . . . bring anyone back."

It wasn't quite an admission, but it was good enough for me. "Billy, come on. I know this has been weighing on your conscience. If you tell the truth, you'll be free from the burden of a terrible secret." He remained silent, so I pushed on. "Has Viper threatened you about keeping quiet?"

"No. He knows I would never break the pact."

"The pact has already been broken! Denise wanted the truth to be known . . . and now I know it. Erik has been trying to contact her spirit as well. Denise won't rest until justice is served. She won't allow her death to have been in vain." I heard myself speaking in clichés, but it seemed to be working. Billy took a step back as if I'd slapped him, and his face underwent a series of contortions.

"Justice? For Denise's death? What are you saying? You think *I* killed her?"

"You and Viper had a lot to lose if she came forward. And I saw Viper's comments on the Witches' Web. They sounded very threatening."

"Hold up, hold up. You're way off base. Whatever you think you know, I had *nothing* to do with Denise's death."

"What about Viper?"

Billy shook his head. "No. Viper didn't touch her. I mean, yeah, he wanted her to drop the issue, so he did what he always does. He cast a spell and asked his patron gods to handle it. Then he let the Universe take care of the rest. That doesn't mean her death was his fault. That's not the same thing as . . . as murder."

Clearly agitated, Billy was breathing heavily and shifting his weight from side to side. I took a quick assessment of my surroundings. A lone fisherman sat on the bank at the far side of the pond. A young couple lounged on a blanket several yards away. From somewhere behind the trees, I heard the repeated *thwap* of a tennis ball in an impressively sustained rally. Then it fell silent.

"How can you be so sure?" I asked gently. "Denise was killed sometime between eight-thirty and nine o'clock. Viper wasn't picked up by the cops until nine-thirty or so."

Billy didn't respond, so I continued, "By the time he was booked and allowed a phone call, you were already in Edindale with Erik. So, you dropped off Erik at Moonstone and turned around to go bail out Viper. What time did you pick up Erik, anyway? That was probably around nine-thirty, too, wasn't it?"

I didn't say it, but the implication was clear. Billy would have had as much time as Viper to poison Denise that morning. So would have Erik, for that matter.

"No way. I think I'd know if Viper had done something so heinous. He wouldn't do that. Neither of us would." Billy gave me a plaintive look. "You have to believe me."

Suddenly, I didn't know what I believed. I began to wonder if I'd rushed to judgment. While I was still fairly confident that Denise, Viper, and Billy had some involvement with the armored truck accident,

I realized I had no proof to connect the incident with Denise's murder.

I squeezed my eyes shut and rubbed my forehead. When I opened them, Billy was staring across the pond.

"I gotta go, Billy. I'm sorry about the Witches' Web thing. I'll delete the bogus account."

He turned to me with pleading eyes. "What about— I mean, are you going to tell anybody about—"

I shook my head. "It's none of my business. You do whatever you think is right." Without another word, I did an about-face and hurried away, hoping he wouldn't follow me. He didn't. When I spared a glance over my shoulder, he was gone.

When Wes returned home, he found me up to my elbows in yard work. I'd mowed the lawn, pulled weeds, planted carrots and beans, filled the bird feeders, and washed out the birdbath. I was watering the flowers when he came out of the house. Scratching his head, he remarked that the garden seemed to be rubbing off on me—literally. I looked down at my clothes and saw that he was right. From my dirt-covered gardening gloves and grass-stained jeans to my mud-caked boots, I was quite a sight. I had to use my inner forearm to push the hair out of my eyes.

"I guess I lost track of time," I admitted.

"How did it go at the police station?"

"It didn't. I didn't go." I set down the garden hose and walked over to the faucet to turn off the water. Wes followed me.

"Why not?"

"Well, for one thing, to avoid making a false accusation." I pulled off my gardening gloves and met his eyes. "I had a surprise visit from Billy this morning."

"What? He came here?" With a dark look, Wes scanned the yard as if Billy might be lurking behind the bushes.

I told Wes everything, including the doubts I had after talking with Billy. "The whole thing left me more confused than ever. I couldn't think straight, let alone speak coherently. I was in no condition to go to the police. Knowing Langham, he'd probably suspect me of making up stories to deflect attention away from myself."

"Aw, babe, I'm sorry. I should have stayed with you today. I'll go with you to the station tomorrow. You still need to file a police report."

"Yeah, I suppose. But today turned out all right, after all. The fresh air and physical exertion cleared away the cobwebs in my mind. I think I've finally fig-ured out the thing I've been overlooking all this time."

Wes frowned as his phone jangled in his pocket. "Dang. That's the security people. They're probably at the front door."

"Do you mind meeting them without me? I need to clean up and make some phone calls."

"Of course not. You go ahead."

We went inside, and I trotted upstairs before Wes answered the front door. As I peeled off my dirty clothes and turned on the shower, my mind returned to the pivotal question I'd been mulling over for the past few hours. It was the one question I'd neglected to ask until now: *Why me?*

Why was I targeted after Denise's death? Someone was interested in me from the very beginning. Some-one took it upon him- or herself to find out where I live, where I work, and what my phone number is. They'd kept tabs on me enough to know I'd be a guest on a radio call-in show—and they disliked me enough to sabotage my law practice, scare me with bizarre, threatening phone calls, set a fire outside my back door, and try to frame me for murder.

Oh, and they left a dead bird on my doorstep, too. *Why?*

It was tempting to imagine the murderer thought I was getting too close to solving the case. Some of the episodes certainly felt like threats to back off. But it didn't really make sense, if I thought about it. The first music box phone call had happened the day after I'd found Denise's body. I hadn't even started asking questions about Denise yet, let alone found any clues or pieced together any useful bits of information. No one could possibly have called me a meddling kid at that point. Later maybe, but not then.

Having scrubbed my body and lathered my hair, I now let the hot water stream over me as my mind continued to wander. I recalled all the descriptions I'd heard of Denise's moodiness, and the email to Poppy in which Denise had said something had been bothering her. And then there was the banishing spell she'd left in the fire lookout tower. When I'd put two and two together about the armored truck accident and the three teenaged witches, I'd assumed that was the cause of Denise's poor attitude. I figured she felt guilty over the incident and frustrated that Billy and Viper didn't agree with her desire to come clean. And maybe that *was* part of her problem. Yet all the evidence, such as it was, pointed to something else—something a little closer to home.

I had pondered this idea once before, and now it seemed all the more compelling. Could Denise have been experiencing the same kind of harassment that was happening to me? We both wrote banishing spells, after all. Evidently we both had someone dogging us and trying to make our lives miserable. If someone out there didn't like me, someone *really* didn't like Denise.

But again, why me? What did I have in common with Denise? I had never even heard of the woman before I met Erik.

And there was my answer. *Erik.* He was the common denominator. He was the only thing—or person—connecting me to Denise.

As soon as I toweled off and pulled on a robe, I sat on the edge of the bed and called Erik. He didn't answer, so I left a message asking him to get back to me. A scratch at the door drew me out of my brooding thoughts. I let Josie in and listened for a moment to the sound of men's voices drifting up from downstairs. Evidently, Wes was still working things out with the security guy. I hoped he wasn't turning our home into a second Fort Knox.

I gave Farrah a call and filled her in on my brilliant deductions and not-so-brilliant charade on the Witches' Web.

"OMG, Keli! Why didn't you call me first? I would have told you to send the message from a computer at the library. Then he couldn't have traced you to your house."

"That would have been smart," I said sheepishly. "But it's just as well that Billy tracked me down. It gave me a chance to hear his denials firsthand. I have to say, he sounded pretty convincing."

"Hmm. I don't know, Kel. I don't think we should underestimate sweet, young Billy Jones. Viper told me Billy's a shrewd operator when it comes to money matters. Part of the reason he can afford to be so generous is because he's a wise investor. According to Viper, Billy doesn't even need to work for a living.

That job he has at an electronics store? It's purely for fun."

I considered this bit of information. "That's interesting, but it doesn't really change anything. I already know—or strongly suspect—where Billy acquired the money to invest in the first place."

"All I'm saying is, no matter what he told you, we can't rule him out. I mean, he's super cute and witchy—Viper said Billy used to go see Denise for tarot readings like some people go to the salon—but he's also very practical. He's not going to risk his neck if he can help it."

"Yeah, well, we can't rule out Viper either. I was thinking about the time line again, and Viper was arrested well after Denise was killed. He didn't have an alibi that morning."

"Now you tell me."

"Have you heard from him since, uh, the other night?"

"You mean since the grand rescue op you masterminded? No. And I doubt if I will. I'm sure he's decided I'm a hazard to his health."

"That's probably not a bad thing."

"I suppose . . . though, I was really looking forward to seeing him play the bongos—or is it the congas? Percussion instruments are so sexy, don't you think?"

I snickered. "Sure, if you say so."

We chatted a few more minutes, then I let her go with a promise not to post any more clever bluffs without consulting her first. Erik still hadn't returned my call. I wondered if he was miffed after our last phone conversation. Maybe I had been a tiny bit cold.

I paced to the bedroom window and looked outside. Shadows lengthened in the late-afternoon sun as birds flocked to the highest branches. Josie wound herself around my legs, and I reached down and absently pet her.

Erik had said he wanted to try to contact Denise's spirit again, but it hadn't exactly gone well the last time. The air in that tower had been thick with heavy emotions. I had thought it was anger, but it could have been more than that. Jealously, loss, regret?

Denise had loved Erik. Based on the attraction spell she'd penned, I knew she was the one who had pursued him—even though he was apparently involved with someone else at the time. And they had been together for about two years—"off and on," according to Erik. But I had the impression they were close during that time. In spite of how things ended, I was sure Denise had cared deeply for Erik. Wouldn't she have confided in him?

Erik had to know more than he'd told me. To give him the benefit of the doubt, perhaps he didn't even realize it himself. But something told me he possessed the key to unlocking this mystery. Maybe he *was* the key.

For the rest of the evening, I kept checking my phone, anticipating Erik's return call. I texted him twice, sent him an email, and left another voice message. Eventually I concluded he must be avoiding me.

Oh, well, no matter. I knew where to find him the next day.

CHAPTER TWENTY-SIX

I was up with the dawn on Saturday morning. Moving quietly so as not to awaken Wes, I slipped outside for a solitary sun salutation. The damp grass prickled my bare feet, and the gentle breeze cooled my face, but the vivid crack of sunlight breaking above the horizon promised a warm, beautiful day.

Standing among my flowers and shrubs, I pressed my hands together and raised them to the sky. Feeling like a priestess, I murmured words that came to me in the moment.

My body awakens like the greening earth;
My blood quickens like the rushing river;
My heart fills with the soul of Gaia,
Divine Mother
Divine Feminine
Divine Lady, who today joins with the Lord, in the
  sacred dance of life.
Blessed be.

I was excited about witnessing the Beltane Festival. Of all the sabbats, this was the one that seemed most to call for a communal celebration. But I was nervous, too. Gazing around the backyard, I spied a pair of white butterflies performing a fluttery pageant in the purple phlox. Their movements mirrored the subtly anxious dance in my heart. I took a deep breath.

"This will be a good day," I said firmly. In my experience, affirmations were often as effective as magic spells. As long as I kept telling myself everything would be fine, it would be. Probably.

Besides, whatever might happen today—with Erik, Billy, Viper, or anyone else connected with Denise—I wouldn't be alone. Not only would I have lots of friends and acquaintances at the festival, but Wes had promised to meet me there later. He had to go into the newspaper office for only a few hours this morning.

I was only sorry Farrah couldn't make it. She had been toying with the idea, but when I phoned her after breakfast, she bowed out.

"Are you feeling okay?" I asked.

She sighed. "Yeah, more or less. My leg is acting up today. I think I twisted it in my sleep. Also, I Googled the festival to look at pictures—you know, to see what people wear to these things—and I learned all about the private nature preserve that hosts the festival every year. The place is huge! It's on this huge swath of grassy, hilly property—probably muddy in low areas. It's not a good place for crutches. I would just be a drag."

"Are you sure? I don't mind walking slowly."

"Yeah, it's fine. Tell Wes to take lots of pictures."

I knew I wouldn't have to tell Wes. He always took lots of pictures. However, as I wound my way "over the hills and through the woods," taking back roads

I never even knew existed, I hoped he wouldn't get lost. I had the detailed directions Erik had sent me days ago, and I still had to backtrack twice after missing my turn. Luckily, signs pointing the way began to crop up along the side of the road. I knew I must be getting closer as traffic picked up. Vehicles merged from left and right onto the same country road I traveled.

More than once, I thought I must be taking the very definition of *scenic route*. At one point, trees gave way to meadows, and, soon after, I passed a tidy, sprawling apple orchard. A faded pastel archway bore the words *Red Gate Hollow*.

So this is where it is. It was the organic farm for sale by Gretta Harrison and coveted by Neal Jameson. I'd tried to help Neal acquire the property at a fair price—and instead wound up being blamed for his dashed plans. I still bristled at the unfairness of it all.

Pushing aside the unwelcome recollection, I focused instead on the colorful old van in front of me. It was painted in swirling paisley and bold splotches of red, purple, and yellow. *Groovy.* I followed the hippie-mobile the rest of the way, until we both turned into a narrow gravel driveway and through the open gates of the Spring Creek Nature Preserve. A young man in an orange vest directed us past the already-full paved lot and into the grassy overflow parking area. As I parked and walked toward the entrance, I realized a lot of people had probably camped here overnight. Small wooden trail markers pointed to campsites, picnic areas, and bathroom facilities.

After paying the suggested donation price for admission, I bypassed the clapboard bungalow that housed the preserve's office and welcome center and headed straight for the festival grounds. Fragrant flower gardens and blooming trees bordered the meandering path, which occasionally branched off to other intriguing destinations: a koi pond to the left, a Zen labyrinth to the right, and, in the distance, a white-washed gazebo gleaming in the sunlight. *This place just might be the best-kept secret in the whole county,* I mused.

Strains of lively Irish music grew louder, and I found myself smiling at the motley assortment of festival-goers. While many, like me, were dressed in casual weekend wear (I'd opted for an embroidered white blouse over denim leggings and faux-leather ankle boots), a good number showed true Beltane spirit. I saw plenty of flower crowns and fairy wings, painted faces and gauzy dresses—and not just on the children. Women and men alike had decorated themselves in festive, flowy, flowery garb.

"Keli! Over here!" It was Arlen the necromancer, waving his arm and beaming from ear to ear. He grasped the hand of a short, muscular man in a kilt and bounded over. "Gregory, meet Keli Milanni, counsel to the Witches and lawyer extraordinaire." He presented me with a flourish that made me blush. As usual, he was dressed in black, this time in renaissance breeches and a leather vest—with no shirt underneath. I tried not to stare at his thick mat of chest hair.

"Hello, Arlen. Nice to meet you, Gregory."

"Miss Keli, I'm so glad I saw you. The bones gave me a message for you."

"For me?"

"Well, for a wise woman who helped me in a time of need. I figured it must be you—especially since I've just run into you."

"Okay." I still wasn't sure quite how to take Arlen. His enthusiasm was a bit overwhelming. As he proceeded to describe his divination rite in great detail, including his method of ritual purification—a complicated process that involved smudging deer bones in the smoke of handcrafted herb bundles—I found myself watching people glide by. They must have come from far and wide, I realized. At first, I didn't recognize anyone. Then I caught a glimpse of one familiar face. Several yards away, Erik walked by carrying a large wooden hand drum. He was the picture of a modern-day Green Man, I thought, in brown cargo pants and a forest-green T-shirt. His dark blond hair, flecked with silver and gold, had become shaggy since we'd first met. Somehow it seemed to suit him.

I would have called out, but Arlen was still talking, and Erik was soon lost in the crowd. *Oh, well, it shouldn't be too hard to find him.* I would just follow the sound of the drums.

"So, then he spoke to me," Arlen said, drawing me back into his monologue. "I was deep into a trance state by this point, you understand. But I saw the spirit of the stag clear as the silver moon. He said, 'The truth is within. You have all the answers you need inside you.'"

"Mm," I murmured. Apparently the spirit of the stag spoke in platitudes.

"Then he said, 'You won't always remember this. Even the wise forget. Carry this message to the wise one. Tell her to listen to her heart. She knows the truth. Jealousy blackens the heart. The motive was personal.'"

I jerked up my head with a start. "What did you say?"

"He told me to tell 'the wise one.' That's you. You must listen to your heart."

"No, the last part. About a motive?"

"Yeah, I'm not sure what he meant by that, but that's what he said. 'The motive was personal.'"

"And 'jealousy blackens the heart'?"

Arlen nodded, a pleased look on his face. "Profound, right?"

Gregory, who had been people-watching like me, touched Arlen's shoulder. "The first maypole dance starts soon. Do you want to join this one or the later one?"

"The later one," answered Arlen. "I'm hungry. Keli, would you like to join us at the food tent?"

"No, thanks. I'm supposed to meet a friend at the maypole."

He pointed the way, assuring me I'd find it on the other side of the "big hill." I thanked him and hurried off, his message still reeling in my head.

What an odd thing to say. For a moment I entertained the possibility that the message wasn't even meant for me. I hardly considered myself a "wise woman." After all, I'd barely reached the "mother" stage (figuratively speaking) of a woman's journey from maiden to mother to crone. I still had much to learn and experience. But I was definitely searching for answers. And Arlen's—or the stag's—mention of jealousy and a personal motive gelled perfectly with the theory that had been crystallizing in the back of my mind.

A small crowd blocked my view of the maypole, but I knew I had reached the right spot. A Celtic banner waved near a trio of musicians who strummed an upbeat Irish folk song, as the lively gathering formed a large circle. I squeezed my way to the front. I didn't want to miss the show.

I spotted Mila, dressed like a queen in a flowing white dress. Catrina was next to her, in white genie pants and a rainbow-striped T-shirt. I recognized a few others from Mila's coven, as well as another familiar face: Carol Peters. She waved at me and gave me a big thumbs-up. I gathered that her husband had agreed to switch weekends with her after all. She and her daughter, Dorrie, also sported white dresses and wore matching butterfly barrettes in their golden brown hair. The little girl was petting a young gray and white cat. It tolerated her attention for a moment, then darted away to chase a butterfly. I smiled. Everyone looked so beautiful and radiant. I couldn't help feeling swept up in the gaiety, as my eyes roved from person to person, to the pole itself, tall and bright, and topped with a green, flower-studded wreath.

Someone touched my arm, and I turned to see Catrina. She handed me the end of a violet ribbon and pulled me forward. "Come on, we're about to start."

"Oh, I'm just a spectator."

"Yeah, right. Come on. It's fun."

"But I've never done this before. I don't know what to do."

Ignoring my protests, Catrina left me holding the ribbon. Mila stepped forward and held up her hands. The band stopped playing while she spoke.

"Welcome to the maypole dance! Take your places now. Let's arrange ourselves with alternating masculine and feminine energies—whatever you're feeling today. Feminine will go clockwise, masculine will go the opposite way."

There was a small bit of shuffling, as a few people traded spots. I stayed put. Mila started moving in a clockwise direction as she continued, in a measured, singsongy voice:

> *"Over and under, the ribbons we braid,*
> *Around the pole and in the glade.*
> *Lasses and lads do dance in time,*
> *Colors blend to life's sweet rhyme."*

Over and under. I can do this. The man to my right nodded at me as he brushed past my shoulder. I had no choice but to follow the woman who had been next to him, lest I be bumped from behind. As Mila repeated her verse, a few other voices joined in. After the third time through, I saw her nod at the band. The instant they broke into their lively Irish melody, the dancers picked up the pace. Laughter bubbled forth as people tried not to bump into one another.

It was a large circle. Previously, I hadn't seen all the participants on the other side. As we met up with one another, lowering and raising our ribbons, I was pleased to recognize a few more friendly faces, including Steve, the new part-time clerk at Moonstone Treasures. And right behind Steve was Erik, going one direction, and Thorna going the other. Erik's face lit up when he saw me.

The music seemed to grow louder and faster, and the laughter more raucous, as dancers became tangled and untangled. I tried to stay in the rhythm of the dance, raising and lowering my entire body with my ribbon. For a while, it worked pretty well. We seemed to move as individual parts of a larger whole—like painted animals rising and falling on a giant merry-go-round. But as the ribbons became shorter, and we drew ever closer to the pole, things got trickier. At one point, I found myself face-to-face with Erik.

As I moved to raise my ribbon over his head, I failed to notice the lowered ribbon of the person in front of me. I tripped and fell on Erik. Startled, he opened his arms to catch me, dropping his ribbon in the process.

"I'm sorry!" I tried to find my footing without pushing Erik to the ground. He laughed good-naturedly and gave my shoulder a squeeze. Then he reached for his ribbon and moved along. Soon afterward, I noticed Mila at the base of the pole collecting the ends of everyone's ribbons. As the dancers let go of their ribbons, they backed up to take their places in the circle once more. After I surrendered my ribbon, Carol touched my elbow.

"Would you mind holding Dorrie's hand for a moment? Her brother's in the kids' tent with a friend, and I need to help Mila tie off the ribbons. Celtic knots are my specialty."

"Of course! I'd be happy to."

"Stay with Miss Keli," Carol said to her daughter.

Dorrie dutifully walked with me back to the circle. But once we took our places, she began to wiggle. With her exuberant energy, I was afraid she would break away and run off. I took her other hand. "Let's dance," I suggested.

The band continued to play, so we twirled in place. "This is fun!" cried Dorrie.

"It sure is," I agreed.

Mila said a few words about the symbolism of the maypole and declared the dance a success. We all applauded, and the group dispersed. When Carol came to retrieve her daughter, I thanked Dorrie for the dance. Then I turned to look for Erik. I hadn't forgotten my original purpose for coming here. I wanted to talk to him about Denise.

Unfortunately, he was nowhere to be seen. Neither was Thorna.

I wandered down the hill, keeping a lookout for him. I came upon a line of vendors and decided to purchase a cold lemonade. All that dancing had made me thirsty.

As I sipped my beverage, I shot off a text to Wes and tried to explain how to find the festival. I told him it was near Red Gate Hollow, if that helped. He replied that he would be leaving work soon and was sure he could find the place.

"Why did you run off?" said a teasing voice. I looked up to see Catrina, with a smirk on her face. "Was it so you wouldn't have to hear me say 'I told you so'? Well, I told you so!"

I grinned and shook my head. "You were right. I had fun."

"I'm heading over to the face painter. Want to come?"

"I would, but I'm trying to find somebody. Do you know what time the drum circle starts?"

Catrina checked her watch. "Right about now. Hurry if you want to join in."

"I just want to watch. And this time I mean it!"

"Sure you do." She laughed and gave me a backward wave as she headed across the lawn. I started off in the other direction. My ears had picked up the low, steady beat of the drums. Soon I could not only hear it, but also feel it, throbbing like a heartbeat in the earth.

The drummers, mostly men with a few women interspersed throughout, sat on logs and tree stumps arranged around a fire pit. Many wore costumes: I noticed a few feathered headdresses and lots of suede fringe. Billy and Viper sat next to one another, the former in a tunic and linen pants, the latter in brown leather. Billy also wore a hammered silver Viking helmet, with horns that were sharpened to a deadly point. Viper wore antlers attached to a brown bandanna.

I scanned the circle for Erik, but he wasn't there. *That's odd.* I had seen him carrying his drum earlier. Maybe he was letting someone borrow it. I searched the crowd. The spectators were as into the music as the drummers. Several danced around the edges, powwow style; others bobbed their heads as they stared into the fire or at the drummers' hands, beating like birds' wings against the drumheads.

Without realizing it, I had become transfixed. The thumping and pounding had become a vehicle, carrying the listeners to another state—an altered state, for some. I glanced at Viper. Sweat glistened on his brow, and his eyes gleamed with an intensity that was mesmerizing in itself. As I watched, I could almost feel his animal magnetism, and I understood what Farrah—and other women—had seen in him. He had a certain kind of appeal, at least when he wasn't drunk.

Had Denise been caught under his spell, too? Did the *V* on her final card stand for *Viper*?

He must have felt me staring. His eyes locked on mine, and his lips curled in a slow, wicked leer. I willed myself not to look away, as if doing so would be a sign of weakness. Eventually, he grew bored of me and let his eyes slide away. Without missing a beat, he tilted his face toward Billy, who turned in response. Almost imperceptibly, Viper jerked his chin in my direction. Billy's eyes narrowed when he caught sight of me. I took a step backward. So much for my assertion of dominance.

Billy the Viking wasn't always the sweet, kind-hearted nerd he appeared to be. I'd learned that yesterday. Could his name be the one in Denise's datebook? Wes had speculated it was a five-letter name ending in *y*.

I backed farther into the crowd, eager to distance myself from *DredShaman* and *BalderBoy*. Unfortunately, I backed right into another spectator.

"Ouch!" she yelped.

"Sorry!" I spun around and reached out to offer an apologetic pat on the arm of the person I'd stepped on. I froze as I recognized another suspect whose name ended in *y*.

"Poppy! Are you okay?"

"Oh. It's you."

With further apologies, I edged away. To my surprise, she followed me.

"Are you okay?" I repeated. I didn't think I'd bumped her that hard, but she seemed annoyed.

"Can I talk to you?" she asked.

"Yeah. Sure." I followed her away from the drum circle to a quiet spot near a grove of pine trees. In the distance, I spotted a cluster of standing stones and forested land beyond.

Poppy crossed her arms and scowled at me. "I want to apologize."

I thought I must have misheard her. "Sorry?"

"You heard me. I'm sorry I was rude to you. Wes told me you're trying to figure out who murdered Denise." Her face softened and she bit her lip. "I don't know why it's taking the police so long. Do you have any ideas?"

"Yes, I have a couple ideas. Do you?"

"None! Denise could be so secretive. It was kind of her thing. Something was bugging her, but she never confided in me."

"Did she talk about Erik much? Or their breakup?"

Poppy shook her head. "That's another weird thing. I don't think she really wanted to break up with him. She thought he was it, you know? She talked about being his soul mate. She even talked about having babies with him."

"She did? What happened?"

"To be honest, Erik can be a little clueless. And kind of self-absorbed. I don't know if he was as serious about the relationship as she was. I mean, he could've tried to work things out with her instead of just accepting the end of it."

"I got the impression Denise was pretty angry at him."

"Probably because she wanted him to try to win her back."

I didn't know what to say to that. It seemed so childish and sad. "I'd like to talk to Erik. Have you seen him around?"

"Yeah, I saw him a little while ago. He was with Vanny."

"Who?"

"Vanny—Vanessa Attley. I guess she goes by Thorna now."

"Why did you call her Vanny? Is that her nickname?"

"That's how she was introduced to me. I met her through Denise. They worked together for an insurance company a few years ago."

"Huh. I didn't know that. Was that the office job Denise had in high school?"

"Yeah. She didn't work there for very long, just a few months. Evidently, she didn't need the money."

I could hear the bitterness in Poppy's voice, but that wasn't my concern. Poppy would find out about the source of Denise's influx of money soon enough. I was sure the truth would come out, one way or another. Right now, I had a bigger concern.

"So, Denise knew Thorna as 'Vanny.'"

"Uh-huh. It's a cute name. I don't know why she changed it to Thorna. I guess she wanted to be seen as tough instead of cute." Poppy paused and cocked her head. "What's wrong? You look funny."

"Which way did Erik and Thorna go?"

She looked around, then pointed. "They were walking that way, toward those stones."

Suddenly, I was seized with an overwhelming sense of urgency. "Poppy, will you do me a huge favor? Call Wes, then meet him at the entrance and bring him here."

"You want me to call Wes? But I don't have his number."

"Where's your phone?"

She handed me her cell phone, and I punched in Wes's number. "He should be here soon. Please hurry."

Poppy appeared confused. "What are you going to do?"

"I don't know. I just have to find Erik. He might be in danger."

With wide eyes, Poppy looked at me as if I might be crazy. But she nodded and ran off.

The drummers were still hitting their drums, harder than ever. The audience had doubled in size. For a split second, I was torn. I wanted to run over there and snatch Billy away to help me. But I also didn't want to waste any more time. The sense of urgency won out. I spun on my heels and sprinted to the standing stones.

Maybe I'm wrong, I told myself. *I hope I'm wrong*. It was all too incredible. Did I really believe Thorna was a demented, cold-blooded killer? Maybe my theory was dead wrong.

Except I knew in my heart it wasn't. Everything fit. Thorna's feelings for Erik had been clear from the beginning. I'd bet my scrying bowl Erik had been dating Thorna when Denise came along and charmed him away. Thorna must have become wild with jealousy, though she hid it and pretended to be Denise's friend. Secretly, she probably tormented Denise— just like she tormented me after she thought Erik and I had become a little too friendly. Erik's apparent interest in me was ruining Thorna's plan to get him back.

Like Arlen said, jealousy blackens the heart.

The stone circle was empty. As I passed around and between the tall, rough-hewn slabs, I noticed that the air felt different. It was almost electric— which didn't help my already-jittery nerves. I hurried away from the stone circle and examined the nearby tree line. A dirt-packed trailhead gaped invitingly. Treading softly, I entered the woods.

CHAPTER TWENTY-SEVEN

The trail was lovely. Sunlight streamed through the branches, lighting up the purple and white spring flowers dotting the ground. Thoughts of murder and vengeance were incongruent with the chirping birds and newly budded trees. I began to calm down. If I was right that Thorna loved Erik, then he shouldn't be in any danger. If anything, I might come upon the two of them in a lovers' embrace. That would be embarrassing.

I had been walking for several minutes, and becoming more and more complacent, when the caw of a crow snapped me to attention. I peered into the trees, trying to spot the bird. Instead, I glimpsed the corner of a building. On a hunch, I left the trail to investigate. Picking my way around boulders and fallen trees, I finally reached the building and saw that it was an old, weathered barn. The back side had no openings except for a single window set high up near the peak of the roof. Moving along to the side of the building, I had better luck. There were two small, dirty windows. Instinct told me to remain silent, as I peeked through the nearest window.

I gasped and clapped my hand over my mouth, hardly believing my eyes. Erik was sitting on the floor, propped against a bale of hay. His hands and feet were bound with gold-colored rope. His eyes were open, but they appeared glassy. As I watched, his head nodded forward and jerked up, as if he was struggling to stay conscious.

Thorna was there, too. Standing before a worktable-turned-altar, she looked like a Gothic priestess, dressed in an ankle-length lacy black gown and a black veil. The altar was covered in an assortment of lit candles surrounding a red crystal carafe and two goblets filled with a dark burgundy liquid. Thorna's lips moved as she wrapped another gold rope around her own wrists.

What is this? A handfasting ritual? Was Thorna forcing Erik to marry her?

She's even crazier than I suspected.

I retreated from the window and pulled out my cell phone. There was no service. *Dang it!*

My earlier sense of urgency was back and stronger than ever. I scuttled to the front of the barn. One of the doors was open a crack. I eased it open a few more inches and slipped into the dim interior.

By the hazy orange light filtering through dingy windows, I made out a snow blower, a wheelbarrow, and some sawhorses. Staying in the shadows, I inched my way toward the back of the barn. As soon as I caught sight of Thorna, I ducked behind a stack of hay bales. The whole scene made my skin prickle, from the deranged look in Thorna's black-lined eyes to the proximity of the candles to the hay.

While muttering an incantation, Thorna ground something with a mortar and pestle. I strained my ears to make out her words.

> *Ashes to dust, and dust to ash,*
> *With love's first breath,*
> *We'll breathe our last.*

I didn't like the sound of that. Was she doing what I thought she was doing?

She lifted the bowl as if making an offering to the gods.

> *Destiny foretold it. Our fate is sealed.*
> *My wounded heart shall now be healed.*
> *We'll wet our lips with nightshade wine*
> *And bind our wrists with golden twine.*
> *Together forever; no cause to weep,*
> *We'll lie as one, in eternal sleep.*

She poured the powdered contents of the bowl into both goblets, then turned and moved toward Erik. Kneeling down, she set the goblets on an overturned crate and proceeded to tie her wrists to Erik's.

I couldn't let this go any further. Without warning, I charged forward and knocked over the goblets, splashing the poisoned wine onto the dirt floor.

Thorna looked up in surprise. Then she started to laugh.

"Perfect! This is exactly what was missing: a witness to our union. You'll be the witness."

"Give it up, Thorna. It's not going to happen."

She smiled at me in a sickening, simpering way. "Poor Keli. I know you wanted Erik for yourself.

You should have stayed away from him. I tried to warn you."

"You told me he was bad luck. Did you tell Denise the same thing?"

"Of course I did," she snapped. "I tried everything to break them apart. I told Denise that Erik was cheating on her. And I told Erik that Denise had cursed him."

"You mean Denise never actually cursed Erik? You're the one who left the dead birds on his doorstep?"

"Birds and snakes. I also put sugar in his gas tank and a laxative in his beer." She laughed wickedly. "I didn't do anything to hurt him—only to make him think he was under a hex."

I glanced at Erik, whose head had drooped forward. "What did you give him this time?"

"Nothing special. Just a little sedative." She grabbed his hair and lifted his head. "Are you still in there, lover? I need you to wake up for our hand-fasting ceremony. We have a witness now."

She's out of her mind. I tried to think. What could I do? I didn't have a weapon, and I wasn't at all sure I could overpower her. She was bigger than me. I might be able to run away, but I didn't want to leave Erik behind. If Thorna was intent on committing a murder-suicide, she could still find a way. For all I knew, she might have more belladonna stashed away nearby.

My best hope was to stall for time. Poppy would tell Wes where I'd gone, and he'd come find me. He would get help, and he would find me. He had to. And I had to converse with a murderer.

"Why did you kill Denise? She'd already broken up with Erik."

"She did, yes. But she wanted to reconcile. I told her she was better off without him, that he wasn't the one for her. She wasn't convinced. Then she caught me stealing a picture of Erik from her photo album. I told her I was planning a surprise spell to help her get over him, but she was suspicious. She accused me of breaking into her house and leaving anonymous messages on her phone."

"Did you play 'Smoke Gets in Your Eyes' for her, too?"

"Aren't you the clever girl? Yes. It was part of my plan to blind her to Erik's charms."

"But it didn't work. Instead, Denise cast a spell of her own to banish you."

"Did she now? Well, it's clear who the most powerful witch is. The one still standing."

"Because you poisoned her! What did you do, invite yourself over for tea?"

Thorna stood up and glared at me. One of her wrists had pulled free from the rope, but the other was still attached to Erik. His arms rose from his body, as she moved her hand. She spoke in a low, deadly voice. "Denise got what she had coming. She used magic to steal Erik from me. She tripped up one day and confessed to using a love spell to attract him to her. I acted like there were no hard feelings. I moved next door to her and pretended to be her friend. All the time, I knew I would get him back. And she would get what she deserved."

Twisting around, Thorna took a step toward the altar, so I seized the chance to peek at my phone. There was still no service. What was taking Wes so long? I wasn't sure how long I could keep Thorna talking. And I had a terrible foreboding about what she might try next.

With one eye on Thorna's back, I reached down for the twine that was lashed around Erik's ankles. It was no use. She turned around, as I quickly pulled back. "Well," I declared, "I never cast a spell on Erik. You were all wrong about us. I already have a boyfriend."

"Liar! You inserted yourself into his life like the slimy worm you are."

"Hey!"

"I saw what you did. You lured him with your eyes and your coy ways. He's weak. He always has been." She kicked him in the leg and grabbed his hair again. "Wake up, lover man! Look at your bride. Look at me!"

She let go of his hair, and his head lolled back to his chest.

I spoke in a rush. "Thorna, I still don't get it. Were you trying to scare me away from Erik? Is that why you left the dead bird on my porch and kept calling my house? Is that why you called in the threat to the radio show?"

"Of course! It was all part of my curse."

"What about the hidden camera? Why did you spy on me in my office?"

"What?" She looked at me as if *I* were the crazy one.

"Never mind. Why—"

"No more questions! I know what you're doing, and it won't work. It was never going to work. Our destiny is already written."

"What do you mean?"

Instead of answering, she spun to the altar, grabbed a candle, and tossed it onto the stack of hay behind me. It burst into flames.

"No!" I yelled.

Before I could stop her, she grabbed another

candle and threw it on the hay bale behind Erik. Then she used her free arm to sweep the remaining candles onto the floor.

We were surrounded by fire. A wall of prickling, scorching heat rose up behind me, blocking the exit. It spread faster than I would have imagined. I lunged for Erik and dragged him away from the flames. With a wild look on her face, Thorna threw herself on top of him.

"With this ring of fire, I thee wed!"

I stared at her in horror. Sweat poured down her face and mingled with her eyeliner, causing black streaks to stripe her face like war paint. As smoke filled the barn, I felt a surge of panic. The fire seemed to be everywhere—devouring the spilled wine on the ground, eating up the hay, creeping up the walls, and spreading throughout the barn. It wouldn't be long before it reached the snow blower near the door. If there was gasoline in the machine . . .

Frantically, I leaned down and yanked at the rope around Erik's ankles. Luckily, the golden cord was looser than most fiber ropes. It fell away more easily than I expected. But this didn't help much with the larger problem. We were still trapped.

Too bad I don't have my bandanna, I thought deliriously. In the next instant, I pulled off my shirt and used the sleeves to tie it around my face. Then I crawled as far as I could away from the fires. With burning eyes, I cast around for a means of escape. There was no way out.

My heart sank, as I realized our only hope was for someone to come to the rescue. Preferably someone with superhuman powers. And a fire hose.

I lay facedown on the dirt floor and wondered if this was it. With a tinge of sad acceptance, I waited for my life to pass before my eyes. Instead, I had a vision of the barn. As clear as a memory, I saw a crate of tools under the altar. Had I noticed it before? Was it really there?

I had nothing to lose. I crawled over to the altar and reached underneath. My hand hit a wooden box. I pulled it out and grabbed the first thing I touched. It was a hammer. Staggering to my feet, I looked up to the spot where I had seen a glass window high on the rear wall of the barn. It was obscured by smoke, but I knew it was there. Whispering a prayer to the Goddess, I hurled the hammer as hard as I could. The shatter of glass told me I'd hit my mark. At least now the released smoke might attract help.

I reached into the box a second time. This time, I pulled out a hatchet.

Thank you!

Coughing and wheezing, I rushed to the only section of wall as yet untouched by the fire. Crouching on my knees, I hacked at the wood with all my might. As soon as I'd made a hole large enough to fit my head and shoulders, I crawled over to Erik and Thorna. Neither of them moved. When I tried to push Thorna off of Erik, she let out a strangled wail and clung to him tighter. I doubled down and tried to wrestle him from her grasp. In the back of my cloudy mind, I found it hilariously ironic that we were literally fighting for this man.

It probably took only seconds, though it felt like an eternity. Finally, I managed to free Erik from Thorna's clutches. I dragged him to the hole in the wall. Then I crawled out and pulled him through after me.

The air outside was filled with acrid smoke, but it was heaven compared to the thick smoke in the barn.

After dragging Erik to safety, I wrenched my shirt from my face and took a deep, gulping breath. From somewhere in the forest, I heard voices call out my name. "Keli!"

I had no energy to answer. Instead, I rushed back to the hole and used my last burst of strength to holler inside.

"Thorna! Over here! Come on!"

It was difficult to see, but I could have sworn I saw her retreat farther into the barn. An ominous creaking sounded from the timbers above. I jumped backward and scrambled away as the barn collapsed in on itself, raising a cloud of dust, smoke, and sparks that matched the stars before my eyes.

CHAPTER TWENTY-EIGHT

Standing at the window of my hospital room, I watched the full moon rise over the trees and felt a strange sense of melancholy. What was wrong with me? Usually the sight of the magnificent white orb—ancient symbol of beauty, mystery, and power—filled me with hope and inspiration. I could gaze at the moon in any of its phases and feel close to the Goddess and in touch with my own divine spirituality. But now everything was off-kilter.

Of course, I was extremely grateful to have survived the fire. All things considered, I actually felt quite well on a physical level. In the ambulance, and again at the hospital, I was given oxygen and examined for smoke inhalation. The doctor even said I could go home if I insisted, though he recommended I stay overnight for observation. Wes strongly seconded the opinion, so I agreed to stay—on the condition that he bring me some healthy vegan comfort food. He was more than happy to make a quick run to the Good Karma Bakery.

At first I had no qualms about being left alone at

the hospital. Besides the fact that I felt fine, I knew
Wes wouldn't be gone long—the café would be
closing soon. But the minute he left, I started feeling vulnerable and uneasy. Now, as I stood by the
window, I started shaking for no reason. *Must be a
delayed reaction from the earlier trauma.* I dropped into
a chair and squeezed my eyes shut.

Melting heat . . . choking smoke . . . the terrible
sound of cracking wood and frantic shouts . . . It all
came back in a flash, as suddenly as the barn had
crashed to the ground. On top of Thorna.

They told me I must have fainted from the exertion. All I knew was the first thing I saw when I opened
my eyes was Wes—shirtless and glistening—framed
against the fiery sky. I thought I must be dreaming.
He looked like a Greek god as he hovered over me,
his face filled with love and concern. Later I learned
that he had begun to administer mouth-to-mouth
resuscitation when I came to. Too bad I didn't remember that part! He then gave me water and slipped his
shirt on me. My own top had disappeared.

Much of what happened next was a blur. However,
there was one image I would never forget: a long line
of fierce-looking women and men, feverishly passing
buckets of water from hand to hand. I recognized
Mila and Catrina and several others from their coven,
as well as Billy and Viper, and Arlen and his friend
Gregory. It was an amazingly colorful and witchy
bucket brigade. Thanks to their dogged efforts, the
fire didn't spread to the trees.

Through the haze, I also noticed Erik being fitted
with an oxygen mask and carried away on a
stretcher—but not before he lifted his head and
waved at me. He seemed confused, and understandably so. But he would be okay. When I asked about

him at the hospital, a nurse told me he was resting and in good condition.

Thorna was not so lucky. After the fire was extinguished, I overheard a first responder say a body was recovered from the charred debris.

Thinking of it now made me light-headed. I clutched the windowsill and tried to draw strength from the soft glow of the moon. After a moment, I became aware of a woman's voice softly uttering my name. For a crazy second, I thought the Goddess was speaking to me. Then I realized it was Mila. I looked up to see her walking toward me.

"Shouldn't you be in bed?" she asked gently.

"Probably. I guess I'm not as strong as I thought."

Catrina entered the room behind Mila. "Yo, Keli! Just so you know, the Beltane Fire Festival doesn't usually feature *that* much fire."

"Catrina, let's help Keli get back to bed." Mila's calm, quiet voice had a grounding effect, as did her light touch on my shoulder.

"I'm okay," I muttered, but I let them lead me back to the hospital bed. Once I was situated, and they had pulled up chairs, I took a good look at them. They must have come straight from the festival grounds—their hair and skin were streaked with soot, and their white clothing was gray. "Look at you two *she-roes*. You saved the nature preserve."

"Mila spotted the smoke first," said Catrina. "She sounded the alarm, and then we all pitched in. But talk about *she-roes*—you're the life saver! You saved Erik's life and your own."

"I didn't save all the lives."

Mila and Catrina exchanged a glance. "You called it," said Catrina, addressing Mila. "How did you know?"

"Know what?" I asked.

Mila gave me one of her perceptive, motherly looks. "I had a feeling you might be specially troubled by Thorna's death."

"She was a murderer!" said Catrina. "Plus, she's the one who started the fire, right?"

I nodded grimly. Catrina and Mila had both been nearby when I gave my statement to the police. They knew about everything that had happened in the barn.

"She'd already killed one person," Catrina continued. "And she would have killed both you and Erik."

"True," I said quietly. "She was also on the receiving end of my counter-curse."

"It was self-defense!" Catrina insisted.

I looked at Mila. It was her view I wanted to hear.

She didn't hesitate a beat. "I agree with Catrina. Thorna suffered the consequences of her own actions. You bear no blame for her death."

I let out my breath. I had already believed as much on an intellectual level, but it meant the world to hear Mila say it. Now I could let go of the moral guilt that had been gnawing at the back of my mind. Yes, I directed a curse at a person who tried to harm me—and she was now dead. But it wasn't my fault.

As a rule, I still wasn't especially keen on the idea of curses and hexes. But if I'd learned anything over the past few weeks, it was that in magic, as in life, things were rarely black and white. Instead, there was a whole lotta gray.

I was having the same philosophical thoughts at Denise's memorial service a few days later. Poppy had arranged a lovely private ceremony on the bluffs behind the Fynn Hollow High School. After scattering the ashes, she unveiled a large three-dimensional artwork she'd created as a tribute for Denise. Bordered in multicolored mosaic, the piece featured shimmering silver stars and golden moons against a purple backdrop. Poppy invited each guest to contribute a trinket or a personal note, which she fastened to the piece. When it was my turn, I brought out the slender, purple ribbon from Denise's datebook. As I added it to the artwork, I noted how it was like a miniature version of the violet ribbon I'd wrapped around the maypole. Wherever Denise was now, I hoped she could feel the joy and delight of May Day.

Poppy told us she'd obtained permission to install the artwork in the lobby of the high school. That seemed like a perfect place to me—especially considering the sweet epitaph Poppy had inscribed in the center of the piece. Beneath Denise's name and the dates of her birth and death, the flowing, cursive words declared:

The magic of friendship surpasses all earthly bounds.

A few people lingered on the bluff at the conclusion of the service. Wes and I meandered, hand in hand, through the tall grass and wildflowers. A stiff breeze ruffled my hair and my dress, but the warm May sun felt so pleasant I didn't want to leave.

As we circled back to where we'd started, Erik walked over to us. He shook our hands and thanked us for coming. His manner struck me as oddly formal, considering the unusual experiences we had shared. Then he cleared his throat, and I could tell he had something on his mind.

"Keli, I, uh, don't think I ever thanked you properly for rescuing me from the, uh, burning barn. You risked your life for me. I can't thank you enough.

And I . . . I'm just so thankful you weren't hurt. I feel responsible for the danger you were in . . ." He trailed off, raking his fingers through his windblown hair.

Wes squeezed my hand and let it go. "I need to go talk to Poppy for a minute," he said softly. As I watched him saunter away, I marveled at how lucky I was to have Wes for a partner.

Turning to Erik, I smiled and shook my head. "I've managed to put myself into danger more times than I'd like to admit. You have no reason to feel responsible for that."

"I don't know. I feel like I should have known, or at least suspected . . . I mean, I had no idea! I only dated Thorna, like, two or three times before I met Denise. I'd forgotten this, but Denise once told me that Thorna had implied she and I were a serious couple. Denise and I had already hit it off, and she was determined to make a go of it. She was all prepared to steal me away from Thorna." Erik laughed self-consciously. "It sounds silly now. And I guess I treated it as a joke at the time, because I never really thought I was in a relationship with Thorna. I had no idea she was so crazy!"

"If it's any consolation, you're not the only one she duped. And at least now you know Denise never cursed you."

"Yeah. It's bittersweet, but I am glad to know she still loved me." We fell silent and watched the cottony clouds float across the vivid blue sky. "Anyway," Erik said, after a moment. "Thank you for everything. I'm glad I had a chance to know you."

"That almost sounds like a good-bye," I said, somewhat startled.

"Actually, I haven't told anyone yet, but I received

a job offer in Springfield. I think I'm gonna take it. Get a fresh start, you know?"

"Congratulations, Erik. That's good news!" I reached out and gave him a spontaneous hug.

"Thanks. I'm gonna miss this place. I'm sure I'll be back to visit."

I smiled at him, wondering if we'd ever really meet again. In spite of the circumstances, I was glad I'd gotten to know him, too. "Don't be a stranger," I said, punching him softly on the arm.

CHAPTER TWENTY-NINE

In the days following Thorna's death, my life had taken on a new level of hectic. The fire at the Beltane Festival was big news even before people learned about its connection to the Fynn Hollow murder. It didn't take long for the stories to start swirling, especially on the Witches' Web. Then, because of my account of Thorna's confession, the cops searched her house and found a host of incriminating evidence—from a diary-like grimoire outlining her plans to a terrarium filled with belladonna.

When the Sheriff's Office issued a statement officially naming Thorna as the murderer, I hoped people would forget all about my involvement. I should have known better. I wound up in the spotlight even more than before. Everyone wanted to hear about my experience with the "bad witch" and how I escaped from her "evil clutches." I was flooded with interview requests from all sides—from print, radio, television, and even Internet news media. I declined them all. But the attention didn't stop until something else grabbed the headlines. It wasn't so much a new story as an addendum to an old one: the Fynn Hollow armored truck robbery.

It was the confessions of Billy and Viper (both of them!) that had everyone talking. The two young men took full responsibility for their crime and stated they wanted to make amends. I wasn't sure what had caused their change of heart, but I suspected Denise had something to do with it. When I had told Billy her spirit wanted the truth out, part of me believed it to be true.

Ironically, the pair chose not to disclose Denise's involvement in the theft. In fact, they didn't mention her name at all. I couldn't say I blamed them. Protecting her reputation was the decent thing to do. In telling their story, they also omitted the part about the money spell—which also seemed like a good call to me.

Reporters weren't the only ones ringing my phone off the hook. In the aftermath of the fire, I also heard from plenty of friends, acquaintances, and clients. I even received a call from Neal Jameson. After I'd learned that the breach of his confidentiality *did* happen in my office (albeit through a hidden camera), I felt a measure of responsibility. At a minimum, I'd stopped expecting to receive an apology from him. Imagine my surprise when he practically begged for my forgiveness. I was sitting in my home office when he called out of the blue.

"Keli, I was way out of line," he said without preamble. "When I found out my intention to buy Red Gate Hollow had been leaked, I jumped to conclusions without thinking. I had absolutely no evidence to suggest you did anything improper."

"Actually, I don't blame you for assuming—"

"But you should blame me. This impulsive nature of mine has been more of a curse than a blessing. As it happened, it was a good thing my plans were scuttled."

"I don't understand," I said, trying not to be distracted by his use of the word *curse*.

"It was impulsive of me to try to buy that property for my friend without discussing it with her first. When she caught wind of it, she was—well, let's say she was far from grateful. She's the type of person who labors hard for everything she earns and likes to make her own decisions."

Who wouldn't? I thought. Out loud, I said, "I'm glad it all worked out, Neal."

"If you're not too annoyed with me, I do have another matter I could use your help on."

"Oh?"

"Yes, another property transaction. When can I stop by your office?"

"My office? Er, how about we discuss it over lunch next week?"

I couldn't avoid my office forever. While I could accomplish a fair amount of work from home, I had to go back to my rented office space eventually. Not only was it my official place of business, but I also had files there and mail to pick up. Finally, I bucked up the courage and made the five-minute drive downtown. It was Monday morning, two weeks after May Day.

As I unlocked my office door and pushed it open, I prepared myself for stale air and dusty furniture. I wasn't prepared for the enormous May basket in the center of the coffee table. *What the—?*

The sight filled me with apprehension. Besides the fact that all the flowers were dead, there was the small matter of the locked door. No one had a key to my office besides myself and my absentee landlord.

Then there was the familiar-looking plain white card sticking out of the basket.

With a resigned sense of inevitability, I extracted the card and held it up to the light. I wasn't a bit surprised to see the neat, black cursive writing—exactly like the writing on the card that had accompanied the fairy figurine. This time the message was slightly more aggressive.

Well done, Miss Milanni. Another mystery solved.
   Good luck solving this one.

All of a sudden, my fear turned to ire. Very calmly, I walked over to the supply closet and selected a blank manila folder. I inserted the white card in the folder and snapped it shut. Then I grabbed a black marker. After a moment's consideration, I labeled the folder "*Giftster.*"

My anonymous gift-giving nemesis was quite the trickster.

After making sure there was nothing left in the basket besides crumbling, dried-up flowers, I dropped the whole thing in the garbage. Then, narrowing my eyes and pursing my lips, I circled my office like a panther.

Where can I hide a witch bottle in here?

* * *

"I have to say, as stressful as it can be sometimes, I do enjoy the freedom of being my own boss."

"I'm liking it, too," said Wes. "We didn't used to get to enjoy afternoons together like this."

"Mm-hmm. I never fully appreciated the advantages of the flex time you're allowed at the newspaper."

"Here's to flexibility," said Wes, raising his beer bottle toward me.

"To flexibility and freedom." I clinked his bottle with mine and took a gratifying sip. We were sitting on our newly finished deck, looking out over a backyard that grew lusher by the day. It felt a little decadent to take a break like this at 4:00 on a Monday afternoon. But I didn't feel too guilty. In defiance of the nefarious giftster, I had put in a few productive hours of work at the office—including a lengthy phone call with Carol's ex-husband's attorney. Using all my powers of reason and persuasion, I convinced him that his client, as well as the children, would be better off with a renegotiated custody arrangement. A bitter courtroom battle would have produced uncertain results and certain negativity. Ultimately, he admitted his client was having second thoughts about fighting for full custody. We worked out a settlement I knew would make Carol very happy.

I was feeling happy myself when I hung up the phone. This was the part of my job I liked best— helping people resolve their problems. As a side benefit, I also gained a healthy perspective on my own problems, which weren't so bad after all.

"Penny for your thoughts?" Wes reached out and tucked a wisp of hair behind my ear.

"I was just thinking about how fortunate I am, all things considered."

"You and me both, babe."

He took my hand and turned it over, exposing my wrist and the freshly inked tattoo emblazoned on my skin. One of the reasons I'd left work early today was to meet Wes at his favorite tattoo parlor. "I'm still a little shocked you did this," he said, as he lightly stroked my forearm with his thumb.

I grinned. "Me too! But I have no regrets."

The idea of getting a tattoo had been circulating in the back of my mind ever since I'd drawn the ankh on my chest. Symbolism was important to witchcraft, so it seemed fitting to mark myself with a symbol of my beliefs. Of course, there were several to pick from. Besides the Egyptian ankh, I could have chosen a pentagram, like on the necklace I often wore, or a triquetra, like the one tattooed on Mila's inner wrist. Or I could have gone with something more innocuous, like the stars and moons favored by Denise.

Yet, at the same time I was contemplating a permanent representation of my Wiccan identity, I also seemed to face challenges to that identity at every turn. I had encountered a lot of Pagans recently who seemed to hold values at odds with my own—including a willingness to use dark magic and, yes, dreaded curses. Then there was that newspaper article connecting me to the Fynn Hollow witches. The resulting lost clients and judgmental attitudes of people like Crenshaw had upset me more than they should have.

With those cheerless thoughts swirling in my mind over the past weekend, I had gone for a morning run on a tree-lined path. It didn't take long to shed the negativity. As often happened, I drew energy from the trees and let my doubts be carried away on the wind.

It doesn't matter what anyone else thinks. The conviction came to me as if conveyed from the earth beneath my feet and the sun shining upon my face.

I looked at the tattoo again, feeling pleased with my choice. Now I would always carry with me the sign of the Triple Goddess: two crescent moons, waxing and waning, on either side of a full moon. The three lunar phases matched the three phases of womanhood—maiden, mother, and crone—and would be a constant reminder of sacred feminine power and the magic in every season.

"And you even let me hire Poppy to come over and photograph the process," Wes continued. "Does this mean you're a public Wiccan now?"

I shrugged. "My beliefs aren't really anyone else's business. I just wanted to support Poppy's art, that's all."

"Oh, is that all?"

I shrugged again and grinned. "Partly."

Wes eyed me thoughtfully, making me wonder what was going through his mind. The trill of a song-bird drew my attention to the flower garden.

"I wonder if my sunflowers have sprouted?" I leaned my arms on the railing of the deck and peered across the yard. "I think I see a green shoot!"

"Do you want to go look?"

I leaned back. "Nah. I'm sure they're growing. I can check on them later."

"There's always something stirring beneath the surface."

I glanced at him in surprise. "You sound like a poet. Or a philosopher."

His eyes twinkled as he edged forward. "Or maybe I'm starting to think like you, and seeing magic all around us."

I smiled, meeting him halfway for a kiss. "Ah, yes. Magic and mystery. It does make life exciting, doesn't it?"

ACKNOWLEDGMENTS

As always, I am exceedingly grateful to my family for their love, support, and unwavering belief in me. Thanks, especially, to my parents and sisters for reading my manuscripts and providing their honest feedback, and to my husband and daughter for their all-around awesomeness. Many thanks also to my agent, Rachel Brooks, my editor, Martin Biro, and the entire Kensington team for all their talent, guidance, and dedication to this series.

Finally, a great big "thank you" to fans of the Wiccan Wheel Mysteries. Your enthusiasm and engagement make writing these books that much more fun.

If you enjoyed *May Day Murder*,
be sure not to miss all of
Jennifer David Hesse's
Wiccan Wheel series,
including

SAMHAIN SECRETS

*It's that haunted time of year,
when skeletons come out to play.
But Edindale, Illinois, attorney Keli Milanni
discovers it isn't just restless spirits
who walk the night . . .*

Keep reading for a special excerpt.

A Kensington mass market and eBook on sale now!

"You know there's no such thing as ghosts!" My words came out in a raspy whisper. I was trying to be forceful enough to get through to the hysterical woman on the other end of the line, while avoiding the attention of the small crowd of businesspeople milling about in front of the converted barn. I failed on both counts.

All eyes looked toward me with blatant curiosity. Among them were those of the park district supervisor, the head of the Chamber of Commerce, and the senior partner at my law firm, all of whom were awaiting the start of their VIP tour through the Fieldstone Park haunted barn. Every year, Edindale's town leaders recruited local businesses to create spooky displays and a funhouse-style maze inside the emptied-out storage barn. This was the law firm's first year participating. As one of the newest partners, I was roped into playing a costumed volunteer. As if that weren't embarrassing enough, now I'd unwittingly placed myself in the spotlight.

With my cell phone pressed to my ear, I looked for an escape route. Instead, I saw Pammy Sullivan, one of the associates at the law firm. She broke off from a small group that included our boss, Beverly Olsen, and made her way toward me with a gleam in her eye. An incorrigible gossip, Pammy probably just wanted the scoop on my strange phone call. On the other hand, maybe Beverly had sent her over to chide me for taking a call right when the tour was about to start.

I offered an apologetic grimace and squeezed out from behind the makeshift ticket booth. Scanning the park for a quiet spot, I landed on a cluster of maple trees beyond the pavilion. As I made my way through the throng, past picnic tables filled with laughing kids and rowdy teenagers, I kept my head down and listened to my client fret on the other end of the line.

Scratch that. She was beyond fretting. She was freaking out.

As soon as I reached the relative privacy of the maple grove, I allowed myself to interrupt. "Mrs. Hammerlin! Wait a minute. Just think about what you're saying. I'm sure there's a perfectly logical explanation—"

She cut me off, leaving me to pinch the bridge of my nose. I took a slow breath in and out and tried again. "Okay," I finally said. "You're right. I agree. We don't know for sure what happens to our spirits after we die. But, really, it's highly unlikely that the noises you're hearing—"

"Keli?" I felt a tap on my shoulder and turned to see a tall man in an old-fashioned tuxedo and flowing black cape. He had slicked, coal-black hair and a matching trim beard. Most striking, though, was the glowing white powder, which rendered his normally pale face even more anemic. Not to mention the two pointy false teeth protruding from his blood-red lips.

In spite of the Dracula getup, there was no mistaking the impatient scowl. It was my fellow junior partner, Crenshaw Davenport III, Esquire.

I nodded and rushed to end the call with my client. "I have to run now, Mrs. Hammerlin, but I promise I'll stop by later this evening. Okay? Okay. Good-bye."

I sighed loudly as I stuffed my phone into my purse.

"I trust everything is under control?" said Crenshaw around his plastic canines. "You gave me quite a start. When I saw you leave your post, I was afraid you were going to abandon your ticket-selling duties."

"I wouldn't do that. I just had to take this call. This client is driving me crazy. We closed on her new house last week, and she's called me every day since—several times each day."

"Ah. Buyer's remorse?"

"I don't know. It's the weirdest thing. She insists the house is haunted, and she wants to go after the seller for failure to disclose."

Crenshaw raised his eyebrows. "You do attract the most interesting people, don't you? But there's no time for that now. Doors will open soon, and those tickets won't sell themselves."

"Fine," I grumbled. "Though I still can't believe we have to do this. I have better things to do with my Friday night."

He ignored my complaint and gave me a nudge. We'd already been through this earlier in the evening, when he'd met me in the parking lot near the ball field. He must have been watching, waiting for me to pull in, because he pounced the moment I opened my car door.

"At last!" he'd said.

"What's the rush?" I asked, checking my watch. "I'm not late."

"People are already starting to arrive, and we need to get changed. Come on."

"Changed? What are you talking about?" I stepped out of the car and stared at his hair. It was different from how it had appeared at the office earlier in the day.

"Here." He thrust a garment bag into my arms and tossed another over his arm. "I brought our costumes, so we can arrive at the barn in character."

"Costume? What costume? I'm not wearing a costume."

He glared at me under heavy dark eyebrows that were normally ginger-colored. "Of course you are. Don't be ridiculous."

Ridiculous? A grown man who dyed his hair for a silly haunted house gig is calling me ridiculous?

"Come along now," he said.

I shook my head and dug in my heels. "I'm only selling tickets at this thing. I don't need to be in costume."

Crenshaw looked down his nose. "You do understand the concept of a haunted house, do you not?"

"I do. But I'm not going to be *in* the haunted house." I had to trot to keep up with him as he led the way toward the restrooms. I realized it was futile to keep arguing. As an amateur actor involved in the local theater scene, Crenshaw fancied himself a true thespian. He loved playing dress-up.

I unzipped the garment bag as we walked. "What is it anyway?" I asked, trying to look inside. "Please tell me I'm not the Bride of Frankenstein."

"Where's your Halloween spirit, Milanni? More to the point, where's your community spirit? You know Beverly's on a big push to raise the firm's visibility. As partners, you and I have a vested interest in promoting—"

"I know, I know. Hey, what is this? A *witch* costume?"

"What's wrong with a witch costume? It's a classic Halloween character."

"Never mind. Here we are. Wait for me?" I dashed inside the ladies' room without waiting for a response.

Luckily, the facilities at Fieldstone Park were well-maintained. Still, I wasted no time in switching outfits. In spite of my protests, I didn't want to disappoint our boss. As it turned out, the gauzy black dress with jagged trim and bell sleeves wasn't too terrible. But the accessories were another story. I cringed as I pulled the bushy, Elvira-style wig over my own chestnut-colored hair. The artificial black mop made my face appear wan and washed out.

Or, I realized as I peered into the mirror above the sink, maybe I just needed to get outside more. Now that I thought about it, I couldn't remember the last time I'd sat outdoors in the sun. What kind of Wiccan was I? I'd been so busy at work; I had let the entire summer pass me by without a single trip to a lake or swimming pool. If I didn't make a change soon, the last mild days of autumn would pass me by, too.

I grabbed the garment bag, now containing my business suit, and joined Crenshaw, who had just emerged from the men's room in full creature-of-the-night formal wear. I did my best not to laugh, but he looked none too happy. "Where's the rest of your costume?" he demanded.

"This is good enough."

"Well, at least put on the hat." He gestured toward a pocket on the outside of the garment bag. "A witch isn't a witch without a pointy hat."

Ha! I thought. Out loud, I muttered, "Shows how much you know."

"I beg your pardon?"

"Nothing," I said, as I donned the pointy hat.

The truth was, in all my years of being Wiccan, from the time I discovered and embraced the path at age sixteen to now, I had never been offended by the image of the Halloween witch. Some might disagree, but I didn't view the stereotypical witch's costume as demeaning to my religion—or even some kind of cultural misappropriation. How could it be, when the "wicked witch" archetype predated Wicca by hundreds of years? Besides, fictional witches came in all stripes. Considering all the pop-culture teenaged witches, not to mention the Harry Potter franchise, witches were as likely to be seen as cool rather than scary. After all, we could wield magic!

Even so, I had to draw the line at the warty rubber nose and sickly green face paint. A girl was entitled to a smidgen of vanity.

Now, as we left the maple grove and made our way back to the entrance of the barn, I was glad to see the business crowd had already gone inside. I took my place behind the cash register. Crenshaw paused at the counter. "Say, do you happen to have a mirror in your handbag? I'd like to check my stage makeup."

"Sure," I said, reaching into my purse. "But it won't do you much good, if you can't see your reflection."

Crenshaw stared at me, evidently not getting the joke. I waved a compact mirror in front of his face as if to clue him in.

While we bantered, a side door opened and a middle-aged man in a charcoal-gray suit came barreling out of the barn. I recognized him as Tadd Hemsley, a local business owner who advocated for small farmers. He was usually pleasant enough, but now his lips curled above his grizzled soul patch as he glared at his cell phone. I could relate to the sentiment. My own phone had buzzed in my handbag at least three times in the last five minutes.

As Tadd passed us, he bumped into Crenshaw and glanced up. His frown turned into a smirk. "I always knew lawyers were bloodsuckers," he drawled. "I guess this proves it."

Crenshaw flushed beneath his white makeup, and I suddenly felt sorry for him. *That was a cheap shot*, I thought. With a strange sense of almost-parental indignation, I stood taller, ready to defend my over-eager colleague. But it was too late. Tadd Hemsley was already halfway down the sidewalk with his phone pressed tightly to his ear.

I looked at Crenshaw and tugged lightly on his cape. "Still want the mirror?"

"Never mind that. I need to join the monsters inside." He straightened his stiff high collar, then disappeared behind the ragged strips of black cloth that blocked the main entry to the "haunted barn."

I shook my head as I peeked at my own reflection, then tossed the mirror back into my purse. While I appreciated the fun factor, Crenshaw was right that my spirit was lacking tonight. Halloween was usually one of my favorite holidays, especially since it coincided with Samhain, one of Wicca's most important festivals. I was probably just too tired to be in the mood tonight. I still had a week before the big day. I'd find the spirit before then.

As I unlocked the cash register, I became aware of a man loitering near the picnic tables. He appeared to be alone, some distance apart from the group of teens clustered a few feet away. He caught me eyeing him and ambled up to the counter.

"Open for business?"

"Uh, sure." I glanced at my watch. "Doors will open to the public in about five minutes."

"I'll take one ticket," he said.

I took his cash and handed over a ticket. He accepted it but didn't leave right away. He seemed to be studying me, which made me slightly uncomfortable. He had a friendly enough face and wasn't bad-looking—with his blue-gray eyes and smattering of freckles, he reminded me of my mother's Irish cousins—but wasn't it odd for a fortysomething-year-old man to hang out at a place meant for kids?

Perhaps he read my mind. He cleared his throat and looked away. "I haven't been to one of these things in ages. Guess I'm feeling a little nostalgic." He flashed me a small grin. "Is it very scary?"

"Oh, I'm sure it's a fright fest in there." I smiled. "You'll be fine."

A small line had formed behind him, so he finally stepped aside. I sold tickets to several teenagers and a number of giggling tweens, then looked up in surprise at the last two people in line—a bubbly blonde with a large smile and a sharply dressed man with a glint of amusement in his warm brown eyes. If I didn't know better, I might have mistaken them for a couple.

"Hey, you two." I looked from my best friend, Farrah Anderson, to my colleague, Randall Sykes.

Although Farrah was a lawyer, too, she had left the traditional career path to become a legal software salesperson, which perfectly suited her outgoing personality. Randall, on the other hand, was cool and laid back with a wry sense of humor. Catching a glimpse of Randall's single gold earring, it occurred to me that he and Farrah might not be a bad match after all. "What are you guys doing here?"

"Oh, my God," said Farrah, lifting the ends of my black wig. "This . . . is . . . awesome."

Randall chuckled. "Your friend stopped by the office just as I was heading over here. How is everything?"

"Peachy," I said drily. "There's nowhere I'd rather be right now."

Farrah whipped out her cell phone and snapped a picture of me. She probably had several shots before I realized what she was doing and held up my palm. She laughed. "What's the matter? You make a perfectly lovely witch. There's something so, I don't know, *natural* about seeing you this way."

I wrinkled my nose at her. Farrah loved that I was Wiccan and that she was privy to my secret. While I trusted her like a sister, I sometimes feared that, with her overabundant enthusiasm, she might inadvertently spill the beans. Given how judgmental some people could be about unconventional lifestyles and lesser-known religions, I felt I had to be discreet to protect my job. Not that I thought Randall would care, but he wouldn't be above some good-natured teasing. And that wasn't the kind of attention I wanted at work. Heck, even my family back in Nebraska didn't know I was Wiccan.

Luckily, at that moment a skeletal arm beckoned the group inside, and I was left alone with my thoughts.

I exhaled softly as I gazed across the empty ball field at a line of trees in the distance, the shadowy branches swishing in the breeze. It was a quiet evening. The low rumble of ghostly sound effects emanating from the barn, punctuated by the occasional bloodcurdling shriek, made for an eerie backdrop. My mind flickered briefly to Mrs. Hammerlin and the strange noises she'd been hearing in her new home. I was sure they'd turn out to be as innocent as the ones within the barn.

Thinking of Mrs. Hammerlin, I reached for my phone to check my messages. Sure enough, I had missed another call from the anxious woman. The other missed calls were from my office and from my boyfriend, Wes. I felt a twinge of guilt for not checking in with Wes sooner, but he knew I was working tonight. I shot off a quick text to let him know where I was. I would have added that I planned to stop by Mrs. Hammerlin's on my way home, but I was distracted by another person coming up the sidewalk. She wore a colorful kaftan with matching head scarf and walked with short, deliberate steps. For a moment, I wondered if she was another volunteer.

"Keli Milanni?"

"Yes?"

"I was told you would be here. I recognize you from your photograph." She spoke with a Caribbean accent and gazed at me with earnest ebony eyes. "I must speak with you. Please. It is urgent."

I glanced around the empty barnyard. *Who told her I'd be here? And where did she see my photograph?*

"What can I do for you, Ms. . . . ?"

"My name is Fredeline Paul. I need to speak with you about Josephine."

Josephine. Ms. Paul didn't provide a surname, but she didn't have to. There was only one Josephine she could mean: Josephine O'Malley—Josie, to her old friends, Aunt Josephine to me. The name brought up a rush of conflicting feelings: affection, curiosity, exasperation. Coating it all was a sense of frustration. Aunt Josephine was a mystery. I had never met her, yet I felt like I knew her—or at least a part of her. At one time, I'd even thought I might take after her. But, for some reason, she never let me find out.

"What about her?" I asked.

"She is missing."

Connect with

U **S**

Visit us online at
KensingtonBooks.com
to read more from your favorite authors, see books
by series, view reading group guides, and more.

Join us on social media

for sneak peeks, chances to win books and prize packs,
and to share your thoughts with other readers.

facebook.com/kensingtonpublishing
twitter.com/kensingtonbooks

Tell us what you think!

To share your thoughts, submit a review,
or sign up for our eNewsletters, please visit:
KensingtonBooks.com/TellUs.

Grab These Cozy Mysteries
from
Kensington Books

Follow P.I. Savannah Reid
with
G.A. McKevett